The EXTRAORDINARY ADVENTURES of Alice Tonks

The EXTRAORDINARY ADVENTURES of Alice Tonks

EMILY KENNY

ROCK THE BOAT

A Rock the Boat Book

First published by Rock the Boat,
an imprint of Oneworld Publications, 2022

Text copyright © Emily Kenny, 2022
Illustration copyright © Flavia Sorrentino, 2022

The moral right of Emily Kenny and Flavia Sorrentino to be identified as
the Author and Illustrator of this work respectively has been asserted by
them in accordance with the Copyright, Designs, and Patents Act 1988

ISBN 978-0-86154-205-5
ISBN 978-0-86154-206-2 (ebook)

Typeset by Hewer Text UK Ltd
Printed and bound in Great Britain by Clays Ltd, Elcograf S.p.A.

This book is a work of fiction. Names, characters, businesses,
organisations, places and events are either the product of the author's
imagination or are used fictitiously. Any resemblance to actual
persons, living or dead, events or locales is entirely coincidental.

Oneworld Publications
10 Bloomsbury Street, London, WC1B 3SR, England

Stay up to date with the latest books,
special offers, and exclusive content from
Rock the Boat with our newsletter

Sign up on our website
oneworld-publications.com/rtb

MIX
Paper from
responsible sources
FSC
www.fsc.org   FSC® C018072

CHAPTER 1

Alice Tonks was having the worst day ever.

"What kind of school holds its Welcome Day on a beach?" she grumbled. She trudged down the steep cliff steps, Gran's polka-dot cool bag over one shoulder and her battered copy of *The Life and Times of Beatrix Potter* wedged under her other arm.

"Come on," Gran said, flashing her a smile. "Give it a try. You might even enjoy yourself?"

"Hmph." There was nothing enjoyable about sitting on a too-hot beach with a bunch of strangers. In fact, Gran really ought to have known better than to force her to attend her fancy new secondary school's Welcome Day. There were two things in life that Alice really, really hated: school and

1

beaches, and somehow today's 'fun family event' at School Bay managed to combine both.

It did not bode well.

Finally they reached the foot of the steps and a sign-in desk surrounded by lavish gold balloons. "Welcome to Pebblewood School!" cried an overexcited teacher in a too-tight blazer. Further around the bay, a small group of teachers huddled round a tartan rug gave them energetic waves.

"Hi," Alice said, not lifting her eyes from her flip-flops.

While Gran signed them in on the teacher's clipboard, Alice gazed moodily at the other Year Seven students and their families splashing in the waves and sunbathing on the sand. Everyone was wearing designer trunks or bikinis and Alice tugged self-consciously at the bobbly swimming costume Gran had dug out of her wardrobe. It was too tight and clung in all the wrong places. The letter had just said 'wear swimwear'. How was she to know that meant something new and expensive?

"Let's pick a spot, shall we?" Gran said, striding off across the strip of golden sand. "Then maybe we can go for a swim."

"You can forget about me going in the sea," Alice muttered. Just the thought of not being able to see her feet in the murky English water made her feel all iffy. "You go. I'll just sit here and read . . ."

She glanced down.

Seaweed.

Alice hated seaweed. Slimy stuff that squelched under her toes. She hated it even more than she hated sand and she really, really hated sand. Sand felt scratchy and she worried about it grating all the skin off the soles of her feet if she stood on it for more than a minute or two, but seaweed absolutely stank. And now there was a long, gloopy green rope of the stuff curled round her right foot . . .

She closed her eyes. *Don't panic. Don't panic.*

She had tried really hard to be Nice Alice today. Nice Alice was smiley. She'd shaken hands with the teacher who greeted them at the train station (even though the teacher had sweaty palms and smelled faintly of boiled ham). Nice Alice tried not to worry about whether all the other students would already know one another, and when the worries did creep into her brain to moulder there, she tried not to upset Gran by talking about them. It was hard work being Nice Alice but somehow she'd managed it.

When Gran had packed her creaking trunk with endless new uniform items, announcing there was no space left for her precious animal encyclopedias, she'd not said a word. She'd kept her Nice Alice act going on the train down to school, even when the carriage got super busy and she was squashed against a window that was home to three dead flies (and those were just the ones she could see).

But now there was the matter of the seaweed. Congealed. Limp. Coiled round her foot.

3

"Come on," Gran said. "You promised you'd give today a go. Please, for me?"

Time slowed down. Alice felt the familiar tickle at the back of her throat. Her fingers began to twitch. She'd tried so hard to hold it all together but the octopus who'd been squirming in her belly all day had finally had enough and was rearing up, fierce and angry, waving its tentacles.

"UGH!" she exploded. "I hate this beach, I hate this school . . . and . . . and I HATE YOU!"

Gran's mouth formed a tight, round 'O' of shock. "Alice," she gulped. "I . . ."

Suddenly Gran was no longer the only one looking at Alice. All along the bay her new classmates had stopped what they were doing to stare. Conversations halted. A hundred pairs of eyes gawked.

"I'm sorry," Gran said. "I just wanted . . ." But Alice didn't hear the rest. Her lip wobbled and she blinked very hard and very fast. All her worst nightmares were coming true. She'd known all along that Pebblewood School wouldn't be the fresh start Gran had promised. She should never have let Gran talk her into coming today.

Alice had to get away. But where? Everywhere she looked families were goggling at her from their picnic blankets and inflatables. The waves smashed behind her and her nose filled with the stench of salt. Overhead, seagulls wheeled in dizzying circles up and up and up . . .

Her eyes fixed on the towering black cliffs and the steep stone steps that led to the school. Surely Gran wouldn't try to follow her all the way back up there?

Alice opened her mouth to say something, anything, but the words lodged in her throat like lumps of gristle so instead she turned on her heel and ran. Welcome Day? More like Disaster Day! Her cheeks burned with fury, shame and embarrassment. She'd been so determined to give this new school a try but it had all been for nothing. Everyone would think she was stupid. No one would be her friend. Even the teachers would think she was weird.

Sometimes being autistic really sucked.

Alice ran back past the Welcome Desk and pounded up the winding stone steps. About halfway there was a flat shelf of black rock. It was shady here and no one could see her cry. She flicked her fingers as quickly as she could against her thumbs. Sometimes, if she did it super fast, it made her feel better, but today wasn't one of those days. She just felt miserable.

Alice sat and watched as the other kids and their families went back to enjoying the sunshine. One family darted in and out of the crashing waves, hooting with laughter as the sea yanked their legs from under them. Another boy and two younger girls with the same podgy cheeks and chestnut-brown hair dug a giant hole, sand flying in all directions.

From her hiding place, Alice kept an eye out in case Gran or any of the teachers tried to come after her. Although Gran was always trying to make things better, even she couldn't mend today. After a few minutes, Alice guessed she'd probably decided to give her some space. Gran was good like that.

A girl around Alice's age was sunbathing on the sand in an emerald-green bikini, her blond hair splaying out beneath her as if she was a mermaid. She'd fry to a crisp lying there like that in this heat, Alice thought, wondering if she should go and warn her. But Alice's eyes still felt itchy and sore and she wasn't in the mood to talk to anyone, especially not the boy she'd just spotted stomping up the steps towards her with a slightly drippy ice cream in his hand . . .

"I, er, thought you could do with this." He thrust the cone in Alice's direction.

Alice looked the boy up and down. He was tall and gangly with an Afro and big brown eyes made still bigger by his spectacles. Bizarrely he was the only student dressed in the full Pebblewood uniform, his boater hat clutched under one arm and chocolate ice cream smeared on his collar. Hadn't he got the letter?

"Thanks." Alice forced the word out and accepted the ice cream.

The boy watched her catch the chocolatey drips with her tongue.

"My name's Alice," she said between slurps. Ice cream always cheered her up.

"I know," he said. "I heard when your gran, er, shouted . . ."

Alice's cheeks flushed.

The boy shrugged. "Don't worry about it. My mum can be pretty embarrassing too. I'm Timothy Crossley-Herbert the Third." He held out a slightly sticky hand for Alice to shake. Alice gave it a quick wobble and then discreetly wiped her own hand on the back of her swimming costume.

"Hello, Timothy Crossley-Herbert the Third."

He gave a hiccup of a laugh. "Most people just call me Tim."

"Why are you wearing your uniform?" Alice asked.

There was an awkward silence. "Mum must have forgotten," he eventually mumbled. "Anyway, better be getting back. See you around."

Tim mooched down the cliff steps and back across the beach, his heavy school shoes dragging in the sand. Alice watched as he picked his way past the newspaper-readers and Frisbee-throwers to the circle of teachers standing stiffly in their smart trousers and blazers, clipboards in hand. One of the teachers greeted him, ticking his name off on her register. Alice wondered where his family were. Maybe they'd gone off to get fish and chips or something. Tim plonked himself down on the tartan rug and started poking about in the sand with a stick.

Alice sat back down on the rocks and stared up at the school, perched high on the clifftop like a bird of prey about to swoop. Tomorrow she'd be a student there. She tried to imagine herself hurrying between the buildings, her schoolbooks under her arms, but she could only see herself cowering in a corner, lost and afraid.

Just as Alice finished her ice cream, a seagull flew over and swooped down to land beside her. It was white with grey wings and tail. There were actually loads of different types of gull and if Gran hadn't made her leave her encyclopedias at home she could have looked up which type this one was when they got back to the hotel. The bird dipped its head and pecked at the furry black lichen growing in the cracks between the rocks. Taking in the red on its bill, Alice figured it was probably a herring gull.

The gull had a good look around, peering over its shoulder as if checking whether anyone was about.

"I've no chips to give you," Alice warned.

The bird cocked its head to one side, looking at her the way teachers did when they were working out whether or not you could be trusted. "It's not your chips I'm after, Alice Tonks," the seagull said sternly. "We've got a job for you."

Alice sat up a bit straighter. Had that seagull just spoken to her? She put a hand to her hot forehead. Perhaps it was sunstroke . . . She did feel a little queasy. She rubbed her eyes but the seagull was still there, watching her.

"Alice? Alice! Where are you?" Gran was calling. "We can get the bus back to the hotel if you like?"

"We'll be in touch," the seagull hissed. "We know where to find you." Then he gave Alice a one-winged salute and flew away.

CHAPTER 2

That night, Alice dreamed of seagulls.

She tossed and turned on her lumpy hotel mattress until morning slid its impatient fingers round the room's beige curtains. Gran was stirring too and for a brief moment as she lay in bed stretching and rubbing her eyes, Alice considered telling her about the talking gull. But she quickly decided against it. She didn't want Gran to think the bird was part of some silly, made-up game. She hadn't imagined the gull . . . had she?

Alice slipped her feet into her lovely fluffy slippers and boiled the hotel-room kettle. As she stood in the thin grey morning light stirring a spoon and a half of sugar into Gran's mug of tea, Alice convinced herself that the talking gull must have been down to sunstroke. What else could it be? Nevertheless something about the bird still seemed so real. Perhaps it was the clipped tone the seagull had used or the way it had known her name . . .

"You're a good girl," Gran sighed, sitting up in bed. Alice handed her the tea and she took a long, grateful slurp. "You know, Alice," she said. "You don't have to go to Pebbles if you don't want to. Just because me and your mum went there, it doesn't mean you have to too. We can get the next train home and find a different school for you, one not so far away?"

Alice's eyes flitted over Gran's crumpled nightie and her tired, puffy face. Gran had been working really long hours recently and going on more and more work trips, leaving Alice in the care of their terminally boring next-door neighbour Miss Pinkerton.

"It's okay, Gran," she said. "I'll give it a try." She paused, dropping her gaze to the carpet. "And I didn't mean what I said yesterday. You know that, don't you?" There was a tight, sharp feeling in Alice's chest at the idea of Gran thinking she hated her. It had been just her and Gran for as long as Alice could remember.

"Oh, don't worry about that!" Gran flapped the thought away with a gnarled hand. "We all say things we don't mean when we're upset." She put a finger under Alice's chin. "I am very, very proud of you, my darling girl, and your mum and dad would be too."

Alice fiddled with one of the lacy frills on Gran's nightie. She never knew what to say when Gran mentioned her parents. The only reason she even knew what her mum and dad looked like was because of the photographs that sat atop Gran's Welsh dresser.

They'd disappeared while on holiday in the Amazon rainforest, back when she was just a baby. The other kids at school said having no parents made her an orphan but she certainly didn't feel like one. In the books she'd read, orphans were always poor, measly children begging for more gruel, or sad, lonely creatures shut away in attics. Her bedroom at Foxden Cottage was snug and sunny, and the kitchen was warm and full of the sound of Gran's great shaggy mutt Roger snoring on the rug. Alice loved waking each morning to the sound of the chickens clucking outside her window. The thought of waking up somewhere new filled her with a sadness so thick and heavy that wading through it felt impossible.

"Goodness me, is that the time?" Gran cried, gawping at the chunky round face of her watch. "We'd better get a move on. You need to be there for noon."

While Gran rushed around the hotel room gathering Alice's uniform together and collected a heavy wooden tray of breakfast things from the room-service boy, Alice squeezed her pyjamas and toiletries into her new maroon rucksack. Her heaving trunk had been sent ahead a few days ago and the rucksack was all Gran would let her carry on the train down.

"Come and have something to eat," Gran said. "You can't be going off to school on an empty stomach."

Alice smiled weakly as Gran lifted the shiny metal lid from the plates and they sat down at the fold-out table to eat. The air in the muggy hotel room clung to Alice like a too-tight sweater and the cold, greasy eggs and burnt toast did little to settle her stomach. The window overlooking Pebblehampton-on-Sea refused to budge so Alice peered through the frosted glass. The bright sunshine of Welcome Day had been replaced by a smudge of grey rain clouds. *Not long*, Alice thought, *and we'll be saying goodbye*.

Once Alice stopped picking at her breakfast, it was time to get changed. She pulled on her summer dress, straightening the collar, and tugged at the ridiculous knee-high white socks that pinched her calves. Gran brushed her hair, taming it into two long plaits before handing Alice her new blazer. She wriggled into it and checked herself out in the wardrobe mirror. Her arms had disappeared inside the sleeves. She looked like a turtle with an oversized burgundy shell.

"You'll grow into it, love." Gran popped Alice's straw boater on her head before she had a chance to dodge out of the way. "Now hurry up or we'll be late!"

After a short drive past the harbour, up the high street and along the twisty cliff road, the bus ground to a halt outside two tall black wrought-iron gates.

"Righto, here we are," the bus driver said as the doors opened with a hiss and a fart.

Alice stepped down on to the grass verge, her rucksack bumping against her back, and stared up at the gates. 'Pebblewood School. Established 1902' the large black metal letters announced.

"Ready?" Gran said, giving Alice's hand a squeeze.

The gates swung open and Alice followed Gran up a long and winding driveway, gravel crunching underfoot. They passed a smart stableyard overlooking a sawdust-strewn arena full of show jumps. A little further up the drive, sleek white dinghies floated on a silver boating lake like overgrown swans. It was a far cry from her tiny village primary with its grey concrete playground and rusty climbing frame.

By the time they reached the top of the driveway, black clouds were threatening to pour rain on to the crowd of new students and their families gathered on the neatly manicured lawn. Alice stopped to stare up at the sprawling grey stone buildings that loomed before her, with their beautiful arched windows that reminded her of cathedrals and steep roofs that disappeared into the mist.

Atop the school's enormous clocktower, the brass hare on the clock's hour hand edged ever closer to the moment Gran would have to leave. So this was Pebblewood School, or Pebbles as it was known to its students. Her home for the next seven years. No turning back now.

"And you're quite sure this is what you want?" Gran asked, twiddling her hands the way she did whenever she was worried.

Alice nodded, afraid that if she opened her mouth to speak the truth would come flying out before she could stop it.

"Well, then, best we get it over with." Gran looped her arm through Alice's and strode off to peruse the cream cakes and brightly coloured macaroons that had been laid out on long trestle tables. Alice wished she was more like Gran. Nothing ever seemed to faze her. She shoved up the sleeve of her blazer and gave her elbow a quick scratch.

On another table were flutes of golden bubbles for the grown-ups and glasses of strawberry lemonade for the kids. The lemonade looked delicious but Alice eyed the other Year Sevens warily, too self-conscious to take a glass. Everyone else already seemed to have made friends, and were standing around chatting in groups. Although she recognised one or two faces from the beach, Alice stuck close to Gran as serving staff in smart black-and-white uniforms bobbed about, refilling glasses and offering canapes from large silver trays.

"Look, there's Mr Marlowe, your headmaster," Gran said between mouthfuls of flaky pastry.

Alice looked up. She'd refused to attend the Open Day with Gran but had heard there was a new headmaster. She'd expected him to be an old man with a wise, friendly face, half-moon spectacles and silvery hair but Mr Marlowe's face was neither friendly nor wise. He had overly white teeth, slicked-back hair and a champagne flute balanced between two pink fingers.

The headmaster was busy talking to a blond lady in a lilac suit. As Alice watched, he slid an arm round the woman's back and whispered something in her ear. She smiled demurely, one perfectly manicured hand resting on her pearl necklace. Alice decided she didn't like her new headteacher very much. He reminded her of a peacock, prancing about in his expensive suit.

Gran slipped a couple of cakes wrapped in a napkin into Alice's blazer pocket. "In case you get peckish later," she said.

Alice couldn't imagine ever eating again. Her stomach clenched as the toast and eggs from breakfast threatened to resurface. She'd give anything to go home with Gran and forget all about this fancy school and all the people in it.

The boy from the beach stood in front of a pyramid of cream cakes, his cheeks puffed out like a hamster's. His eyes lit up when he saw Alice and he swallowed quickly, licking the last of the icing from his mouth. He was about to say something when the sombre echo of a gong rang out. Alice and Tim looked at one another wide-eyed. The hare on the clock face said it was twelve. There was no going back now.

Standing at the top of the flight of marble steps leading to the school's atrium was a tall, dark-eyed woman. She was smartly dressed in a pinstripe suit with long red talons that tapped impatiently against her leg. If this teacher were a bird of prey, she'd be a buzzard, fierce and quick. Alice could imagine her swooping down and carrying off an unsuspecting Year Seven for her tea. A hush descended over the crowd.

"If all new students could kindly make their way inside, please." The woman's tone made it clear this was not a request.

Just then, the rain began to pour down.

"Would you look at that!" Gran exclaimed, her bright yellow umbrella springing open. She was never wrong about the weather, just like she always knew when to have a bag of toffees in her coat pocket for Alice to dip into at desperate times. Alice would miss Gran's jam roly-poly and the way she did all the voices when she read stories aloud. But most of all she'd miss knowing she always had Gran to fall back on. How on earth was she going to manage at this great big school without her?

"Ottoline! Ottoline!" The lady in the lilac suit and pearls dived under a gazebo for cover. "Wherever has she got to?"

"Here, Mother," a quiet voice said and Mermaid Girl stepped forward.

"Oh, there you are," her mother said, straightening her daughter's blazer and rearranging her boater. "Come out of that rain. You know how limp your hair goes! Have you been mingling like I told you? Networking is key, remember."

"Yes, Mother," Mermaid Girl intoned.

The lady smiled, her teeth perfectly neat and square. "Right, then, off you go," she said curtly, giving her an air kiss on either cheek. "And make us proud. No one remembers runners-up, do they?"

"No, Mother." Ottoline turned and went to join the line forming at the bottom of the marble steps.

"Quickly now!" the buzzard-like teacher barked. "No dawdling!"

There wasn't time for Alice to say a proper goodbye to Gran. She stepped back and studied every part of Gran from her chunky green Doc Marten boots to her snuggly red jumper, not wanting to forget a single detail.

"Bags over here!" called an old man with a flat cap covering his shaggy white hair. "Leave your bags here!"

Alice gave Gran a hug that didn't last nearly long enough. She smelled deliciously of toffee and Alice breathed the yummy scent in, unsure when she'd smell it again. Not trusting herself to speak, Alice released Gran and ran over with Tim to put their bags in a pile with everyone else's. The old man said the porter would bring them along later. Alice felt grown-up but also slightly worried about someone else bringing her luggage to her room. The maroon schoolbags all looked the same. What if they got her bag mixed up with someone else's?

As Alice joined the line of pupils surging forward, she glanced back at Gran's distant figure, waving and blowing kisses from beneath her yellow umbrella. Then the heavy wooden doors to Pebblewood School slammed shut. Alice realised too late she hadn't told Gran she loved her, like she usually did each morning. If something bad happened, she'd never forgive herself . . .

A chorus of *ooh*s and *ahh*s reverberated around the school's oak-panelled atrium as the crocodile of Year Sevens filed past gilt-framed portraits of previous headteachers, whose beady eyes stalked Alice all the way. At the far end of the corridor hung a particularly massive gold frame housing a portrait of a ginger-haired man with a terrier on his lap and a twinkle in his eye. The inscription below read 'Sir Rudyard Jessops. School founder and headmaster'.

Ornate chandeliers dangled from high ceilings and a plush plum carpet muffled the students' steps. A faint smell that Alice could not quite place lingered in the air. It smelled a bit like the stinky cheese and mulled wine the old lady next door served up at Christmas. Alice sped up, keen to get out of the corridor as quickly as possible.

The students were herded into the school's magnificent glass-domed hall and Alice and Tim squeezed on to the end of a packed bench. Alice felt hemmed in on all sides. The other kids were too close and one of them smelled of pickled onion. The students around her had bright, excited faces so Alice tried to arrange her own expression to mirror theirs.

"Good afternoon, Year Sevens. My name is Mrs Salter and

I am the housemistress here at Pebblewood School," the teacher announced, one red talon twitching against her skirt. "Please stand for your headmaster."

All the students rose smoothly to their feet and Alice stumbled after them.

Mr Marlowe strode across the hall, his shiny shoes squeaking on the wooden floors, his black gown flowing, and stepped up to a huge golden lectern with some kind of bird carved into it. Alice took in its claws and massive wingspan. Eagle, she decided. Golden eagle.

"Welcome, scholars, to this most exceptional of schools," Mr Marlowe boomed. "Do take a seat as we embark on this adventure together, setting sail in search of academic excellence."

Embark? Alice felt more like she'd been shoved off a short plank into a very deep sea.

Alice sat down quickly, determined not to be the only one standing. The last thing she wanted was for anyone to notice her. Mr Marlowe was saying something about opportunities and the school's great time-tested traditions.

"Witness all around you the accomplishments of your predecessors." Mr Marlowe gestured to the wooden plaques decorating every wall of the hall. Alice scanned them – Rugby Team, Lacrosse Team, Sporting Excellence. There was even a board recognising Choral and Orchestral Talent but there didn't seem to be a plaque for most books read.

"I can't wait to check out the school band," Tim whispered. "I've been practising all summer. Did you see the music studio on Open Day?"

Alice didn't want to admit that she had refused flat out to attend Open Day but she tried to smile encouragingly. Gran always said the right thing was to cheer other people on but Alice found it hard to feel excited about anything at the moment. In this huge, grand hall she felt like the tiniest ant, miniscule and unimportant.

Mr Marlowe wished everyone the very best of luck and implored them to 'make Pebbles proud'. Then it was time to go for their tour of the school and the boarding house.

Alice and Tim got to their feet. As they shuffled forward, Tim nudged Alice. "Cool, huh?" he mouthed, nodding in the direction of the stained-glass window that stretched the full length of the far wall.

Alice stopped and looked up. In rich autumn colours of russet and amber, the window depicted the school crest: a fox, a badger, a hare, and a white bird looking out from beneath the branches of a mighty oak tree at an expanse of blue ocean. The gull had the same grey-tipped wings as the bird from the beach.

Just as she was about to look away, Alice spotted movement out of the corner of her eye. There! She gasped. The gull's wing was moving. It was waving at her, she was sure of it.

"Did you see that?" Alice said, turning quickly to Tim. But he was already lining up with the other boys to go on their tour of the school with the headmaster, while the girls queued up with Mrs Salter.

When she looked back, the stained-glass window was perfectly still, as if nothing had happened at all.

CHAPTER 3

"And here we are, girls," Mrs Salter announced at the end of her two-hour-long tour. "Home sweet home. The boarding house."

Alice and twenty-nine other girls stared up at the large stone building. "I wonder which room will be ours?" one blond-haired girl said to her identical twin but Alice's thoughts were elsewhere. The gull in the stained-glass window really had waved at her, she was sure. If only Tim hadn't disappeared off on his tour with Mr Marlowe before she'd had the chance to show him . . .

"Follow me inside, please," the housemistress instructed, leading the group into a neat, cream-painted lobby with a black-and-white-tiled floor and a doormat that implored you to 'Wipe your feet!'.

Alice passed three old-fashioned dial-up telephones mounted on the wall. For a moment, she considered ringing Gran to tell her about the talking seagull and the stained-glass window before realising what a terrible idea that was. 'Telling porkies' Gran would call it and Alice didn't think she could bear the shame. She'd never lie, especially not about something like this. *Magic*, Alice whispered to herself, the word tingling on her tongue like a tiny, flickering fire.

"And this," Mrs Salter said, "is the common room." She pushed open the door to reveal a large, open space crammed with squishy sofas and tatty armchairs piled high with cushions. School flags fluttered from the rafters and the walls were adorned with dog-eared film posters and sign-up lists for sports clubs. "Consider it your space to relax in at the end of a busy school day, though all Year Sevens are expected to be in their dormitories by nine o'clock sharp. Do I make myself clear?"

"Yes, miss," the girls chorused, Alice joining in half-heartedly.

"Excellent. Lights out is at a quarter to ten." Mrs Salter's eyes settled on every girl in turn. "No exceptions."

"Are those for us?" asked one particularly brave red-headed girl, staring hungrily at a huge platter of cookies resting on the kitchen counter.

Mrs Salter glanced at the platter, her lip curling. "I assume so," she said sniffily. "I do not eat sugar. It does not agree with me."

No sugar? Alice thought. *That explains a lot.*

The housemistress strode out of the common room, leaving the girls to it. The feeding frenzy that followed would have put a pride of lions to shame. Alice watched from a safe distance.

"Look!" a pretty, dark-haired girl cried on discovering jugs of creamy chocolate milk and freshly squeezed orange juice in the gigantic fridge. As the others gathered round, Mermaid Girl brought out some beakers from one of the cupboards. While everyone was distracted, Alice took the opportunity to help herself to the last of the cookies.

When everyone had finally eaten and drunk their fill, the crowd splintered off to play table football or flop on the squishy beanbags. While the other girls laughed and chatted, Alice stared up at the skylights in the high, vaulted ceiling, hoping to see a white flash of wings soaring past.

"Chop-chop, girls!" Mrs Salter announced, reappearing in the doorway a few minutes later. "We've dormitories to sort before dinner."

Sighing, Alice took one last look up through the skylights before following the housemistress up the narrow staircase. First the seagull on the beach and now the moving window. In stories, magical things always happened in threes. What would be next?

The long line of girls filed past the boys' dormitories on the first floor and carried on up another flight of steep stairs to their own landing on the top floor. "Strictly no boys allowed up here," Mrs Salter said sternly, only to be met with a chorus of rousing cheers. The housemistress glanced around, unnerved. It clearly wasn't quite the reaction she'd been expecting.

Alice stepped on to the landing and gasped. It was perfect. All along the corridor, nooks and crannies were tucked beneath the rafters – a bookcase here, a table there – and cosy window seats nestled under curtains. The light was soft and shadowy and for the first time since arriving, Alice thought she'd found somewhere she could truly feel at home.

As the other girls ran over to the bannisters to peer down at the boys' corridor and the common room below, Alice wandered over to a little square window and pressed her nose to the glass. She could just make out the domed roof of the school hall and the stained-glass window sparkling in the post-storm sun. There, at the end of the line of animals, was the seagull. Tingles of excitement rushed up and down her arms, giving her goosebumps.

Alice scoured the school roofs for the gull, her eyes peeled for a flash of white wings. But the only birds in sight were a posse of plump pigeons and a handful of starlings.

"Alice Tonks?"

Alice jumped, turning from the window with a start. Mrs Salter was glaring at her, hands on hips. "Come along, Tonks! I haven't got all day," she snapped.

The landing had emptied and Mermaid Girl stood alone outside the furthest door on the landing. Alice hurried to join her.

They hovered awkwardly while Mrs Salter checked their names off a list and fumbled with her keys. Mermaid Girl's long blond waves were neatly pinned back today but she still looked as fresh-faced and immaculate as she had sunbathing on the beach. Alice gave her elbow a nervous rub, wishing Gran hadn't put her hair in plaits like she was still in primary school. Standing around with nothing to say was another of Alice's Pet Hates. The pressure to make small talk always made her feel like a spotlight was burning down on her.

"So have you got brothers and sisters at Pebbles?" Mermaid Girl asked when the silence became unbearable.

"No," Alice said flatly.

For a moment, Mermaid Girl looked taken aback. Asking a question and then acting surprised by the answer was something neurotypical people did a lot, Alice thought. It was very odd.

A smile tugged at the corner of Mermaid Girl's mouth. "Me neither," she said. "It was a stupid question really."

Finally Mrs Salter unlocked the door. "Well, in you go."

Alice stepped forward tentatively. To her delight, the room was much homelier than she'd been expecting. The walls were painted a cheery yellow and there was a set of wooden bunk beds, a pair of desks, two wardrobes and a stripey rug. It looked a bit plain compared to her bedroom at home, with its animal posters and her collection of soft toys piled on the bed, but it was still much nicer than the damp, gloomy dormitory she'd been picturing.

"You'll find your trunks already here," Mrs Salter said, nodding in the direction of the two huge boxes sitting on the rug. "Unpack before dinner, please." Then she turned and left them to get on with it, her footsteps fading away down the corridor.

Mermaid Girl stuck out her hand. It was tanned and slender, her nails neat pink squares, shiny and clean. "How do you do?" she said. "I'm Ottie."

"Alice." Ottie gave her hand a very energetic shake. Alice tugged her hand free and gave it a wipe on her dress. Ottie didn't seem to notice.

"Would you mind if I have the top bunk?" Ottie asked.

"Not at all!" Ever since Alice had seen the bunk beds in the school prospectus, she'd been tormented with visions of toppling out in the middle of the night and cracking her head open.

Ottie deftly swung up and started making herself at home while Alice stared out of the nearest window, keeping her eyes peeled for seagulls.

"Want to know a secret?" Ottie said, jumping down to land beside Alice with a thud. She pointed to the quad and the spectacular fountain that sat directly below the window. "There's a path that goes all the way down to the beach. Look, can you see it?"

Alice peered down and could just make out a narrow alleyway running alongside the boarding house.

"It's just for sixth-formers, of course!" Ottie rolled her eyes. "More's the pity."

On the other side of the dormitory, a second window looked out on to the kitchen gardens behind the boarding house and the dark woods beyond. Suddenly Alice noticed a flash of gold.

"Ottie, look!" she cried as a dog burst out of the bushes. "It's a golden retriever!"

The two girls watched the large dog gallop a loop around the garden. Then a second dog, much smaller and white with a brown patch by its ears, shot out of the hedgerow and tore after the retriever, yapping all the while. The terrier had a slight limp like it had hurt its back leg, though it wasn't letting that hold it back!

"That's a Jack Russell, I think," Ottie said. "My old housekeeper had one."

The dogs chased each other excitedly in and out of the vegetable patch, barking, before disappearing off in the direction of an old shed. No one told her they had dogs at Pebbles! Things were starting to look up.

"Come on," Ottie said, throwing open the lid of her white-and-gold trunk. "We'd better start unpacking."

Alice immediately pulled the lilac-and-white chequered curtains shut. It was much nicer without the bright sunshine flooding in. Too much light gave her a headache. Ottie was humming to herself as she rifled through her trunk and only now did Alice remember she had a roommate to consider. She was used to having her bedroom all to herself. What if Ottie liked the curtains open? Alice knew her habits would probably seem petty to other people but she really wouldn't get a wink of sleep unless the window was wide open and her body wrapped tight in her favourite blanket. It was just one of the many things that worried her about boarding school.

Ottie placed her shiny rose-gold tablet on the nearest desk and switched it on. With a sudden blast of horns and a thumping beat, pop music blared out. Alice cringed, fighting the temptation to cover her ears. Maybe Gran had been right and she should have brought her ear defenders after all. Alice didn't know much about pop music but the song was one she remembered her classmates loving at the Year Six leavers' party. She'd spent most of the disco out in the playground listening to the thunderstorm crackle overhead, the summer rain pattering against the tiles of the school roof. That was her kind of music.

"Oh, sorry," Ottie said. "Is that a bit loud? I was always getting into trouble at my last school for making a din in the dorm."

"Your last school?" Alice asked.

"Oh yes," Ottie said casually. "This is my third boarding school."

"Wow, you must have been young when you started boarding!" Alice said.

"I was seven when I first went." Ottie shrugged. "You get used to it."

"Oh," Alice said. It had been bad enough leaving Gran at eleven.

Ottie shrugged again. "Boarding makes you independent, that's what Mother says. She believes in 'standing on your own two feet'. My whole family do."

Alice shuddered, grateful she had Gran to look after her and not the lady in the pearls she'd seen Ottie with earlier.

"Here, I'll give you a hand with your posters," Ottie said, changing the subject. She helped Alice fish out her crumpled animal posters from the bottom of her trunk and pin them to the corkboard beside her bunk.

The girls stepped back to admire their handiwork. "That looks better already, doesn't it?" Ottie beamed. "We'll have you feeling at home in no time!"

Alice watched as Ottie started to put her clothes away in the wardrobe. As well as her school uniform, Gran had packed Alice's favourite jeans and her comfiest T-shirts and hoodies, while Ottie seemed to have a different outfit for every occasion. Each dress was protected by a clear plastic bag and she hung them carefully, arranging them by colour. Alice felt a sinking feeling in the pit of her stomach. Was she supposed to have brought fancy dresses too?

Ottie looked up and noticed her watching. "Oh, ridiculous, aren't they?" she said, gesturing at the rainbow of dresses. "My mother doesn't believe in travelling light. Most of them never even come out of their bags but don't tell her that. Oooh!" Ottie squealed as she caught sight of Toby, Alice's threadbare toy dog, in her almost emptied trunk. "Can I look?"

Alice nodded shyly, hoping Ottie wouldn't think she was babyish. She'd had Toby for as long as she could remember and he was the only cuddly toy Gran had let her bring. Nuzzling up to his super-soft ears almost always made things better when she was feeling stressed or worried.

"I am SO glad someone else brought a cuddly toy!" Ottie said. "I thought I'd be the only one." She held aloft a zebra who was missing one ear. "Meet Stripcy!"

"Toby," Alice said, grinning.

"You don't mind lights, do you?" Ottie asked, retrieving a long line of fairy lights from the bottom of her trunk and swinging back up to the top bunk to arrange them along the wall.

"Not at all," Alice lied, her spirits falling again. Fairy lights were for Christmas. If Ottie left them on at night, she would get no sleep at all. Maybe she should just come out with it and tell Ottie she was autistic? There had never been anyone she'd trusted enough at primary school to tell but maybe, just maybe, things at Pebbles were going to be different . . .

Ottie glanced down from her bunk. "You know, if they're too much, I can switch them off?"

"No, it's all right," Alice said, surprising herself.

She had been dreading the thought of sharing a bedroom but Ottie actually seemed really nice. She wasn't sure how to say she was glad Ottie was her roommate without sounding like what the kids at her last school called 'a crawler', so instead she climbed halfway up the ladder to Ottie's bunk

31

and helped her hammer in the last few pins into the corkboard beside her bed.

Suddenly there came a *tap*, *tap*, *tap* at the window.

"What's that?" said Ottie, jumping down from the top bunk and grabbing a spare hanger. She edged towards the window, tiptoeing closer, brandishing the hanger in her outstretched hand as a makeshift weapon.

The tapping came again.

Ottie leaped forward, flinging back the curtain with the hook of her hanger.

There, perched on the windowsill, was the seagull, *tap*, *tap*, *tapp*ing with its beak. Alice froze. It was the same bird from yesterday, she just knew it. It had come to find her.

"Shoo!" Ottie shouted, waving her arms. "Go away!"

The gull turned its head to look Alice straight in the eye then flew off, soaring in the direction of the cliffs.

"Gross," Ottie said. "We'll have to keep the windows shut. Mother says they carry loads of germs."

"Your mum's thinking of pigeons. Seagulls are actually really clever," Alice murmured, half to herself. "They trick worms into coming out by stamping their feet. It makes the worms think it's raining."

She had the distinct sense that this seagull was an especially clever one and that he was back because he had something to tell her. Something important. Alice was determined to find out what that something was.

"I just need to nip out," Alice said. "There's, er, something I need to ring Gran about . . ."

"Good luck asking Mrs Salter for permission!" Ottie laughed.

Alice raised her eyebrow. She was going to need all the luck in the world for what she had planned. "I won't be long," she promised, hoping she'd be back before the housemistress noticed she'd gone.

Alice ran downstairs and out of the boarding house into the large stone courtyard. Thankfully all the other Year Sevens were probably still unpacking so there was no one about. Now she just had to find the alley Ottie had pointed out. After a couple of minutes, Alice spotted a narrow path sandwiched between the boarding house and a red-brick wall.

Time to be brave, she told herself, taking a deep breath and ducking into the gloomy passageway. A few seconds later she was spat out on to a sandy path winding all the way to the cliffs and the steps down to School Bay.

She was going to find her seagull.

CHAPTER 4

The cliff steps were crooked and crumbling and with every hesitant step Alice had visions of tumbling all the way down to the jagged rocks below. *You must be mad*, she told herself. *Disappearing off on your own to talk to a seagull!* But there was something about the way the seagull had looked at her that made Alice sure he wanted her to go after him. She'd just have to be quick. If she didn't hurry up, Ottie might go looking for her and realise she hadn't gone to speak to her gran at all.

The tide was on its way in, the white-crested waves rushing to meet her as Alice clung to the rickety metal rail, the wind tugging at her uniform and whipping her plaits up into the air. The bottom steps were thick with seaweed.

Shoes or no shoes, she'd know she was treading on the damp green furls. She stopped where she was and picked at her elbow, unable to go any further. The seagulls wheeled and looped over the beach, squawking and screeching to one another, bickering over the fish swept in by the tide. It was impossible to tell one bird from another at this distance. How ever would she know which one was *her* seagull?

She'd come this far. If she was going to get thrown out of school on her first day she at least needed to make it worthwhile. She closed her eyes so she didn't have to look at the webbed tentacles of seaweed clinging to the steps ahead. Tightening her grip on the rail, Alice shuffled on down, her eyes squeezed shut. One step. Two steps. Three . . . Her foot skidded and she lurched forward, catching herself just in time.

Very slowly Alice opened her eyes. There on the rail sat the same seagull from earlier, his head cocked to one side. He opened his beak and spoke.

"You took a risk coming here today, Alice Tonks." Instead of squawks, Alice heard the voice of a traffic warden, fussy and officious.

The seagull beckoned her closer with his wing.

"Y-you can talk? You're a seagull and you can r-really talk to me?" Alice tried to calm her breathing. *In one, two, three. Out one, two, three.* That's what Gran had taught her to do when her nerves got the better of her but this wasn't like worrying about school or being in a crowded shopping centre. There was a real-life seagull talking to her and, what was more, she could understand every word!

"Of course I can!" the seagull blustered, clearly affronted. "You didn't actually think humans are the only ones who can talk, did you?"

Alice gulped. Maybe she really was going mad after all! But herring gulls have a much wider range of discernible calls than other species, she recalled. There was a section in her encyclopedia about their vocalisations: the soft baby talk they used with their chicks and the long, mewing sounds for mating. What if they were even more sophisticated than humans thought?

"W-what do you want with me?" she asked, her hands shaking. "It was y-you, wasn't it? At the window?"

"I had to warn you. It couldn't wait."

"Warn me?" Alice asked, her chest tight. "W-warn me about what?"

The seagull shifted uneasily from one webbed yellow foot to another. "It's not safe to talk here," he said, looking back over his shoulder and standing tall in the kind of defensive body stance Alice had seen in a nature documentary. "Anyone could see us." He edged closer. "We are living in perilous times."

"Perilous? Perilous how?" Alice's palms were sweaty and her pulse hammered. Magic wasn't always exciting, she remembered. It could be scary and dark and dangerous . . .

The gull swivelled his head, glancing nervously at the

other seagulls spiralling above them and the waves that were now lapping at the foot of the rocks. "I can't tell you much now. All you need to know is that my name is Agent T and I've been keeping an eye out for you. I came to find you earlier but that other girl was there, the one brandishing the hook . . . Strange things are happening in Pebblehampton. Keep your wits about you. Stay alert."

Alice's hands were scrunched into tight balls of anxiety. "Why? What's wrong?"

The bird flexed his wings as if he might have to fly away at any moment. "Animals are going missing."

"What do you mean 'missing'?" Alice asked.

"Disappearing. Vanishing. *Taken*." The gull's dark beady eyes fixed fiercely on her own. "Trust nobody. Do you hear me? Nobody at all."

Alice nodded, though her mind was spinning faster and faster like a fairground ride. Pebblehampton was a small, sleepy seaside town. Surely nothing bad could happen here?

She glanced back towards the school. Any minute now it would be time for dinner and Mrs Salter would begin getting the students to line up. She'd soon notice one was missing and it wouldn't take the housemistress long to work out who . . . Alice still had so many questions but she was running out of time. "Will I see you again?"

The bird nodded solemnly. "Of course. Us animals are very excited that you're here at Pebbles, Alice. Very excited, and very glad."

"When?" Alice demanded. "When will you come?"

"I can't say," the bird told her. "Keep your eyes open. My comrades or I will be in touch."

"But—" Alice said.

"Go!" the seagull insisted. "And remember what I said: *trust nobody*."

Reluctantly Alice turned. Clutching the rail, she climbed the steep steps back to school and then hurried up the path, the screeching of gulls echoing in her ears.

CHAPTER 5

Alice tumbled out of the alleyway and into the quad, her hands still shaking. She'd taken a big gamble, breaking the rules on her very first day. She glanced around in case anyone was watching but the courtyard was deserted. Alice smoothed down her uniform and straightened her boater. *Just act normal*, she told herself. *You were just going to find your housemistress, remember?*

Following the sound of excited chatter, Alice made her way through the stone archway and into the main corridor, her heart thumping in her chest as she slid into place beside Ottie at the back of the dinner queue.

"There you are!" Ottie cried, then lowered her voice so they weren't overheard. "You've been gone ages."

"Sorry," Alice said. "I, er, got a bit lost."

The queue lurched forward and Mrs Salter and Mr Marlowe came into view. They stood in the dining-room doorway, ticking off each student on a list as they entered for dinner. Alice's palms began to sweat. *Don't say anything, Ottie*, she silently begged.

"Ah, the stragglers." Mrs Salter said and narrowed her eyes as Ottie and Alice passed by. "Fifty-nine . . . and sixty. Better late than never, I suppose."

"Have a wonderful evening, sir, miss," Ottie said breezily, flashing the headmaster and housemistress a cheerful smile and steering Alice towards the servery. She handed Alice a wooden tray and as she leaned in close whispered, "Next time, tell me if you're sneaking off somewhere. I *love* adventures."

Alice's mouth fell open in shock. Had she really been that obvious? "H-how did you know?" she spluttered.

Ottie tapped her nose mysteriously. "Intuition! I've learned from the best."

Alice stared at her, awed.

"Not really!" Ottie giggled. "Look, you have sand on your shoes!"

Alice glanced down at her shiny black school shoes and sure enough they were encrusted with telltale grains of sand. "Oh," she said sheepishly. She stamped her feet.

"Don't worry, your secret's safe with me!" Ottie grinned.

Alice stood in line, waiting to be served, the delicious smell of apple crumble and custard wafting over. Her stomach rumbled loudly, making both her and Ottie giggle. *Maybe it really is true what people say about sea air*, Alice thought.

When they reached the servery, Ottie leaned into the kitchen, waving excitedly to a tall, dark-haired man in a chef's chat who was stirring a gigantic pot of mashed potato. "Hello, Felix!"

"Ottie!" the chef cried, waving his wooden spoon in greeting. "Good evening! And who have you brought to meet me tonight?"

"This is Alice Tonks. She's my dormie. Alice, meet Felix, chef extraordinaire."

"Err, hi," Alice said shyly. She couldn't believe Ottie was already on first-name terms with the school's chef. They'd only just arrived!

"Any friend of Miss Ottie is a friend of mine," the chef said, giving her a wink, before loading both their trays with dinner and a dessert. "Voilá! Bon appetit!"

Alice stared down at the neat rectangle of flaky pink flesh on her plate. *Ugh, fish!* A little knot of panic tangled itself in Alice's throat. Without Gran, who would trim the slimy grey underlayer from her salmon?

"Looks delicious, Felix," Ottie said briskly, yanking Alice away before she could say anything to the contrary. "You're the best!"

Alice's lip curled in horror at the lemony scent of the fish.

"Don't even *think* of complaining!" Ottie whispered as they weaved their way round the tables with their stiffly starched tablecloths and candelabra. "*Never* insult the chef."

"And you know him how . . .?" Alice asked.

"I make it my business to know all the staff," Ottie said as if it was obvious. "It's just good manners, really."

Alice shook her head in amazement. She'd never met another child as confident as Ottie. Boarding school really was turning out to be a whole new world.

Alice pulled out a velvet-padded chair opposite Ottie and sat down. She stared at the soft pink fish for a moment, revolted. Carefully, she manoeuvred the fish off her plate with her knife and wrapped it in a paper napkin, sliding it out of sight behind the salt and pepper. However hungry she was, nothing was going to make her touch that!

Ottie looked up. "Try the mash," she suggested. "It's divine."

Cautiously Alice used her fork to pick off a tiny lump of mashed potato and took a wary nibble. "Mmm," she said. "That's lovely." It was smooth and creamy, just like Gran's. Alice also approved of the way Felix had served the peas, carrot and sweetcorn separately, each in their own neat pile.

"Told you!" Ottie smiled. "There's school dinners . . . then there's Felix's meals."

Alice wolfed down her apple crumble and custard, thankful that the lump of hard, dry sponge that she'd grown to dread at primary school was nowhere in sight.

Ottie leaned in conspiratorially. "Midnight feast tonight," she whispered, her blue eyes sparkling. "I've got chocolate biscuits and crisps."

Alice froze. As much as she liked a chocolate Bourbons, she'd been hoping for an early night with *The Life and Times of Beatrix Potter* and the chance to make sense of her first day at boarding school. After all, it wasn't every day that a talking seagull tracked you down to tell you to be careful! *Perilous times*, Agent T had said. Now she was in the busy dining hall, the gull's message seemed ridiculous. She glanced around at all the other students chatting and munching contentedly. Why would anyone in a sleepy little seaside town like Pebblehampton want to steal animals?

Alice looked up to see Ottie staring at her with eager eyes. Her roommate was clearly expecting an answer. "Er . . ." she said, playing for time. In every boarding-school story she'd read, there'd been a midnight feast. Clearly you were supposed to be thrilled about the prospect of getting up in the middle of the night to eat a lifetime's worth of sugar by torchlight. "Sounds great." She flashed Ottie what she hoped was a convincing smile.

"It's going to be so much fun!" Ottie beamed back. "You know, we're really lucky our room is at the end of the corridor.

Much less chance of getting caught!" She lowered her voice. "Mrs Salter's just the sort of teacher to creep about outside our rooms, don't you think?"

Alice's dinner turned to rocks in her belly. She glanced over at the housemistress, now seated beside the headmaster on the top table, and remembered how Mrs Salter had been looking at her in the queue. Did she already suspect that Alice had broken the rules?

"Who's that boy over there?" Ottie said.

Alice followed Ottie's gaze to where Tim sat, two tables over, staring down at his cutlery morosely while the other boys laughed and joked. "Oh, that's Tim. I met him on Welcome Day."

"Hmm," Ottie said. "He doesn't look very happy." Her eyes lit up. "I know! Let's invite him along!"

"To the midnight feast?" Alice asked. "Boys aren't allowed on our floor. Mrs Salter said so."

Ottie laughed. "Not to our dormitory! You sneaking off earlier gave me an even better idea." She reached into her blazer pocket and retrieved a gel pen, quickly scribbling down a note on one of the paper napkins.

Alice squirmed, really not liking the sound of this.

Quick as a flash, Ottie was out of her seat and halfway across the dining hall. "Meet me in the corridor," she told Alice. "And don't be long!"

Alice groaned.

Ottie made a beeline to Tim's table and just as she passed

44

his seat, she tripped and stumbled. "Ow!" she cried, just loud enough to catch Mrs Salter's attention. "My leg!"

The students at the neighbouring tables turned round to look.

The housemistress looked up sharply, her eagle eyes scanning the room. "What's going on?" she snapped. "Why are you out of your seat, young lady?"

"Sorry, miss," Ottie moaned, clutching her right leg. "I must have tripped. May I go and see to my leg? I think I've grazed it."

Mrs Salter sighed. "Quickly, then!"

Ottie hobbled out of the dining hall. "Come on!" she mouthed to Alice, just before the doors swung shut behind her.

Alice sighed. She'd already had a really lucky escape getting back on to the school grounds earlier and the last thing she wanted was to get into trouble now. Perhaps she ought to just finish her meal in peace . . .

Across the dining hall, Tim caught her eye. Ottie was right, she realised: he did look thoroughly miserable. Suddenly she wanted to do something nice for him, like he had by bringing her ice cream on Welcome Day. But first she had to get out of the dining hall. From the way Mrs Salter had reacted to Ottie, Alice guessed getting up from the table wasn't encouraged and she didn't fancy a public telling-off. Then she had a brainwave. The kind of brainwave that meant being unnaturally brave. Alice took a deep breath and slowly raised her hand.

It took a lifetime for the housemistress to spot her but eventually she put down her cutlery with a roll of her eyes and beckoned Alice over. Alice felt all the blood in her body rush to her cheeks. The walk across the dining hall seemed to go on forever as one student after another paused eating to stare.

Cheeks glowing, Alice stood before the teachers' table and stretched up on tiptoe. Even though it made her feel all icky, she made sure to look Mrs Salter in her eye. Usually, eye contact was the kind of icky experience she tried to avoid but people always thought you meant something more if you were looking at them. People were weird. "Excuse me, Mrs S-Salter, but m-may I go to the toilet?"

Shooing Alice away with a flap of her hand, Mrs Salter continued her conversation with Mr Marlowe. Alice couldn't help but notice the headmaster appeared to be eating a totally different dinner to everyone else. A much fancier dinner. A dinner that came with wine and after-dinner mints.

Alice made a point of staring at Tim as she walked out of the room, her eyes boring into him. If he had any sense, he'd find a way to follow her.

As the doors closed behind her, Alice was certain Mrs Salter would come bursting through them any moment, bellowing at her to sit back down.

"Quick!" a voice urged. "Over here!" Ottie peeped out from behind a trophy cabinet.

Alice glanced over her shoulder then hurried to join her roommate.

"Well done!" Ottie said as if Alice had won a race. "I wasn't sure you'd make it. Do you think your friend will come?"

Alice shrugged, thinking of how sad and lonely Tim had looked at his table. "I hope so," she said, crouching down beside Ottie in the dimly lit corner.

The girls hid behind the glass cabinet for several long minutes. Alice's calves were beginning to cramp and she was about to give up and go back when she heard the sound of someone choking. Suddenly the dining-hall doors flew open and Tim burst out into the corridor, coughing and spluttering.

"Fish bone," he wheezed to the teacher holding the door open.

Just in the nick of time, Ottie yanked Alice down out of sight.

The teacher, an older man in a spotty waistcoat, frowned. "I think I'd better come with you," he said. "Make sure you get to the nurse."

"I'll . . . be all right with . . . some water . . ." Tim said between hacking coughs. "Really, sir . . . don't trouble yourself."

"All right, then," the teacher said, glancing back at his half-eaten pudding. "If you're sure." He retreated inside, the heavy wooden doors slamming shut behind him.

Alice got up to go and check on Tim but Ottie pulled her back down again. "Not yet," she whispered.

Poor Tim was still bent over almost double in a coughing fit but after a few seconds, he straightened up. "Okay," he said, his cough completely gone. "You can come out now."

CHAPTER 6

"I got your note." Tim waved the scribbled-on paper napkin.

"Hello," Ottie said, stepping out from behind the trophy cabinet and sticking out her hand. "Lovely to meet you. I'm Ottoline but you can call me Ottie."

"Tim," he said warily, looking over at Alice. "What's going on?"

"You looked a bit glum," Ottie said. "I've just the thing to cheer you up but we'll have to be quick about it."

"I'm not sure we should, Ottie." Alice glanced in the direction of the dining hall. "The teachers might come looking for us . . ."

"Nonsense! They've probably forgotten all about us by now. Didn't you see the wine on their table? As long as we get back to our dorms before lights out, we won't be missed in the common room." Ottie checked her watch. "An hour and a half's aaages!"

Tim and Alice exchanged worried looks.

"Don't worry," Ottie promised. "I'll get us back in plenty of time so long as we get a move on!" She sprinted off down the corridor, her patent-leather school shoes squeaking on the polished tiles.

Tim shrugged. "I'm in if you are?"

Alice chewed her lip. "All right," she said slowly.

Ottie led Tim and Alice on a mad dash out into the cool late-summer air of the quad and down the alley.

"I don't think this is a good idea," Alice mumbled but it was too late. Ottie hurtled out on to the sandy path but instead of turning right to the beach as Alice had done earlier she instead forked left, sprinting across the grassy clifftop.

The sky was fading to violet as the sun set over the sea. Along the coast, the last few fishing boats were heading back to the harbour before darkness closed in.

"How much further?" Alice puffed, not used to running on such uneven ground.

"Not far!" Ottie shouted back. She zigzagged past picnic benches and down winding paths until they were right at the edge of the cliff, staring down at the jet-black rocks and crashing surf of the bay. "We're here," she said, slowing to a halt. "What do you think?"

"Would you look at that?" Tim sighed, his eyes wide with awe.

A huge oak with great curving arms stood before them, its head almost up in the mist.

"And that's not the best bit," Ottie said. "Look!" She led them round to where the tree faced out to sea. Nimbly, she leaped from foothold to foothold, before climbing down the steep soil bank. She dusted the earth from her hands and pushed back tall grasses to reveal a hollow in the base of the tree. "It's a den!"

"Cool!" Tim cried as he watched Ottie crouch down low and crawl inside.

"I'm going after her," he told Alice, scooting down the earthen slope on his bottom. He clambered over the oak's thick, gnarly roots, nowhere near as light-footed and catlike as Ottie, then squeezed through the hole in the trunk, disappearing from view.

"Hold on!" Alice eyed the steep bank with its thick tufts of grass warily. She was never going to make it down in one piece. "Wait for me!"

"Alice, you've got to see this!" Ottie called up, her voice echoey and distant.

Alice edged closer to the bank. There was only one thing for it. She unbuckled the stiff new school shoes Gran had bought and pulled off her socks. Gripping the thick, rope-like roots for purchase, she manoeuvred herself down towards the oak. Just when she thought she'd done it, she lost her footing and slid the final couple of feet, bumping to a halt against the thick trunk. "Ow!"

In the thinning light, Alice looked down at her brand-new blazer, now streaked with dirt, and thanked her lucky stars that Gran wasn't here to see it. *What am I doing?* she wondered, shaking her head. But as she got to her feet, she swelled with pride. She'd done it. She'd made it down.

Pushing her way through the undergrowth, Alice wriggled through the hole, the smell of earth and dry leaves filling her nostrils and making her cough. The hole opened up into a small, wooden chamber, wider and taller than it seemed from the outside, yet small enough that her nose almost collided with Tim's knees.

He was sat on the mossy ground, his legs drawn up under his chin. Beside him stood Ottie, who was squirrelling through a blue-and-white-striped carrier bag. "Here!" she said, tossing Tim and Alice a bag of sweets each.

"This is awesome," Tim nodded, helping himself to a handful of sweets. "How did you find it?"

"I got here earlier than everyone else this morning," Ottie said. "I was bored." Alice noticed her look away quickly, the way Alice did whenever she wasn't quite comfortable.

Tim wriggled a little, rearranging his legs. "Thanks," he mumbled. "You know, for inviting me . . ."

Ottie smiled. "We couldn't leave you looking miserable. What was the matter, anyway?"

"Oh," Tim said quickly. "I was just a bit homesick. You know how it is."

Alice glanced from one of her new friends to the other. Something told her neither of them were quite telling the truth.

"It's really cool, Ottie," she said, unwrapping a sweet. "Thanks for showing us. We should probably get back to the boarding house, though. It'll be lights out soon."

Ottie sighed, deflated. "I suppose you're right."

"But we can come back another time?" Tim said enthusiastically. "Can't we?"

"Of course!" Ottie beamed at him. "It can be our secret. Right, Alice?"

Alice nodded. "Right."

"I'll hide some tuck here," Ottie said, wedging the carrier bag back into a little nook. "But mine has almost all gone now. Can you both try and bring something next time?"

Alice and Tim nodded. "Yeah, sure," Tim said. "My mum sent enough to feed the five thousand!" He rolled his eyes. "I think she reckons I'll waste away otherwise!"

As they wriggled back through the hole, one after another, Alice felt giddy with happiness. She'd been dreading starting at Pebbles but perhaps Gran had been right after all. Being here was an amazing opportunity. She was just clambering to her feet, thinking about how good it felt to have friends at last, when a strange voice – an adult man's voice – shouted, "Is that the lot, Jim?"

Alice gasped and Tim grabbed her arm, pulling her down into the undergrowth.

Ottie put her finger to her lips. "Shh," she hissed. Slowly and very, very quietly she began to climb up the bank, keeping low to the ground. Peeping over the top, she beckoned to Tim and Alice.

Tim pulled himself up by the tree roots and slipped into place beside Ottie but as he did, his foot brushed a clod of loose earth and sent it rolling down the bank. Alice's breath caught in her throat. What if the men heard? Without thinking, she shot out her leg and the clump of soil rolled to a halt against her foot.

"Phew!" Tim mouthed.

"What was that?" the man's voice called sharply.

Alice froze, her skin prickling.

A second man said something in reply but his words were lost over the sound of breaking waves.

"Let's get out of here!" the first voice said. An engine suddenly choked into life and began to chug rhythmically.

"Alice," Tim hissed. "Come and see this." He helped her haul herself up to crouch beside them.

Over the cliff edge, Alice could make out a light down in the depths of the cove. Holding her hands up to shield her eyes from the glare, she peered down over the cliff. A small boat was cutting through the waves away from School Bay. Two men were standing at the prow, their collars turned up against the wind, facing out to sea.

"Gosh!" Ottie breathed, her eyes growing large. "What do you think they're up to?"

"Maybe they're smugglers?" Tim whispered back excitedly. "Look!"

His outstretched finger pointed to the rear of the deck where a tarpaulin covered something big and bulky . . .

Alice gulped, the taste of bile bitter in her mouth as she remembered the seagull saying animals were going missing in Pebblehampton. What if these men were *animal* smugglers?

CHAPTER 7

In the middle of the night, Alice awoke screaming. A strange figure was watching her from the darkness of the dormitory.

"What is it? What's wrong?" Ottie shot upright, bumping her head on the eaves before leaping down from her bunk. There was a thud as she landed on the rug.

"There's someone in our room!" Alice whispered. With a trembling hand, she pointed to the person crouched just in front of the closed door. "Can't you see him?"

Ottie squinted into the darkness. "Alice," she groaned. "There's no one there!"

"No, look!" Alice squeaked, cowering beneath her bed sheets. Her dreams had been full of shadowy boats slicing through black water. "It's one of the men from the bay!"

"That's just my dressing gown!" Ottie laughed. She gave the 'man' a kick and he slumped to the floor. "Try not to worry so much."

Ottie climbed back into her bunk. Before long, her breathing deepened as she drifted back to sleep.

Alice listened to the quiet rattling of the bed frame and to the creak and groan of the landing floorboards. Her fingers clutched the sheets in panic each time footsteps passed the dormitory door and her lungs ached from holding her breath. *It's only Mrs Salter, checking everyone's in bed*, Alice told herself. But she longed to be back at Foxden with Gran snoring in the room next door.

The next morning, Alice woke up early. She was full of jitters, her eyes itchy and red. Ottie was still sound asleep so Alice pulled on her uniform in the semi-darkness of the dormitory, grabbed her schoolbag and went to splash water on her face in the huge, echoey bathroom at the end of the corridor. Her reflection in the mirror looked drawn and pale but there was someone she had to find. It couldn't wait.

Out in the quad, a thin grey mist had settled like cobwebs over the benches and flowerpots. Two jet-black crows eyed her watchfully as she ran past the boarding house, continuing until she saw the domed roof of the school hall rising before her. Alice slowed as the stained-glass window came into view. It wasn't as good as the beach but she couldn't risk that again.

The window had to be at least a little bit magical, didn't it? She'd seen it move yesterday just before the gull had come to talk to her, after all. Maybe if she waited beneath it, Agent T would somehow know she was looking for him.

"Agent T?" she whispered. "Are you here?"

The wind whistled through the trees but no seagull appeared.

"Agent T!" she called, a little louder this time. "It's me, Alice. I need to talk to you."

The sun was a red ink spill, spreading across the sky. "Come on . . ." she muttered impatiently. "I've got something to tell you. Something important."

Four pairs of eyes stared down at her from the stained-glass window, warning her not to be too loud. Alice's fingers flicked restlessly at her side.

The tower's clock ticked as the hare raced closer to seven. The other students would be waking soon. "Agent T?" she tried one last time. "Please come and talk to me!"

She stood on tiptoe, peering up at the great glass dome of the school hall and the grey tiles of the roofs beyond. Her heart sank. It was no good. He wasn't coming and she had no way of warning him about the men she'd seen in the boat. Alice turned and ran back to the boarding house, unease swelling in her belly like waves gathering before a storm.

"Morning," Alice mumbled, hurrying across the crowded dining hall and dropping into a spare seat between Tim and Ottie.

"Take this," Tim said, handing Alice a rather squished pain au chocolat. His own plate was piled with hash browns, bacon, sausages, fried eggs and French toast. "You look like you need it."

"Thanks," Alice said, taking a giant bite out of the sugary pastry. "I didn't get much sleep."

"You can say that again!" Ottie said, topping up her glass with fresh orange juice from one of the jugs on the table. "You . . ."

Alice widened her eyes, pleading with Ottie to stop talking. She already felt like such a baby, still being scared of the dark.

". . . Disappeared this morning," Ottie corrected herself, giving Alice a discreet nod while Tim was focused on pouring himself a mug of hot chocolate.

"Oh, where did you go?" Tim asked through a mouthful of bacon and egg.

Alice's throat tightened. What excuse could she give this time? She could hardly tell them she'd gone to find a talking seagull! "I, er, just needed some fresh air." She smiled sheepishly. "Nerves, you know? I get a bit . . . jumpy."

"I get it." Tim nodded sagely. "My mum's the same."

Ottie fiddled with her place mat and glanced at Tim. For the first time since Alice had met her, she seemed

59

almost . . . nervous. "Look, Alice," she said. "Tim and I were talking before you got here. You seemed pretty shaken up last night. If you're really worried, we can tell an adult, if you like. I know we'd get into trouble for being off site but—"

"No!" Alice interrupted, almost choking on her pastry. Agent T had told her that she should *trust no one* and the teachers were most definitely *someone*. "I mean, let's just keep an eye out ourselves for now," she added quickly. "No one's going to take us seriously, anyway. We're just kids."

"Fair point," Tim said, dunking his sausage in ketchup and munching it thoughtfully. "At the end of the day, what did we actually see? Two men on a boat? It's hardly the crime of the century."

You wouldn't be saying that if you knew there's an animal thief on the loose, Alice thought. She couldn't shake the feeling that the men had something to do with the seagull's warning. *Be careful. Keep your wits about you. Stay alert.*

"We should go back to your tree soon, Ottie," Tim whispered. "It'd make a really cool hideout." He took a long slurp of hot chocolate.

Just then, two girls walked by, arm in arm. Alice recognised the taller of the two as the red-haired girl who had asked Mrs Salter about the cookies on the first day. She knocked hard into Tim, sending his hot chocolate splashing all over his bright white school shirt. Instead of stopping and apologising, the girls just smirked at one another and kept walking.

"Hey!" Alice shouted, pushing back her chair and standing up. "Aren't you going to say sorry?"

The redhead paused, her eyebrow cocked indignantly. "Is she talking to us?"

"It's all right, Alice," Tim said quickly, tugging her back down into her seat. "It doesn't matter."

"But your shirt . . ."

"I said it doesn't matter!"

Alice shrank back in her chair and an awkward silence settled over the breakfast table.

"Here, use these," Ottie said, sliding a wodge of paper napkins across the table to Tim.

"Thanks," Tim said, forcing a somewhat watery smile. "And sorry, Alice, I didn't mean to snap."

"S'okay." Alice shrugged. "Do you know them or something?"

"They were at my last school." Tim pushed his half-eaten breakfast away. "Kelcie Maloney and Lexi Khan."

"Ah," Alice said. She knew a bit about not-so-friendly classmates and figured Tim might appreciate a change of subject. She leaned forward across the table. "About that boat we saw . . . Do either of you know if there's a lot of fishing off School Bay?"

"I don't think so," Ottie started to say. "Boats don't usually come so—"

Suddenly the shuddering clang of the school bell rang out across the dining hall and chaos descended.

"Chop-chop, everyone!" Mrs Salter's voice trilled. "Straight to period one lessons! Don't be late!"

Alice blanched. "I don't where I'm meant to be going!" She rifled through her blazer pockets. "My timetable! It's gone."

"It's all right," Ottie said calmly, retrieving a plastic wallet from her rucksack and checking her own timetable. "We've got geography. Room twenty-three."

"Twenty-three?" Tim said, fishing a scrap of paper out of his blazer pocket. He unfolded it carefully. "Just a sec . . ."

Ottie peered over his shoulder at the hand-drawn map. "Where'd you get that?"

"Made it myself last night before dinner," he said, tracing the scribbles and arrows with a finger. "I like knowing where everything is."

"I could do with one of those," Ottie admitted. "I only bothered learning where the exciting stuff is!"

"Come on," Tim instructed, giving the map a satisfied tap. "It's this way." He strode off down the corridor looking more like an intrepid explorer embarking on an expedition than a new student on his first day of school. "I know exactly where we're going."

"I suppose we'd better go after him!" Ottie laughed.

Alice nodded, grateful that at least one of them had a clue how to find their classroom. The school was a sprawling maze of wood-panelled corridors and tightly looping spiral staircases. The two girls had their work cut out keeping up as

Tim marched down corridors and up flights of winding stairs, leading them past ancient statues, suits of armour and old wooden trunks crammed full of lacrosse nets and hockey sticks.

"Slow down!" Alice panted. She'd never learn her way around at this speed! Then again, nothing was worse than arriving at class when everyone else was already sat down and staring at you . . .

Tim turned one final corner and skidded to a halt outside a blue door. "Ta-da!" he said, checking his map one final time. "Room twenty-three. Told you I'd get us here in time!"

Alice looked around. They were in a long, narrow corridor lined with black-and-white photographs of students from long ago. She stared at the serious faces of the smartly dressed young people. One of those faces must belong to Gran, she realised, and that meant somewhere along the corridor there'd be a tiny, smiling picture of her mum. She walked over, wondering if she'd recognise her mum as a girl.

Just then, a throng of Year Seven students came charging down the corridor, shouting to one another, "Is this it?" and "Hope we're not late!" Alice sighed and returned to join Tim and Ottie just as the classroom door flew open.

"Good morning, good morning!" cried an old man in a tweed suit and bright yellow bow tie, a model globe in his hands. His blue eyes sparkled as he took in the huddle of Year Sevens. "Welcome to geography! My name is Professor Biddle."

Slowly the students fell quiet and as they organised themselves into something loosely resembling a line, Alice peered round the teacher into the cluttered classroom beyond. An array of brightly coloured flags fluttered from the rafters. What looked like a lifetime's collection of *National Geographic* magazines stood neatly stacked upon the wonky shelves beside papier-mâché volcanoes and tiny animal skulls, bone-white and hollow-eyed. They stared back at her, their teeth still sharp and jagged. Had the one at the front belonged to a weasel or a stoat?

"Don't stand there catching flies!" Professor Biddle grinned, herding the class inside. "Come in and discover the wonders of the world!" He spun the model globe he was clutching with a dramatic flourish.

As the students began to file into the room, the professor peered at Alice. "Now there's a face I recognise! You, young lady, are a Tonks, if I'm not mistaken? Alison, isn't it?"

"Alice," she mumbled, blood rushing to her cheeks.

"Now the last time I saw you must have been when your pram was running away down the high street towards the harbour!" the professor wheezed. "Your poor gran was in such a state. Luckily I heard her screams and caught you just in the nick of time before you tumbled in, pram and all! You were none the wiser, thankfully."

Alice cringed. She had heard the story of her runaway pram a thousand times. It was a family favourite but she couldn't recall Gran ever mentioning that it had been the geography teacher who'd saved her from a dip in the sea. "Nice to meet you, professor," she said, pulling Tim and Ottie towards an empty table before her cheeks could get any redder.

As they took their seats, Kelcie and Lexi burst into the classroom in a fit of giggles. Tim slunk down in his chair as they barged their way to the back row.

"Sorry we're late!" Lexi said with a toss of her glossy dark hair, but it didn't sound like she meant it.

"Settle down, now!" the professor said, handing each student a scarlet exercise book.

Alice carefully opened hers, giving the front cover a nice stiff, crisp fold. She breathed in deeply. There was nothing better than the smell of new paper.

"We'll be starting the year with a spot of mapwork," the professor told them. He hobbled down the rows, giving each student a magnifying glass and a dog-eared Ordinance Survey map before turning on the dusty overhead projector stationed beside his desk. Slowly the machine whirred into life. "This here is Pebblehampton," he said, pointing with a long wooden stick to the flickering map now projected on the wall. "Here's the school. The woods. That's School Bay and the beach. Just down the coast we find Pebblehampton harbour . . ."

Alice glanced at Tim. He was staring up at the map, his face a picture of concentration.

"I want you to use your own maps to find these landmarks

and record their coordinates." The professor chalked up an example on the old-fashioned blackboard so they could all see how it was done.

Alice reached for her map and unfolded it carefully but Tim was already peering at his through a magnifying glass, totally engrossed. "The cliffs!" he whispered, tracing a line along the beach with his finger.

Just then there was a sharp knock. Before Professor Biddle had a chance to respond, the door opened and Mr Marlowe stepped into the room. A hush fell immediately over the class.

"Ottoline, a word," the headmaster said, tapping his foot impatiently. As an afterthought, he nodded curtly in Professor Biddle's general direction. "If you don't mind, that is, professor."

Ottie got to her feet and hurried out of the room, twenty pairs of eyes watching her every step. The door clicked shut behind her and the class immediately descended into excited chatter.

Tim turned to Alice. "What was that all about?"

"No idea," Alice said. "You don't think it could be about last night, do you?"

Before Tim could reply, Kelcie's smug, sing-song voice drifted across the classroom. "Ottie's Mr Marlowe's niece," she announced. "Her full name's Ottoline Miranda Marlowe. Apparently the Marlowe family are filthy rich. I read about them in *Star!* magazine."

"Filthy rich *and* filthy gorgeous!" Lexi giggled. "My mum thinks the headmaster's a proper hottie. She kept going all red whenever he passed by on Welcome Day!"

"Yuck," Tim said, pulling a face like he'd just stepped barefoot on a slug.

Of course! Alice thought. Suddenly it made sense that Ottie was already friendly with Felix the chef.

"Did you know he was her uncle?" Tim asked.

Alice shook her head. "No," she admitted, giving her elbow a scratch. "Ottie didn't tell me." She felt a bit deflated. Why hadn't Ottie mentioned that she was Mr Marlowe's niece? They were meant to be dormies.

"For what it's worth, I don't envy Ottie much," Tim whispered. "I wouldn't want Mr Marlowe for an uncle. He's seriously smarmy!"

As Alice and Tim went back to their work, fragments of conversation drifted over to their desk.

"It's just such a shame that Ottie has to share a dorm with *her*," Kelcie told the group of girls sat round her table. "She's so weird."

Alice froze, humiliation crawling all over her like a colony of red ants.

"Talk about bad luck," Lexi agreed. "Poor Ottie."

A lump rose in Alice's throat. It was just like primary school all over again. She'd known this was going to happen! It never took other kids long to start saying she was weird. She stared straight ahead. *Don't cry. Don't cry.*

67

"Don't let them know they've got to you," Tim whispered before raising his voice unusually loud. "I've got that map reference for the church when you're ready, Alice." His voice carried across the classroom.

Alice blinked. "Sorry, what?"

"That map reference you wanted," he repeated, giving her a nudge. "For the church, remember?"

Out of the corner of her eye, Alice saw Kelcie and Lexi look up. "Oh yeah," she said, catching on in time to feign a casual, carefree tone. "Thanks." With a trembling hand, she wrote down the coordinates as Tim read them out.

When the class had lost interest and turned back to their work, Tim flashed her his lopsided smile. "Friends, right?"

Alice smiled. "Friends."

CHAPTER 8

"What do you think her uncle said to her?" Tim pondered, chewing the eraser on his pencil.

It was their last lesson of the day and their English teacher, Mr Whadworth, a young man with a nervous cough, was pretending not to notice the chatter that had erupted across his classroom in the final few minutes of class. They were supposed to be studying nature poetry but almost no one was.

"Dunno," Alice said, staring at the back of her dormie's head and wondering if she ought to try to get Ottie's attention. "Maybe he just told her she needs to get good grades or something. Whatever it was, she doesn't seem herself."

Although Ottie had reappeared towards the end of geography, she hadn't said anything to Tim or Alice about what Mr Marlowe had wanted with her. And for the rest of the afternoon's lessons she had sat alone at the front of the class. Alice watched her roommate studiously taking notes in her elegant, looping handwriting, her blond waves of hair shielding her face from view.

"Apparently the Marlowe mansion has an indoor and an outdoor swimming pool," Kelcie told the gaggle of girls sat round her table. "*And* a cinema room."

"I've heard they don't just have one chauffeur," Lexi added, "but two." She closed her eyes dreamily. "Imagine having two chauffeurs to drive you wherever you wanted!"

Tim looked at the girls as if they'd just said they liked to roll around in horse manure. "Imagine being as shallow as the Gruesome Twosome!" he scoffed.

"Good name!" Alice commented. "Why does it matter who her uncle is, anyway? Ottie can't help who her family are."

The bell rang, its shrill clang making Alice shudder. As soon as Mr Whadworth said they were dismissed, Ottie got up, pushed in her chair and headed out of the door, her head held high. Like the surface of the school boating lake, her face was a picture of calm. It was like she hadn't even heard the other girls talking about her.

"You think we should go after her?" Tim said.

Alice thought about it. "No," she concluded after a moment. "Maybe she wants some space. Fancy heading to the common room? I've heard Felix puts cakes and biscuits out for teatime."

"Can't, sorry," Tim said, throwing everything into his bag. "Got to sign up for the band. Catch you later, though, yeah?" He was already halfway out of the door.

"Oh," Alice said, taken aback. She tried to rearrange her face into something resembling a smile. "See you around."

She watched Tim saunter away down the corridor, his long, lolloping strides setting him apart from the other Year Sevens. Sighing, Alice looked down at the blank pages of her exercise book. Here she was, alone again.

"Everything okay, Alice?" Mr Whadworth asked.

Alice nodded quickly. "Everything's fine, sir." She picked up her things and traipsed back to the boarding house but as she got close she heard the buzz of hungry students swarming around the trays of cake. What she needed was a bit of peace and quiet. She decided to go for a walk around the school instead.

Each stretch of corridor looked the same as the last and Alice paused by the trophy cabinet outside the dining hall, afraid of getting lost. On the opposite wall was a large oil painting of a pink shell. A conch, Gran had called it, and Alice remembered her saying once that if you held one to your ear, you could hear the sea trapped inside, like a memory. She scratched at her elbow, unable to get any relief from the constant itch. Once again, she wished she was back at Foxden. There'd be a plate of

Gran's flapjacks on the table by now. Hot chocolate too. And Roger would be at her feet, sniffing hungrily in the hope of some crumbs. Maybe she should have popped into the common room for some of Felix's cakes after all . . .

Alice drifted over to one of the corridor's tall glass windows and watched the hare on the tower's clock face. Yesterday, she'd barely had time to say goodbye to Gran and now the clock seemed to be teasing her, crawling so slowly she was surprised it didn't stop altogether. She wondered what Tim and Ottie were up to and how she'd fill the gaping void of time before dinner.

Then Alice saw it. A narrow wooden sign. A single word. 'Library'.

Her heart soared. Libraries were her favourite places in the whole wide world. She'd whiled away many happy hours at the village library with Gran, picking out stacks of beautiful books. Forgetting for a moment how lonely she felt, she rushed forward. So what if she didn't know her way around the school yet? She couldn't get lost when there were signs to follow!

Alice followed the arrow round a corner and down a long corridor, finding herself outside a wooden door, with three glass panes exactly at her eye level. She pushed her face up against the glass. Books. Rows upon rows of books. She gave the door a nudge and it swung open, welcoming her in.

Wooden beams stretched up into the eaves of the roof, giving the library a light and airy feel. Tall windows flooded the room with a balmy glow. Best of all the room was empty. Alice passed a row of cubicles and clusters of tables set aside for group study, and approached the first of several shelves full of novels. She picked up *Little Women*, one of her gran's favourites, from the section labelled 'A', then drifted over to a circle of mismatched armchairs that filled one corner.

Alice sat down in a navy-blue chair and found herself sinking into its plump arms. She opened *Little Women* and there was Jo, lying on the rug, complaining it wouldn't be Christmas without any presents. Suddenly she was back at Foxden, listening to Gran read aloud to her, wrapped up snug in her fleece blanket . . .

"Whatever do you think you're doing?" a droll voice said.

Alice jumped up from the chair. "I was just . . ." she started to explain but there was no one there. She looked about for the prickly, strict teacher the voice belonged to but the room was empty, its door firmly shut.

"Down here!" the voice said.

A silver-grey tabby cat sauntered into view. She stretched, her long, sleek belly dragging on the floor, as if waking from a deep and wonderful sleep, before her amber eyes pinned Alice to the spot. "Has no one ever told you it's terribly rude to stare?"

Alice closed her eyes and opened them again. The cat was still there. Her skin tingled. It was happening again. So it wasn't just the seagull she could talk to . . . Her imagination began to race. Could Agent T have sent this cat to speak to her?

The cat tapped her paw impatiently. "Cat got your tongue?"

"Oh, er, I'm sorry . . . I . . ."

"Just thought you could help yourself to my favourite chair, did you?" the cat said. "I know. I saw." She licked her paws and set about washing her elegant stripey face.

"I just thought I'd read for a bit." Alice couldn't believe she was explaining herself to a cat.

"Hmm, yes. That happens. You'd be surprised who wanders in here when they think they have the place to themselves." She jumped neatly up on to the arm of the chair Alice had been sitting in and butted nosily at the book she'd just been reading. "Hmm. Alcott. Good choice."

Alice tried to build up the courage to speak. "E-e-excuse me?" she ventured after a moment or two. "Miss Cat?"

The cat laughed, a dry, mocking laugh. "Miss Cat, is it?" she said, one furry black eyebrow arched. "My name, I think you'll find, is Constance."

"Oh," Alice said, feeling foolish. "Well, Constance, then, I was just wondering . . . did a seagull send you?"

"A seagull? Send *me*, a cat?" The cat swished her tail. "Certainly not! Know many cats who are friends with birds, do you?"

"No," Alice mumbled, feeling even more foolish.

"Exactly." The tabby jumped nimbly down into the seat of the chair and walked in a tight circle once, twice, three times before settling herself so that her head was tucked beside her tail. "Now if there's nothing pressing, I am overdue a sleep."

Was Alice imagining things or did the cat seem to want to change the subject? Maybe she did know the gull after all! Smiling to herself, Alice turned to go.

"Ahem." The tabby gave a short cough that was quite uncattish in tone and manner. She flicked her tail casually in the direction of *Little Women*, which still lay open on the arm of the chair. She then tucked her front paws under her head and shut her eyes.

"Sorry!" Alice snatched up the book. She hurried back to the shelf to slot it back in its place and was on her way to the door when she stopped and turned back. Constance was proud, that much was obvious, and proud people tended to like flattery. Maybe animals did too? Alice decided she had nothing to lose. "It was very silly of me to think a mere bird could have sent a cat like you. But I was wondering, if you do happen to see a gull – a very talkative kind of gull – do you think you might be able to pass on a message?"

"A message, hmm?" The cat did not open her eyes. "I suppose that would depend on what type of message it was."

Alice thought carefully. "Perhaps . . . perhaps you could tell the gull that he was right about what he told me . . . and that . . . that I'm worried too."

One eyelid opened. One amber eye looked at Alice. "Yes," the cat said. "I think I can do that." Then the eye closed again.

CHAPTER 9

"Oh, here you are!" Alice cried when she finally tracked Tim and Ottie down in the common room that evening. "I've been looking for you everywhere. Why weren't you at dinner?" She'd been looking forward to telling them about the library cat – even if she did have to gloss over the tiny detail of Constance talking! But instead she'd ended up eating alone.

"Oh, hi," Ottie said, barely looking up from the notebook she was scribbling in.

Tim was slumped beside her on one of the giant beanbags, his headphones on and the volume turned up loud. Spotting Alice, he switched off his music and pushed his headphones down so they hung around his neck. "Wasn't hungry," he mumbled.

"Okayyy," Alice said, raising a sceptical eyebrow. Tim could eat for Britain. She switched her attention to Ottie, waiting for an answer.

Ottie pressed so hard on her pink sparkly gel pen, Alice was surprised the nib didn't buckle. "Uncle Hugo wanted to talk to me again. You know what families are like." She rolled her eyes.

No, Alice wanted to say. *I don't.* The only family she'd ever had was Gran, and Gran was one of the most straightforward people she knew. It was why Alice liked her so much.

"Well, I went to the library earlier—" she started to tell them.

"Sorry, Alice," Ottie interrupted, getting to her feet. "I think I'm going to have an early night. Why don't you tell me all about it tomorrow?"

Alice shrugged, disappointed. "Sure."

Ottie smiled but Alice could tell it wasn't a real one. Her eyes had no sparkle at all.

"See you both in the morning," Ottie said, picking up her notebook and heading out of the common room.

Alice stared after her. What had Mr Marlowe said to put her in such a bad mood?

"I'd better turn in too." Tim yawned. "I said I'd meet the professor before school and have a look at some more of his maps. They're pretty cool, you know. He's got loads. Some are really old too."

"Fascinating," Alice said flatly. "Night, then."

"Night," Tim said, trudging off upstairs.

Alice watched him leave. *Never mind*, she told herself, *who needs human friends when you have talking animals?* It felt good having a secret that was all her own.

When Alice woke up the following morning, the dormitory was still and quiet.

"Morning, Ottie!" Alice called up to the top bunk as she reached out to switch off her alarm.

Silence. Not even the sound of snoring.

Alice sat up in bed and tried again. "Ottie?"

Nothing.

The hanger on Ottie's wardrobe was empty, her uniform gone, and her roommate's schoolbag had also vanished from the chair by the desk. Where was Ottie this early in the morning?

Suddenly, Alice remembered her encounter with the tabby cat in the library and shot out of bed. Bouncing from foot to foot, she grabbed her uniform from the wardrobe and quickly got dressed. Yesterday, Constance had said she didn't know Agent T but from the hasty way she'd answered, Alice was pretty sure she'd been lying. If she hurried, she might be able to find the cat before breakfast.

A few minutes later, Alice shoved open the library door and was met by glorious silence. There was no one in sight so she rushed straight over to the circle of comfy armchairs and began looking for the cat. The tabby wasn't in her favourite navy-blue chair, nor underneath it. Alice started hunting under the bookshelves and along the sun-drenched windowsills. Constance had to be here somewhere . . .

"Here, kitty, kitty," she murmured.

Behind her, somebody coughed. Alice spun round.

"Can I help you?" A librarian with a pen poking through her dark bun stared at her from over the top of a returns trolley.

"Oh . . ." Alice faltered. Her eyes swept the library for inspiration. "I'm looking for a . . . book." She cringed. She really was a rubbish liar.

The librarian raised an eyebrow. "Well," she chortled. "You've come to the right place!"

Alice felt her cheeks glow.

"Don't worry," the librarian said kindly. "I'm just the same. I can't bear not having a book to read. Anything in particular you're looking for?"

"Animals," Alice blurted out. "Anything on animals."

"Ooh." The librarian's warm smile reached all the way to her big brown eyes behind their thick-rimmed glasses. "An animal fan. Follow me." She walked straight over to the non-fiction section. Alice took the opportunity to peep below the bookshelves in case the cat was hiding there but then she hurried after the librarian, afraid she'd give the game away if she was too obvious.

"Here you go," the librarian said, pointing to a huge bookcase labelled 'Nature'.

Alice's eyes widened. From thick encyclopaedias to small field guides on British species, there were enough books to keep her going for months, maybe even years. The village library back home had a much smaller selection. She couldn't wait to get stuck in. Alice scanned the shelves and spotted a title she hadn't read before about her all-time favourite naturalist, Beatrix Potter.

"Ooh, good choice!" The librarian smiled as Alice reached for the book. She rummaged in the pockets of her baggy green cardigan and retrieved a rather crumpled rectangle of card. "Fill that in and bring it to the checkout desk when you're ready to go. We'll have you signed up for a library card in no time!"

"Thanks." Alice liked the librarian already.

"New here?"

Alice nodded.

"Me too – well, sort of!" She stretched out an ink-stained hand, her chipped nails painted green to match her cardigan. "Miss Ada Jessops at your service. School librarian."

"It's nice to meet you," Alice said, and she meant it. Miss Jessops seemed like her kind of person. "What did you mean when you said you're 'sort of' new? Surely you either are or you aren't?"

Miss Jessops smiled. "You'd think so, wouldn't you? I'm kind of a funny case. I've only just started working here but I came here a few times when I was a girl."

"Oh, did you have family at the school?" Alice asked.

"I suppose you could say that!" Two pink spots appeared on Miss Jessops' cheeks. "My great-grandfather was Pebbles' very first headmaster."

Alice gasped. "Your granddad was the school's founder?" She'd seen his portrait hanging in the atrium on her first day.

Miss Jessops nodded. "Well, great-granddad. Sir Rudyard Jessops. I like to think he'd be proud I've come back to work here after all these years."

"Were you a student, then?"

"Oh no!" Miss Jessops laughed. "But the old place is in the blood. I couldn't resist the chance to make the library my own. How are you settling in? Have you had much of a chance to look around the town yet?"

Alice shrugged, remembering ice creams by the harbour and fish and chips in greasy wraps. "A bit. My gran used to bring me here on holiday when I was younger. She went to school at Pebbles too, and so did my mum." Alice smiled shyly. "I'm Alice, by the way. Alice Tonks."

"Well, Alice," Miss Jessops said, checking her watch. "I don't suppose you'd care to join me for a little spot of pre-breakfast?"

"Pre-breakfast?" Alice asked. "What's that?"

"You don't know pre-breakfast?" the librarian gasped. "Why it's the most important meal of the day!"

Alice laughed. Pre-breakfast did sound good but she had really hoped Constance might have some news. She glanced back at the navy armchair but it was still empty. If she searched for the cat again now, the librarian was bound to notice, plus her tummy was beginning to rumble . . .

"So what do you say?" Miss Jessops prompted. "Got time for a hot chocolate with a fellow book lover?"

Alice smiled. "Sure."

Alice followed Miss Jessops over to the library counter and waited while the librarian lifted the hatch. In the poky space behind the counter were two wheelie chairs, a mountain of rather shabby old books and a navy door. "Poor things," the librarian sighed, giving the books a gentle stroke in the way someone might pet a very old and senile dog. "I'm having to get rid of this lot. They've been rather neglected."

Alice had a quick glance at the titles in case there were any she recognised but they were all old tomes about South American countries and not anything she'd be interested in. No wonder Miss Jessops was throwing them out.

"Come in, come in!" the librarian called. "Never mind the mess."

She pushed open the wooden door and Alice was immediately struck by the stench of damp vegetation. The smell remined her of greenhouses and it was no wonder because Miss Jessops' desk was completely consumed by indoor plants. The green vines were so overgrown that they had started to trail across the floor and up the walls. Alice gasped to see the thick creepers coiled around the telephone and hole punch, but the librarian was completely oblivious.

"Drink?" she offered, opening the lid on a little red-and-gold tin and releasing the rich, chocolatey aroma of cocoa into the air.

Tucked between two tendrils was an electric kettle, and the librarian insisted on boiling it and making them both a mug before retrieving a tin of biscuits from the top drawer of her desk. "What'll it be?"

Alice chose two jammy biscuits to dip in her frothy hot chocolate while Miss Jessops flicked through a huge book cataloguing wild plants, one finger drumming on the desk. Alice peered over her shoulder at the elaborate black-and-white diagrams and the long Latin names.

"So you like plants?" Alice said. Although Miss Jessops was a grown-up, there was something about her that made Alice feel at ease.

"However did you guess?" The librarian laughed. "What about you?"

"Hmm," Alice hedged, not wanting to offend her. "I'm more of an animal person. They seem to like me," she explained, swelling with pride as she thought of the seagull and the cat. She still couldn't quite believe they'd chosen to talk to shy, awkward her when they could have chosen anyone.

Suddenly the bell on the library counter rang.

"Better see who that is," Miss Jessops said, getting up with a sigh. Alice drained the last of her hot chocolate, then followed her.

To Alice's surprise it was Tim with a stack of books to check out. "Alice!" he cried. "What are you doing here?"

"Oh," she said. "I was just talking to Miss Jessops." She leaned over to have a look at the books. Quick as a viper going for a strike, Tim whipped the pile away, sweeping them on to the returns trolley.

"Changed my mind," he said.

Miss Jessops and Alice exchanged bemused looks. "Are you sure?" the librarian said. "You can take out up to six books at a time, you know."

"No, no," Tim said hurriedly. "I don't think I need them after all." He turned to Alice. "Are you coming back to the boarding house?"

"Er, okay," Alice said, wondering why he was acting so strangely.

Tim was already headed towards the door. "Sorry, miss," Alice said to the librarian. "Thanks again for the hot chocolate. It's been really nice talking to you. But it looks like I'd better get a move on."

"Seems that way." Miss Jessops smiled, lifting the counter hatch so Alice could leave. "See you soon!"

As Alice raced after Tim, she couldn't help but notice the stack of books he'd abandoned on the returns trolley. The top

85

one was a large blue book entitled *When My Worries Grow Too Big*.

It seemed to be about anxiety. What did Tim want with it? "Hey, Tim!" she called after him. "Wait for me!"

But Tim had already vanished.

CHAPTER 10

Tim was in a funny mood all morning. He made no mention of his visit to the library and instead rabbited on about maps until Alice thought if she ever heard about one again, it would be too soon.

"The professor's got drawers and drawers full," Tim whispered as their history teacher, a stern woman named Miss Hetherington, wrote copious notes about the Battle of Hastings on her blackboard. "He's even got these really old ones that show where smugglers used to store their goods."

"Smugglers?" Alice said, suddenly paying more attention. "What kind of smugglers?"

Tim shrugged. "The professor said that once upon a time

they'd wreck ships off the coast and use the cliff tunnels to carry the loot inland."

Alice thought about it. "But that boat we saw seemed to be sailing away, not bringing things ashore."

Tim checked that Miss Hetherington still had her back to the class. "Maybe that's why they were in such a hurry to leave?" he suggested. "They'd already hidden what they came to hide."

"Hmm." Alice remembered the flapping tarpaulin on the deck of the boat. She was pretty sure the men were taking things with them, not leaving things behind. That would make sense if what Agent T had said was correct and they were stealing animals . . . But where were they taking them?

"You're both overthinking it," Ottie whispered, cupping her hand so no one would overhear her. "They probably weren't smugglers at all."

"There's only one way to find out for sure," whispered Tim. "How about we take another trip back to the oak tree sometime? We're due another adventure."

"Sure," said Ottie absent-mindedly.

Miss Hetherington was still scribbling away on the board, her writing getting smaller and smaller as she tried to cram everything on. Alice glanced over at the neighbouring desk. Kelcie and Lexi were writing notes to one another behind their pencil cases and giggling. Kelcie then folded up one of the notes into a tiny parcel and flicked it over to Ottie.

Ottie snatched it up, unfolding it on her lap beneath the desk where Miss Hetherington couldn't see it. A moment later, she looked up and beamed at Kelcie and Lexi.

Alice hadn't forgotten how they'd treated Tim and the mean comments they'd made about her. The more she saw of the Gruesome Twosome, the less she liked them.

"Pay attention, Year Seven!" Miss Hetherington snapped without turning round.

Immediately the whole class sat up poker-straight in their seats, each pupil certain that the teacher was referring to them in particular.

Alice picked up her pen and began to copy the notes into her exercise book but it wasn't long until her thoughts drifted back to the men on the boat and the missing animals. She really needed to speak with Agent T – and fast.

Alice shoved open the dormitory door, kicked off her school shoes and put a plate laden with cakes down on the desk. The minute the bell had rung for the end of the day, Tim had rushed off to speak to Professor Biddle again and Ottie had gone to try out for the swimming team. Alice had overheard Kelcie and Lexi saying they were going too, and she couldn't help feeling a bit left out.

Luckily today was Felix's day off and once a week the school took a delivery of cakes directly from Hetty's, the teashop on Pebblehampton high street. Alice remembered going there when she was on holiday with Gran. She had fond memories of yummy slices of Hetty's famous 'Chocolate Delight' so when she saw the rose-pink boxes with gold ribbons sitting on the common-room table, she'd helped herself to both a brownie and a slice of lemon drizzle. Now Alice was looking forward to getting into bed, tucking into the cakes and reading some of her library book in peace and quiet.

Alice threw her boater on the floor, climbed into her bunk and was just about to snuggle down under the duvet when a black-and-silver leg poked out from beneath the covers. "Aargh!" she shrieked, leaping up again.

"At last!" The library cat yawned, getting up and stretching her long silver back.

"You're . . . here . . . in my dormitory," Alice whispered. "How did you get in?" She glanced at the door. "I'm, er, not sure we're meant to have visitors. I don't think Mrs Salter would like it."

"That old trout?" Constance sniffed, fishing out an errant sock from beneath the duvet and batting it away. "It'll take more than the likes of that cold fish to tell *me* what to do! I'm the school cat! I'm a veritable *tradition*."

Alice stifled a giggle. Maybe, just maybe, Mrs Salter had found her match in the tabby cat.

Constance gave an indignant humph. "Anyhow, I've not come for an idle gossip. You'd better take a seat."

"Oh, er . . . okay." Alice perched on the edge of her bunk, goosebumps rising on both her arms.

"I'm here on official business," Constance announced grandly.

Alice watched in fascination, amazed at the way the bossy, teacherly voice came from the cat's mouth. "Official business?" she asked. "What do you mean?"

The tabby put her front paws on Alice's knees so that they were almost head-to-head. "We've been watching you."

A current of electricity surged in Alice's veins. They were the exact words the gull had used on the beach! "So you do know who the seagull is!" she cried indignantly. "You *lied*! In the library, you said—"

"I know exactly what I said," the cat snapped. "But these days, one can never be too careful. It doesn't do to talk willy-nilly to strangers, you know. You would do well to keep that in mind."

"Oh, I'd never tell anyone about you!" Alice said quickly.

"Pleased to hear it," the tabby said, flexing her claws. "Make sure you don't." She fixed Alice with her bright amber eyes. "The LSPDA would know if you did."

Alice gulped. "The LSPD-what?"

The cat swished her tail impatiently. "LSPDA. The Loyal Society for the Prevention of Danger to Animals. And I'm here because we need your help."

Alice laughed nervously. "I don't know what you think I can do . . ."

"I don't *think* anything," the cat said. "I *know*. You, Alice Tonks, are a Switcher."

Alice leaned forward. "What did you just say?"

"I said," the cat continued slowly, like she was talking to a very small child, "that you are a Switcher."

Alice stared at the cat, gobsmacked. "W-what's that?"

"A Switcher is that extraordinarily rare thing: a useful human. A human being who has a special affinity with animals and can talk to them. Some say Switchers can do other things besides . . ."

So there was a name for people like her who could talk to animals . . . Switchers. Alice rolled the word around in her mouth, trying it on for size. She was a Switcher. Just the sound of it made her skin tingle.

"To be honest, we'd presumed Switchers had all but died out until you came along," Constance said.

Alice shook her head, unable to believe this was really happening. "But why?" she wondered aloud. "Why me?"

"Why not you, Alice Tonks?" Constance said firmly, her tone clipped and efficient as that of a newsreader. "There's been Switchers at Pebblewood School since it first opened. Rumour has it that Sir Rudyard Jessops himself was a Switcher . . ."

"The school's founder?" Alice gasped, again thinking of the portrait in the atrium of a ginger-haired old man with a terrier on his lap. Now she came to think about it, there had been something rather unusual about the way he was smiling at the dog, like the dog had just said something particularly witty . . .

"Frankly you couldn't have come along at a better time." Constance leaned in close, her voice no more than a whisper. "Agent T told you about the animal snatcher, didn't he?"

Alice nodded.

"There's not a moment to waste." The cat shuddered. "Animals are disappearing. At first it was just the odd pet here, the occasional wild animal there, but now hardly a day goes by when we don't hear of another snatching."

"And it's not just another animal?" Alice asked, trying to avoid Constance's cool, hard stare.

Constance jabbed her front paw into Alice's chest. "Contrary to what most humans think, us animals aren't stupid, you know. We've thought about all the possibilities. The wolves are gone and you don't get wildcats this far south. It can't be poachers or roadkill. We're talking about disappearances on a scale that's never been seen before. This is an emergency!" Her eyes were round and wild and her fur stood on end.

"Okay, okay!" Alice held up her hands in surrender. "So this group you're in . . ."

The cat's fur deflated. "The LSPDA. Thomas – I mean, Agent T – chose the name." She snorted. "That's seagulls for you. Always melodramatic."

"What do you guys actually, well, do?"

"The LSPDA's sole mission is the preservation of animal life. We work collectively for the sake of animal kind. Patrols. Intelligence gathering. Security." Suddenly the cat seemed exhausted and she flopped down on the bed, draping her head over her paws. "Oh, Alice, we've tried everything! Thomas wouldn't have broken protocol to speak to you on the beach the other day if we weren't desperate. He's certain the culprit can't be another animal and, for what it's worth, I think he's right. If there was a large predator around, we'd have seen trails, surely? Picked up the scent. But if it's a human behind the disappearances then we need an insider . . ."

". . . And that's where I come in." Everything was starting to make sense.

"Correct. When Thomas spotted you, he thought all his suppers had come at once! He reckons you're our only hope of getting to the bottom of things."

"No pressure, then," Alice mumbled, her mind buzzing like a beehive. Not only did she have a strange new talent but now it seemed a bunch of animals were relying on her to save them from the mysterious snatcher. What if she ended up letting them down?

"Being a Switcher is an honour. A privilege." Constance paused, drawing breath. "But it comes at a price. Switchers pledge to serve the animal world, to put animals before themselves. Do you think you can do that?"

Alice nodded slowly, trying to make sense of everything she was hearing.

"We're not asking for miracles," Constance said, her front paws resting on Alice's knees. "Just keep your eyes open and your ear to the ground. Look out for anything suspicious. Any odd comings and goings. Anyone unusual in the vicinity. So will you help us?"

It was the first time anyone had come to Alice for help. She was usually the one who needed protecting. The one everyone looked out for. But now she was a Switcher. Even the name sounded impressive.

"All right," Alice said. "I'm in."

CHAPTER 11

Thunder crackled and popped as lighting forked across the sky.

"Are you sure we should be going out?" Alice asked, peering round the corner of the alley at the angry black clouds gathering over the cliffs. Another school day was over and while most of the school was watching football in the common room or hanging out in their dormitories, Tim had somehow talked her into heading back to their den.

"It's perfect!" Tim grinned. "No one'll think we've gone off site in this weather. Anyway, it's only a bit of rain."

"A bit?" Alice pulled her waterproof jacket tighter round her. The thought of sitting in a soaking-wet tree trunk was not an appealing one. And although she'd been eager to have another look for the men in the boat ever since she'd told Constance that she'd help the LSPDA, she was pretty sure even smugglers wouldn't venture out in a storm like this.

"Where's your sense of adventure?" Tim laughed.

"Can you even remember how to get to the tree without Ottie?" said Alice. "Maybe we should wait for her?"

"You worry too much! Anyway, you heard her. She'll meet us there when she's done with swimming practice."

Ottie had made the school team, along with Kelcie and Lexi, and now had training almost every day. Ottie was over the moon and though Alice had congratulated her, she quietly had her reservations. Swimming practice meant even less time with her roommate and it was also another excuse for Ottie to spend time with the Gruesome Twosome.

"Don't look so miserable," Tim said, grabbing Alice's hand and pulling her after him. "We can still have fun without Ottie, can't we?"

Soon Alice and Tim were sprinting down the sandy cliff path, almost blinded by the rain pummelling their faces. Down on the deserted beach, the sea reared and bucked against the rocks.

A bad feeling sloshed around in Alice's stomach. "I think we should go back!" she shouted.

"What?" Tim bellowed over the raging waves. "I can't hear you!"

A hundred sharp needles jabbed Alice's cheeks and hands as the rain plastered her hair to her face. She stumbled after Tim, slipping and sliding on the grass. Finally the old oak came into view.

"Take your coat off!" Tim hollered, removing his own.

Alice wriggled free of her jacket, wondering why she was taking off her waterproof in the middle of a downpour.

"We can slide down," Tim told her. "Look." He ran over to the steep and now very muddy bank, laid his coat on the ground and sat down cross-legged on top of it. Grabbing fistfuls of tufty grass with both hands, he hauled himself to the edge of the bank then released himself.

"Woohoo!" he cried as he whooshed down the slope.

Groaning, and wishing she'd never come, Alice placed her jacket on the edge of the incline, wobbled for a moment and then slid down after him, screaming as she went.

Tim grabbed her at the bottom before she could shoot straight into the tree trunk, then they squeezed inside.

"Never ever make me do that again!" Alice cried but she couldn't help but wheeze with laughter.

"Your face!" Tim hooted, squeezing out his sopping-wet hair.

They helped themselves to the remainder of Ottie's stash of chocolate biscuits and sweets, talking about their teachers and classmates, and how weird it was to think they'd be at Pebbles for the next seven years. Alice wondered about bringing up the subject of the library books Tim had been about to check out the other morning but thought it was best not to mention it unless he did. Maybe he was feeling a bit homesick and didn't want to admit it? She knew that feeling only too well.

Finally the hammering of the rain faded away to a steady drip. "You know, I don't think Ottie's coming," Alice said.

"Don't be stupid," Tim said. "She said she would, didn't she? After swimming."

Alice checked her watch. "Swimming finished ages ago. I think Ottie's just got other friends now."

Tim looked at Alice shrewdly. "You mean Kelcie and Lexi?"

Alice nodded.

"If Ottie's got any sense, she'll keep well away from them," he said, cramming half a biscuit into his mouth in one go. "Trust me, they're trouble."

"Maybe I'm wrong," Alice said hopefully. "Maybe the storm just put her off." She paused, wondering how honest she could be with Tim. "It just seems like she's more interested in them then she is in us."

"What you mean is Ottie's had time now to work out who's popular and who's not." Tim laughed hollowly. "And we're definitely not!"

Alice picked at the mud caked on her jacket. "I didn't think Ottie was like that," she said sadly.

"It's her loss." Tim shrugged. "For what it's worth, I'd much rather be mates with you then the likes of Kelcie!"

Suddenly Alice felt compelled to trust Tim with something she'd never told anyone else. "It's because I'm autistic," she said. "That's why people think I'm strange sometimes."

Tim shook his head. "You're not strange. You're just different, Alice. I like different."

Alice smiled. "I like different too." She checked her watch. "Come on, it'll be dinner soon. We should probably be heading back."

"Yeah, we don't want to be late," Tim said, getting to his feet. He offered her his hand and pulled her up. "Better hide the evidence!" he said, stuffing the wrapper into his jeans pocket. He lowered his voice and put on a cockney accent. "We was never 'ere, right?"

Alice shook her head. Tim was an idiot but he was her idiot.

When they emerged on to the clifftop, the sun had appeared. In the distance, the school roofs gleamed in the golden late-afternoon light.

It proved a lot harder getting back up the steep bank than it had been getting down it but eventually Tim managed to scramble up and helped haul Alice up after him. They then set off at a jog.

In the distance, Alice heard the guttural oink of a cormorant and a moment or two later, a pair of them soared into view, their wings dark against the sun-soaked sky. "Look!" she cried, pointing them out to Tim. "I think they're—"

"Whoa, careful!" Tim cried, catching her arm as she tripped.

Alice steadied herself and looked down to see what she'd fallen over. There on the ground was an empty medicine bottle. "People should throw their litter away properly," she tutted, then giggled, realising she sounded just like Gran.

It was only when Alice glanced at the label that her curiosity spiked. Beneath the mud, she could make out a picture of a rabbit and a guinea pig. She scooped up the bottle and popped it in her jacket pocket. *Could this be a clue?* she thought excitedly.

Keeping a careful eye out for anyone who might report them for truancy, Alice and Tim made their way back along the clifftops. As they reached the main path back to school, they paused, glancing down at School Bay.

"Shh!" Tim hissed, grabbing Alice and pulling her to the ground.

"What are you doing?" Alice snapped but Tim had a finger to his lips.

"Mr Marlowe," he mouthed, pointing down to the beach.

Alice peered round him and sure enough she could just make out the headteacher, striding along the sand. "Who's that with him?"

Alice and Tim leaned in for a closer look. "Ottie!" they both whispered.

Sure enough, there stood the headmaster and his niece, deep in conversation. There was no mistaking Ottie's bright blond hair and maroon blazer.

"At least now we know why she never joined us," Tim said.

Alice's tummy clenched. That was all very well but there was still a big question. What *was* her roommate doing meeting Mr Marlowe down on the beach?

CHAPTER 12

Alice managed to make it back to her dormitory without anyone spotting her. She immediately changed out of her wet clothes and hid her muddy jacket at the very back of her wardrobe. Then she took the medicine bottle from the pocket, before closing the door.

She wiped the label clean. Alice didn't recognise the name of the medicine but she made a mental note to look it up on the library computer. It was clear it was for animals, though. And there was only one person she could think of who'd want to drug animals around here – the animal snatcher. An image flashed up in her mind of the headmaster down on the beach with Ottie – near where they'd spotted the men on the boat on their first trip to the den. Surely those things couldn't be connected?

Suddenly the door flew open and Ottie walked in. "Sorry I didn't make it to the den," she said, dumping her swimming bag on the floor. "Coach kept me behind after training. Did you miss me?"

"Oh," Alice said, struggling to think of an answer. It always made her feel squirmy and uncomfortable when people lied. "W-what did she want?"

Ottie's face broke into a grin. "She wants me to swim for the school in the gala next month. She says I've got real promise."

"That's . . . that's great, Ottie. Well done," Alice said, wanting to believe her roommate.

"Thanks, Alice," Ottie beamed.

Alice smiled back. Ottie seemed genuinely happy at how well swimming had gone. Maybe it wasn't a lie after all . . .

"Ottie," Alice said, turning away and busying herself by tidying a pile of textbooks. "I meant to ask, was everything okay with Mr Marlowe the other day? You looked kind of . . . stressed afterwards."

"Yeah . . . that," Ottie said, the happiness suddenly gone from her voice. "Look, Alice, I'm sorry I didn't tell you he's my uncle. I don't know why I didn't. I guess I was just embarrassed. No one wants to be the teacher's pet, do they?"

"You've nothing to be embarrassed about," Alice said, realising she'd been silly to take it personally. "You can't help who your family are, can you? And it's up to you who you want to tell."

Ottie visibly relaxed. "Thanks, Alice," she said. "I knew you'd understand." She grabbed her boater from the top bunk. "Anyway, I don't know about you but swimming's made me ravenous. Are you coming for dinner?"

"I'll meet you there," Alice said. "I'm just going to pop to the bathroom."

"I'll save you a seat!" Ottie said as she headed out of the door.

Alice listened to Ottie skip lightly across the landing and down the boarding house stairs, not a care in the world. She was so stupid to let herself get carried away. Ottie had nothing to do with the missing animals! She was just an eleven-year-old girl. Maybe her uncle had just wanted to talk to her about doing well in school or even warn her off being friends with the likes of Kelcie and Lexi.

Alice grabbed her boater and straightened her uniform. She was about to nip to the bathroom when there was a tap on the window.

"Agent T!" she gasped, rushing over, but it wasn't the seagull.

Constance was perched precariously on the windowsill, her face pressed to the glass.

Alice thrust the window open. "Constance!" she whispered, glancing at the neighbouring window in case anyone happened to be looking out. "I've found something that might be useful . . ."

"Good," the cat purred. "Because an emergency meeting of the LSPDA has been called. Find me in the kitchen garden at lights out – and Alice? Don't be late!"

Night drew its cloak over Pebblewood.

Alice hid in the flower bed, large pink blooms pressed up against her cheek. Her knees were damp and aching from pressing into the wet soil and her nose tingled, threatening to sneeze. Hands trembling, she peeped over the red-brick wall as two bored-looking prefects herded the final Year Elevens out of the common room and bellowed, "Lights out!" up the stairs after them. A chorus of groans followed and then one dormitory light after another was switched off until the boarding house stood in darkness.

"Come on, Constance," Alice muttered, her fingers twitching nervously at her side. She counted two long minutes in her head, half expecting a teacher's hand to grasp her shoulder at any moment. But the only sound was the singing of a nightingale as it hopped merrily around, poking into the soil in the hope of a worm or grub for its supper.

With a shiver of excitement, Alice wondered whether Constance had sent the nightingale to help her. "Is it safe?" she whispered to the little bird.

"Safe!" the nightingale sang, tip-tapping over on his nimble yellow feet. "Safe! Safe!"

Rising to a crouch, Alice peeked over the wall. She almost toppled over in shock, for there at her very own dormitory window stood Mrs Salter. The housemistress's arms were folded, her buzzard-like eyes scanning the school grounds for miscreants. Alice ducked back down behind the wall, certain she'd been spotted. She turned to the nightingale. "I thought you said it was safe!"

"Safe!" the bird chirped before flying away.

Alice groaned. Of course Constance hadn't sent him! She counted sixty slow seconds then peeped back up at the window. Mrs Salter's needle-sharp figure had disappeared and Ottie was drawing the curtains. She watched as Ottie's slender silhouette moved about inside the dorm, no doubt getting ready for bed.

Alice sucked in a sharp breath. Had Mrs Salter been looking for her? Did the housemistress know she was out of bed?

From the direction of the woods came the low wail of a cat and Constance sauntered into view. "What are you doing down there?" the cat asked disdainfully.

"I didn't want anyone to see me," Alice said, glancing up at the window uneasily, but when she turned back to Constance, the cat was already off, bounding away through the gardens.

"Hurry up!" the tabby called over her shoulder. "We mustn't be late."

Gone was Alice's impression of cats as dozing, drowsy creatures. Constance sped through the garden gate and down the steep ditch to the dense hedge that separated the school from the woods beyond. She slipped easily through the shrubbery. Alice ran after her, wriggling and squeezing her way past spiky holly leaves, the sharp points bloodying her bare legs.

Soon they were scurrying over tree roots and weaving past low-hanging branches that threatened to thwack Alice in the face. She tripped and fell more than once but Constance didn't wait for her to find her feet, zigzagging on through the thick undergrowth. Without the cat, Alice knew she'd soon be utterly lost amid the dense woodland, but she guessed that was probably the point. She had no choice but to wipe the sweat from her forehead and keep running.

"Sorry about that. LSPDA rules," Constance explained when she finally slowed. "You never know who's following."

Alice looked back over her shoulder. In the distance, twigs snapped underfoot and unseen bodies shifted in the shadows. Goosebumps shot up her arms. Was Constance right – could someone be following them?

The tabby cat paused at the edge of a ring of tall oak trees. "We're here," she whispered. "Don't say a word and follow my lead."

Alice was tentatively following Constance into the clearing when something leaped out at her, its jaws snapping inches from Alice's leg.

Alice screamed, remembering to clap her hands over her mouth a moment too late.

When she looked down, yellow eyes glowered back up at her, full of rage. Something low and angry snarled, gums drawn back to reveal long, jagged teeth. Alice stumbled backwards, tripping on a log. She needed to run. Escape. Scrambling for a foothold, she hauled herself up.

Constance jumped forward to stand between Alice and the bright white teeth, her body arched, and let out an almighty hiss. Her fur was on end and her ears lay flat to her head. Alice had never seen the cat look so fierce. However, as swiftly as Constance's fur had puffed up, it started to deflate.

"It's okay, Red. It's me!" the cat said. "It's Constance!"

The sharp teeth snapped shut one last time. A magnificent plume of red fur flashed before Alice's face, its white tip bright and bushy. Alice felt the fox's anger pulsing. "You have betrayed us, comrade!" he barked in a voice both proud and stern. "You have brought a human to our meeting."

Constance held her ground under the fox's fierce stare. "No, I've brought a friend," she said patiently. "This is the girl Thomas told us about."

The fox's yellow eyes looked Alice up and down. "Forget what Thomas said!" the fox growled. "Thomas is gone."

Alice gasped and turned to Constance but the cat was staring at the fox in confusion. "Gone?" she whispered. "What do you mean, gone?"

The fox bowed his head. "Snatched," he said more gently. "We received word late this afternoon from a pair of cormorants."

Constance flopped down in the undergrowth. "It can't be . . ." she muttered. "Not Thomas . . ."

The fox spoke quietly. "There is no mistake. He was taken from the beach yesterday evening."

"I saw them!" Alice whispered in Constance's ear. "I saw those cormorants today, circling the beach . . ."

"Lookouts," Constance explained. She got to her paws shakily. "You have to listen to me, Red," she begged. "This is Alice, Alice Tonks. I've brought her to help us. She's a Switcher."

"Her? A Switcher?" the fox scoffed. "We haven't had a new Switcher in what . . . twenty years? And she's just a child!"

Constance nodded encouragingly to Alice. "Go on. Speak."

Alice gave the fox a short, jerky wave. "Er . . . hi," she said, feeling self-conscious.

The fox narrowed his eyes. "Fine, so she can Switch. That doesn't mean you were right to bring her here."

Constance was resolute. "We can trust her."

The fox snapped at the air inches from Constance's whiskers. "Trust her? Trust a human? Have you lost your mind? Humans hunted my mother with dogs! Shot my father simply for trying to survive." He swallowed, trying to regain control of himself. "How do you know she wasn't followed? Or that next time she won't bring more of her kind with her? You've endangered all of us!"

"Just listen to what she has to say, please," Constance implored. "If the cormorants are right and Thomas really has been snatched –" she gulped – "then it's more important

110

than ever that we have Alice on our side. He believed in her. He thought she could help us."

The fox spoke in a low rumble. "You were wrong to bring her, Constance," he said, striding away into the clearing. "These woods belong to animals, not human folk."

"Sh-should I go?" Alice whispered, the moment the fox disappeared from view.

Constance shook her head. "Follow me," she said. "And stay close."

Forcing her legs forward, Alice pushed low-hanging branches out of the way and entered the clearing. When she looked up, she noticed the wide eyes of a barn owl watching her from a nearby tree. Two grey squirrels scurried up and down a branch, chittering away to each other. At Red's side was a badger, heavy and squat.

A hare glimpsed Alice and froze, its yellow eyes wide with terror.

"At ease, comrade," the fox told the hare gently. "Constance tells me this human is a friend."

The library cat spoke up, her voice firm. "Alice *is* a friend," she insisted. "This isn't just any human. She's a Switcher."

The squirrels squeaked excitedly and though Alice couldn't follow everything they said, she caught the gist of their conversation. "A Switcher?" they squealed. "A real live Switcher?"

Alice looked at Constance uncertainly. Maybe this was a mistake. The squirrels clearly thought she could do something special but she was just a girl, an eleven-year-old girl . . .

"Red just told me the news about Thomas," Constance continued.

The badger glanced at the fox while the smaller animals exchanged terrified looks.

"And if it's true then you should all know that the last thing our comrade did was speak to this human," Constance went on. "He believed Alice could help us . . . and so do I."

The hare, its tall ears erect and listening, shuddered. "But how can we trust a human, Constance? How do we know she isn't one of them . . . one of the *animal snatchers?*" He whispered the words, too terrified to speak properly.

Watching the hare quake, Alice grasped for the first time how truly fearful the animals must be. Their friends and family were being snatched, and no one knew who was taking them or why. She had to do something.

Constance rubbed noses with the hare. "It's okay, Milo. Alice isn't an animal snatcher."

Alice took a deep breath. If she wanted to convince these animals, she needed to fight her own battles and not rely on Constance fighting them for her. She kneeled down awkwardly so she was at eye level with the hare and extended two fingers. "I'm not going to hurt you," she told Milo. "I want to help."

The hare flinched, recoiling from her touch, but Alice held her fingers steady. After a moment, Milo hopped forward again and sniffed her hand warily with his twitching black nose. A wood mouse and two shrews crept out of the shadows to watch.

"You really can understand us?" Milo asked, amazed.

Alice nodded. "It looks that way."

"I've heard stories of Switchers but I never imagined they really existed," the hare said, giving her hand a little nudge. "But you're real, all right."

The wood mice tiptoed closer. "Do you think she can find our brother for us?" said one. "We can't find him anywhere."

"If anyone can do it, a Switcher can," replied the other.

The badger, meanwhile, was rather less impressed by her presence. "Thomas might have thought you were special," he grumbled. "But you look just like any other small human to me. Smell like it too." He turned away to snuffle in the grass, his claws rifling through the old leaves until he unearthed a worm. He sucked it up with his long snout, slurping it down greedily.

"Thomas believed Alice could help us, Henry," Constance said.

"And look where that got him!" Red snapped. "Missing, presumed dead is where!"

The other animals, including Constance, all gasped. Milo shrank back, his head in his paws. In the tree, the owl hooted noisily in protest.

"Come now, Milo, Athena, all of you. We need to face facts," the fox said bluntly. "Thomas is gone. That's where trusting humans got him. Animals have been disappearing for months now. How many more of us have to suffer before you learn that lesson? We trust humans. We get hurt. It's always been that way and it always will be."

"No," Alice said, getting to her feet. She couldn't let Constance stick up for her any longer. "It doesn't have to be that way. I told you, I can help you. I want to help you." She reached into her pocket and pulled out the empty medicine bottle. "Look. I found this today on the clifftop near school. I think that maybe the animal snatcher has been drugging the animals so they can capture them."

A ripple of excitement passed around the group. "It stands to reason that someone at the school must be involved," Red growled. "We've worked that much out ourselves. We don't need her."

Alice shook her head. "If someone *is* snatching animals then you can't stop them on your own. I'm a pupil at the school. I don't face the same dangers you do . . ."

The fox started to turn away.

"Wait!" Constance cried. "This has always been a democratic organisation. The LSPDA stands for cooperation between species. Every animal has a say."

Milo glanced skittishly at the fox. "Th-that's r-right, Constance," he said. "A-all in favour of l-letting the girl help?" He slowly raised his quaking paw.

Alice watched and waited, every muscle taut. The owl hooted. The squirrels and wood mice looked at one another then edged forward, paws raised.

114

Red surveyed them, his expression stony. "The LSPDA has voted," he huffed. "And, unfortunately, tradition says I'm bound to honour that vote." He eyed Alice carefully. "So I'll give you until we meet at the next full moon to track down this animal snatcher and find out where they've taken our friends. Perhaps you'll prove me wrong, show me you're not just another good-for-nothing human . . ."

"She will, Red," said Milo excitedly. "I know it!"

"I have a lead," Alice told the gathering. "The other night I saw a boat, off School Bay. The men on it were acting suspiciously . . ."

The fox shrugged, a smug expression on his face. "We need more than that, small human."

"Then I give you my word." Alice forced herself to look Red directly in the eye. "I'll find the animal snatcher, you see if I don't!"

CHAPTER 13

"Quietly!" Constance hissed.

Alice's hand was slick with sweat as she fumbled for purchase on the heavy wooden frame of the common-room window. The thick glass rattled. She froze, straining her ears for the sound of the housemistress's heels click-clacking down the stairs. "She's going to hear!" Alice whispered, stealing a glance at the only light still on in the boarding house – the one in Mrs Salter's office on the top floor.

"Then hurry up!" the cat snapped. "I thought you said she'd be asleep by now?"

"She should be . . ." Alice said, remembering with a sickening lurch of her stomach how she thought she'd seen Mrs Salter standing at her dormitory window earlier, spying

116

on the gardens below. Had the housemistress seen her hiding in the flower beds? If she had, Mrs Salter might be lying in wait for her . . .

Finally the window ground upwards and a narrow gap appeared, just big enough for Alice to squeeze through. "Right, in you go," Constance told her. "And careful on the stairs. The third—"

"The third from the bottom creaks and so does the second from the top," Alice parroted. "I remember." Carefully she climbed through the window and dropped down into the common room. "Constance?" she said as she began to heave the window closed behind her. "Be careful, won't you?"

From down in the flower bed, the cat purred. "Don't worry about me, Alice."

It was impossible not to. Out there somewhere, lurking in the shadows, was the animal snatcher. They already had Agent T – what if Constance was next? "I meant what I told Red, you know," she whispered, leaning out of the window and giving the cat's ear a rub. "I'll find Agent T and the other animals. The animal snatcher won't get away with it."

Constance nuzzled her head against Alice's hand. "I know you'll do your best to help us," she said. "Now off to bed and remember – not a sound."

"Alice!" Miss Jessops said the next morning as she wandered into the library. "How lovely to see you!"

"Oh, hi, miss." Alice yawned, rubbing the sleep from her eyes as she drifted over to join the librarian at the counter. She hadn't expected Miss Jessops to be there already. Ottie wasn't even up for swimming practice yet. Keeping the library in order must be harder work than Alice had thought!

Miss Jessops put down the borrowing labels she was sticking into the front of a pile of hardbacks and took a sip of her coffee. "So what brings you to the library? I thought I was the only early bird around here!"

Alice's hand drifted to her blazer pocket where she had stashed the medicine bottle. She might not know why someone would want to steal animals or where they might be hiding them, but she did know how to research. She'd been hoping to look up the name of the medicine and find out what it was used for on one of the library's computers but now Miss Jessops was here, that would have to wait. It was time for Plan B.

"Have you got any old newspapers? Local ones?" she asked.

Miss Jessops' eyes lit up. "Newspapers? Why, as a matter of fact, I think we do!" She plucked the biro out of her hair and began to nibble the end. "Now wherever did I put them?"

Alice followed the librarian over to the non-fiction section and watched as she scoured the shelves. Alice drummed her fingers against a nearby bookcase. If wild animals were going missing then maybe pets and farm animals were too and their owners might have seen something suspicious. That seemed just the kind of thing that the local press might be interested in.

Finally Miss Jessops reached the furthest, dustiest corner of the library where cobwebbed stacks of the *Pebblehampton Chronicle* had been piled against the wall. "Aha!" she said. "I knew they were here somewhere."

Alice rushed forward to take a look but as she lifted one crisp and faded corner, her excitement fizzled and died. The pages smelled of mice and rainwater and Alice realised that searching through the yellowed pages for relevant articles was going to be long and painful work. Especially as Red had said animals had been disappearing for months now.

"Anything in particular you're looking for?" Miss Jessops asked.

"Oh, just local news for a . . . project I'm working on." It wasn't a complete lie, Alice consoled herself. She rummaged through the pile for more recent editions, trying not to feel too deflated. Nobody said catching the animal snatcher was going to be easy.

"Oh dear," the librarian said, her gaze dropping to the buckles of her shoes when Alice came over to the counter with a pile of newspapers. "You know, I'm not actually supposed to let students check out the periodicals . . ."

"The . . . what?"

"Periodicals," Miss Jessops said, tapping the newspapers.

Alice groaned. This was all she needed.

". . . But I don't think anyone will miss these too much!" The librarian winked. "So you go ahead and take them."

"Thanks, miss," Alice said, folding the newspapers and packing them into her rucksack. *They're just a starting point,* she reminded herself as her heart began to pound. *Don't get your hopes up.*

As Alice hurried back to the boarding house to hide her stash of papers before breakfast, she almost collided with a sleepy-looking Tim who was hovering by the telephones in the hall.

"Good morning!" She smiled.

"Is it?" he groaned. His hair was uncombed and he was wearing a white school shirt and tie with pyjama bottoms.

"Waiting for a call?" she asked. It was a strange time for phone calls. Usually students rang home in the evenings, not first thing, and Tim was acting shifty.

Tim looked at the telephone and quickly turned away. "Yeah, er, Mum works in the evenings."

"Oh, okay," Alice said, though she was sure Tim had gone to ring home in the evening before. "See you in a bit."

Alice went upstairs to her dormitory, where she squirrelled the newspapers away under her bed, then ran downstairs to get a glass of chocolate milk before breakfast. As she opened the common-room door, she heard giggling.

Ottie was perched on the sofa, her hair still wet from swimming, painting the nails of a girl with long dark hair.

It was Lexi. Immediately Alice wished she'd given the chocolate milk a miss.

"Hey, Alice," Ottie said quickly, before turning back to Lexi's outstretched hand and applying another stroke of bright pink polish.

"Don't encourage her," Kelcie told Ottie. "We don't want Little Miss Boring hanging around."

Lexi rolled her eyes and giggled. Ottie wasn't laughing but nor was she telling them to stop. "Hold still, Lex," she murmured.

Lex? Since when had Ottie had a nickname for Lexi Khan? Alice looked at Kelcie and Lexi, taking in their gleeful faces. An icy sensation slid down her back. She remembered the mean comments they'd made about her the other day in geography, and now Ottie seemed to be friends with them. The bitter taste of betrayal rose in Alice's throat.

Lexi blew on her wet nails then sprang to her feet. "What do you think?" she said, waving her hands right under Alice's nose. Alice took a step back, the chemical stench of the nail polish overwhelming her. As Lexi pouted, an image of a red-lipped batfish from a documentary she had once watched swam into Alice's mind.

"Very nice," Alice mumbled. Her palms were sticky. Was it her fault that Ottie had gone off and made new friends? Maybe Ottie was cross that she'd had to cover for her to Mrs Salter last night.

"Ottie could do yours next," Kelcie said. "Although your hair could do with a brush first," she added cattily.

Alice put a hand to her knotty bush.

Lexi's dark eyes glinted mischievously. "I don't mind helping you."

Where Lexi's hair looked slick and glossy, Alice's felt thick and tangled. Visions of hair straighteners popped into her mind. She looked at Ottie, hoping she'd say something. But her roommate just screwed the lid back on the nail varnish without bothering to look up.

"I'm all right, thanks," Alice said eventually, hating the squeak that had crept into her voice. "See you at breakfast, Ottie."

She turned on her heel, a wave of embarrassment crashing over her. It was clear Kelcie and Lexi thought she was weird – did Ottie think that too?

Alice focused on forcing her legs to walk slowly out of the common room when all they wanted to do was run. She fumbled her way out of the hall and into the quad, her breaths coming quick and shallow. Her chest felt like it was being squeezed by an invisible python and tiny stars flashed and twinkled before her eyes.

Blinking hard, Alice stumbled towards the fountain at the heart of the courtyard and sat down on the edge. The coldness of the hard stone helped her feel grounded again. She closed her eyes, listening to the sound of running water splashing into the basin until the pulse hammering in her ears softened and died away. Her fingers steadied. Her breathing slowed.

After a moment or two, the boarding-house door slammed open and Ottie, Kelcie and Lexi strode out into the quad, their arms linked to form a human paperchain. Behind them came the rest of Year Seven, accompanied by Mrs Salter, with Tim trailing along at the back.

"Hiya," Tim said, coming over to join her. He watched her stare after Ottie and the others. "Come and have some breakfast. I always find a good breakfast sorts me out when Mum is—"

He stopped himself.

"When your mum's what?" Alice prompted.

"When Mum goes to one of her boring antique fairs," he said quickly. "Are you coming or what?"

When they reached the dining hall, Felix was laying out a rack of toast, his handlebar moustache perfectly slick and his tall chef's hat a gleaming white. "Good morning!" he beamed, spinning a tray of cooked tomatoes with a flourish. "What can I get you today?"

"Hi, Felix," Alice muttered, unable to muster any more cheer. She scanned the breakfast options. "Scrambled eggs, please." She waited while Tim collected a bit of everything on offer.

Ottie was seated in the middle of the hall with the Gruesome Twosome. Like Kelcie and Lexi, she was eating a bowl of grapefruit drizzled with yoghurt. Alice turned away, the heat rising to her cheeks, but then she noticed two empty chairs at their table. *Nothing ventured, nothing gained*, Gran's voice reminded her and Alice recalled how brave she'd been at the LSPDA meeting last night, standing up to Red. Maybe, just maybe, this morning had all been a misunderstanding . . .

Alice took a deep breath and headed over.

"What are you doing?" Tim whispered, grabbing her sleeve.

"Going to say hello," she whispered back, wriggling out of his grip. "Want to join me?"

"Are you sure that's a good idea?" Tim said, but it was too late.

"Hi," Alice greeted the girls, interrupting their conversation. "Mind if me and Tim sit here?"

Kelcie looked Tim up and down. "Yes, we do actually," she said, her voice hard. "We mind very much if *he* sits here . . ." She glanced at Lexi and smiled. ". . . But *you* can join us, if you want, Alice."

"I really don't mind sitting somewhere else, Alice," Tim said, staring at the floor tiles so hard he could have burned holes in them.

Alice had stuffed her hands in her blazer pockets to stop them shaking. Kelcie had no right to talk to Tim like that. "No, Tim, you don't have to—"

"Good idea, Crossley-Herbert!" Kelcie said loudly. "Go away. No one wants you here." She turned slyly to Alice. "But what about you, Little Miss Boring? Are you going to sit with him or are you going to sit with us?"

"I'm just going to go," Tim mumbled, turning to leave, his shoulders slumped and eyes downcast. Alice looked to Ottie for help but her roommate was suddenly fascinated by her napkin.

"Bet you Little Miss Boring goes with him," Kelcie whispered nastily to Lexi.

Alice's skin prickled, her embarrassment replaced with fury. Why did people have to be so mean? Suddenly she felt really protective of Tim. She raised her chin defiantly. "Come on, Tim," she said loudly. "Let's sit over here."

"Told you!" Kelcie said smugly. "Freaks stick together."

Alice opened her mouth to retaliate before thinking better of it. She didn't want to give them the satisfaction. She glared at Ottie.

"I hope you're happy with your new friends, Ottoline," Alice said coolly. "You deserve them."

CHAPTER 14

Over the next few days, Alice found it increasingly difficult to focus on her lessons. Everywhere she turned, Ottie seemed to be laughing and joking with Kelcie and Lexi or, worse still, whispering with them in the back row of class or a secluded corner of the common room.

At least she still had Tim. But something wasn't quite right with him, she could see that now. Alice kept catching him staring into space, his eyes red and watery. The incident at breakfast had really upset him but she wondered if there was more to it than that. Alice added it to her list of things she needed to get to the bottom of. She'd been so busy with her investigations into the animal snatcher she hadn't had a chance to ask him what was going on.

She was already starting to regret the stupid promise she'd made to Red and the LSPDA. What had she been thinking? A week had passed and all she had so far was a pile of musty old newspapers and a suspicion about a couple of men in a boat. She hadn't seen Constance since the night of the meeting and a little voice at the back of her head was beginning to whisper *maybe she's been snatched too . . .*

"What's up?" Tim asked her as they made their way out to lunch. "You seem kind of distracted."

"I'm fine," she said vaguely, studying two older boys hauling a black sack of footballs out to the sports field. For a moment she thought she saw the bag twitch, a tiny paw trying to break free. Her heart skipped a beat. The bag could easily hide a small animal . . .

"Hello!" Tim waved his hands in front of her face. "Earth to Alice!"

"Huh? What is it?" she said, shaking herself awake. It was a gloriously sunny day with a powder-blue sky and puffy white clouds sailing overhead, but she'd barely noticed until now. Every day she felt edgier than the one before, her body tense and wary as if danger lurked around every corner. Alice wished she could tell Tim the truth about her fears but Agent T had sworn her to secrecy and Constance had made it crystal clear that the LSPDA would find out if she told anyone.

"Nothing." Tim sighed. "Just stand still a sec, will you?"

Alice paused and looked around. She'd been so deep in her thoughts she couldn't remember walking past the boarding house, but here they were, already headed into the gardens that curved round the back of the building. "What are we doing here?" she asked. "I thought we were going to the dining hall."

"Not today!" Tim grinned. "I've got a surprise for you."

He reached into his backpack and pulled out a crumpled hoodie. "Don't worry," he said. "I won't let you trip." He wrapped the hoodie around her eyes until all she could see were dots of sunshine poking through the fabric.

"I can't see where I'm going!" she protested, clutching Tim's elbow as he guided her down a bumpy stone path. Now was not the time to be blindfolded, not with an animal snatcher on the loose!

"Just a bit further . . ." Tim promised as Alice felt the stones turn to tufts of grass beneath her feet. "Okay," he said eventually. "You can take your blindfold off now."

Alice yanked Tim's hoodie from around her eyes, blinking as the sunlight rushed in. Slowly she looked about. They were standing beneath an archway woven with roses leading into a grassy area bordered by stone walls. The kitchen gardens were home to row upon neat row of vegetables, a herb patch and even a little orchard. Spread out on the grass beneath a cherry tree was a pale pink blanket that Alice recognised from the common room and an assortment of sandwiches, cakes and bags of crisps.

"I, er, just wanted to say thank you for the way you stuck up for me the other day," Tim said shyly. "Not many people would have done that."

Alice was speechless and although she really wasn't much of a hugger, she felt a sudden urge to hug Tim. She leaned towards him just as he stepped back and they ended up in an awkward sort of half hug, Tim's elbow colliding with her stomach.

"Sorry!" Tim said, flustered, but that just made Alice hug him harder.

"You are okay, aren't you?" Alice asked. His face looked gaunt and tired.

"I'm fine," he said, waving her worries away. He nodded in the direction of the picnic blanket. "Do you like it?"

"Like it? Tim, it's perfect!" She plonked herself down and helped herself to a glass of apple juice. "This must have taken you ages to get together!"

He shrugged. "I had a little help this morning from Felix. Here, take a cake." He held out a Tupperware box crammed full of fairy cakes and chocolate brownies.

Alice lay back on the grass and watched a couple of blackbirds splashing in a nearby bird bath. It was so much nicer eating outdoors than in the busy dinner hall with the clatter of crockery and the smell of cooking. She listened to the blackbirds chirping, straining to pay close attention. Among the cheeps she began to hear voices.

"That's better!" one bird said.

"Nice and clean!" the other cheeped. "Nice and clean!"

Alice felt giddy with excitement. There really was a whole world of animals out there, just waiting for her to meet them. She remembered the two dogs she and Ottie had seen on the first day of term. She'd love to have a chat with them! They seemed to have free run of the school grounds and if the animal snatcher was connected to Pebbles, as Red suspected, they might even have some useful information to share. In fact, maybe she ought to start interviewing the animals around school. She sat up, mulling this over, and helped herself to a cheese sandwich.

"I've been thinking about those men we saw on that boat," Tim said, breaking into her thoughts. "And I've got something to show you."

He pulled out a rather battered-looking tourist guide to Pebblehampton and thumbed through its pages to a section that he'd marked by folding down the page. "You're not the only one who can use a library, you know!" He winked. "Listen: 'It takes a skilled sailor to navigate Pebblehampton's treacherous rocky coast. Many ships have not been lucky, with the last shipwreck in 1982 when a tourist vessel sailed too close to the submerged boulders of School Bay.'"

"Okay . . ." Alice said, wondering where he was going with this.

"A skilled sailor? Submerged boulders? Don't you see, Alice? Those men must have known what they were doing, coming right up to the shore the way they did."

130

"Oh," Alice said, nodding. "I see what you mean."

"Exactly!" Tim said. "They must have made the trip before if they had that kind of confidence."

"Hmm," Alice said, lying back in the grass to think about it. Tim knew loads about the local coastline. Red could call another meeting at any moment and currently she had nothing new to tell him. Tim had proved himself pretty trustworthy – would it be so bad if she told him the truth about the LSPDA and the missing animals? Her tummy squirmed like earthworms after rain. Agent T had said to trust no one but Tim was the most reliable person she'd met since arriving at Pebbles.

Suddenly Alice couldn't eat a morsel more. Tim had barely touched his lunch either.

"Tim," she ventured, fiddling with a blade of grass. "There's something I need to tell you."

"Me first," he said. "I haven't been completely honest with you."

"Go on," Alice said, wondering what he was about to say.

Tim took a deep breath. "Look, I've never told anyone before, not properly, but I think after what you told me about being autistic you'll understand . . ."

Alice nodded encouragingly.

"You know those books you saw me taking out in the library? Well, they were for me – kind of, anyway. I wanted to read them to try and help my mum. She's got depression,

131

you see. At least, that's what the doctors say. Depression and anxiety."

"Oh," Alice said. Suddenly everything made sense – the early-morning phone call home, the way he'd been so tired lately . . .

"She's really unwell. I was able to look after her over the summer but now she's at home by herself." He picked up a sandwich and turned it over in his hand, studying it meticulously. His eyes had gone misty. "I feel really guilty being here at school when she's all alone. When I went away for the Year Five residential, Mum got so ill that I had to come back early. What if that happens again?"

"I wish you'd told me earlier." Alice reached over and squeezed Tim's hand. "I can help you find some other books that might help if you'd like. I'm sure Miss Jessops has got loads in the library."

Tim nodded. "That would be really good," he said, his voice much hoarser than usual.

"Maybe you can send your mum a postcard?" Alice suggested. "That way she'll know you're thinking of her."

"Thanks, Alice." Tim cleared his throat. "I'm glad I told you. Now what were you going to tell me?"

Alice chose her words carefully. "You know I like animals, right? Well, it turns out they've been going missing recently all over Pebblehampton. I'm trying to investigate. You're really good at maps and that kind of thing so I wondered if you'd help me?"

Tim looked a bit confused but he nodded earnestly. "Of course I'll help," he said. "There's got to be a logical explanation."

"I think someone's taking them," Alice said, hoping the LSPDA wouldn't be too cross with her for telling another human. "It might even be someone at the school."

"Stealing animals?" Tim said thoughtfully, almost to himself. "Who'd want to do something like that?"

They sat in silence for a few minutes then Tim got to his feet and wandered down towards the end of the garden. Alice drifted over to join him. "What do you think that's used for?" he asked, pointing at a ramshackle old shed. It was perched on the grassy slope where the gardens joined the woods that stretched beyond the school.

"Dunno," Alice said, shielding her eyes from the sun to take a better look. "It's creepy, though."

"That's just what I was thinking," Tim said. "Perfect for hiding stolen animals, right?"

Someone had pinned old sacks and compost bags over the windows. Alice's thoughts drifted back to the men on the boat and she shuddered. Maybe they hadn't been operating alone . . . If someone wanted to hide the stolen animals, this looked like just the kind of place where they could do it.

Mischief glinted in Tim's eyes. "We should check it out."

"I don't know . . ." Alice chewed her lip. She didn't much fancy poking around in some creepy old shed.

"Go on," Tim needled. "Just a really quick look."

"Okay," Alice relented, thinking how angry Red would be if he knew that she'd found out virtually nothing so far. "I suppose it wouldn't do any harm to have a *quick* look."

"Cool!" Tim grinned. "Even if we don't find any captured animals I bet there's all sorts in there. Spiders as big as your hand, maybe even a dead rat . . ."

Alice and Tim crept closer to the shed. Tim went ahead and tugged at the door handle. The door rattled but didn't open. It was locked fast. Alice peered round at the steeply pitched roof and the heavy wooden door. It was bigger than she'd first realised. Maybe whoever owned it had equipment to store, or maybe they needed the space for the animals they'd snatched . . .

She stood on tiptoe to peer through one of the windows where the corner of the plastic compost bag pinned up over the glass was drooping slightly. If she really stretched, Alice could just about see through the foggy, cobwebbed glass. In the gloom she made out a red-and-white-striped deckchair and an old transistor radio.

"Budge up," Tim said, squeezing in beside her. "That's weird . . ."

"What?"

"Down on the floor. Are those cages?"

Alice craned to see through the gap. There, piled up along one wall, were a stack of metal cages, each one big enough to house a small mammal. They were empty apart from some

134

old straw – straw someone might have put in there to lure an animal inside . . .

Alice stepped back from the window with a gasp. Had they found the animal snatcher's lair?

"Oi! You two!" a gruff voice shouted. A moment later, a man with shaggy white hair and a flat cap came into view, hurrying towards them as fast as his limp would let him.

CHAPTER 15

"What do you think you're doing?" the man hollered, shaking his rake at Alice and Tim. "This is my shed. What do you want?"

Alice jumped back from the window. "I'm sorry, sir," she said. "We were just having a look."

"Well, don't," the man said gruffly, leaning his rake against the shed wall. "I've enough to do with autumn on its way without a pair of schoolkids getting under my feet."

Alice looked the man up and down. He was wearing sturdy boots with steel toecaps and the kind of thick gloves Gran used when she was doing the gardening. "Are you the school gardener?" she asked.

"I am," the man said proudly, puffing out his chest. "Ted Turner, head gardener and groundsman."

Tim stepped forward, putting out his hand for the gardener to shake. "Pleasure to meet you, sir," he said. "I'm Tim and this is Alice. We were wondering if—"

"We were wondering if you'd seen a couple of dogs," Alice interrupted, thinking on her feet. "A golden retriever and a Jack Russell. We've seen them running about in the gardens before."

"Course I have!" The gardener laughed a warm, friendly kind of laugh, his gruffness disappearing. "The terrier's mine. A right rascal, he is!"

Either the gardener was a very good actor or he loved animals as much as Alice did. But that didn't explain what she'd just seen . . . "Is that why you have the cages?" she asked cautiously. "For your dog?"

Ted Turner laughed again and fumbled in his pocket for his key. "Put my dog in a cage?" he chortled. "Not likely! Here, let me show you."

Alice and Tim shared wary glances – should they go with him? But then Tim began to follow . . .

The gardener let them in. The shed looked a lot less scary from the inside, with light flooding through the open door. A half-eaten sandwich sat on a dusty fold-down table beside the deckchair and a *Gardener's World* calendar was pinned to the wall.

Ted stooped over and picked up one of the cages. "Rabbits," he said. "They're forever eating the plants."

"So you kill them?" Tim cried, horrified.

Ted laughed so hard he wheezed. "Goodness me, no, young man. I take 'em to the woods, though the little blighters still find their way back!"

Alice breathed a sigh of relief. This wasn't the animal snatcher's lair after all!

"Now," the gardener said, putting a weathered hand on each child's shoulder. "Is that your picnic back there?"

Tim nodded.

"Do me a favour, then, and make sure you take any rubbish with you. You'd be surprised at the harm a can of drink or a cardboard tube can do to an animal. Besides, we want the gardens looking nice, don't we?"

"Of course, sir," Tim said. "We'll go and tidy everything up right away."

"Thanks for showing us around," Alice added.

"All right, then," Ted Turner said, easing himself into the deckchair and giving his left leg a quick rub. "Good meeting you both."

"You too!" Tim and Alice called.

But as Alice turned to head out of the door she saw a medicine bottle on the shelf. There was a rabbit and guinea pig on the label, just like the bottle she'd found on the cliffs.

"Well, he seems nice," Tim said as they walked back to their picnic spot.

"Yeah, he does," Alice said, wondering why the gardener needed drugs for small animals when as far as she knew the only pet he had was a dog. She was glad she'd confided in

Tim and that he was so keen to help her investigate, but she still didn't feel any closer to getting to the bottom of the disappearances.

That evening after dinner, Tim wanted to call his mum so Alice decided to use the couple of hours before lights out to look for Constance. It had now been a whole week since she'd last seen the cat.

She checked all the places she thought the cat might be. But Constance wasn't in the library and there was no sign of her in the school gardens or anywhere else for that matter.

Tired and increasingly anxious, Alice trudged back to the boarding house. Suddenly she heard yapping in the distance and a moment later, the golden retriever and the Jack Russell trotted past the hall in the direction of the gardens, their tails wagging.

Alice's heart beat quickly, her hopes lifting. Maybe the dogs had seen Constance? "Hey! Wait up!" she called to them, hoping they would recognise her as a Switcher, the way other animals seemed to. "I really need to talk to you."

The dogs paused but instead of running over to speak to her, they sped up, breaking into a run.

"Come back!" Alice called, not caring whether anyone overheard her. "It's important!"

The dogs hurtled through the quad and down towards the wood. "Quickly! Let's get out of here!" Alice heard the Jack Russell bark. "It's not worth the risk."

Alice stared after them as they disappeared from view. Not worth the risk? Surely they didn't think *she* was the animal snatcher? Horrified, she thought about going after them but it was getting late and she certainly didn't want to end up lost in the woods after dark. Reluctantly Alice turned into the quad and headed back to the boarding house, vowing to search for Constance again the next day.

CHAPTER 16

The next morning, Alice sat in geography staring out of the window and stifling a yawn. Last night, she'd had the dormitory to herself again and she'd made the most of it by retrieving her secret stash of newspapers from under her bed. Certain there had to be something of use within the inky pages, she had stayed up, scouring the columns for anything on missing pets by the light of the torch Gran had packed for her until her eyes watered.

Alice was woken up a few hours later by Ottie sneaking back in. Shifting in bed, Alice realised something was stuck to her cheek. Peeling it away, Alice saw it was a crumpled newspaper. Once Ottie had swung herself up into her bunk, Alice switched Gran's torch back on under the cover of her duvet. The newspaper was an edition from the spring, open to the advertisements section. Almost every ad was offering a reward for a lost dog. As soon as she was sure Ottie was asleep, she'd rummaged through her stack for the following week's paper and there it was on page twenty: an item about a spate of dog thefts in Pebblehampton. Bingo! It seemed the disappearances had been going on for much longer than she'd realised.

Now the classroom clock ticked on. Instead of answering the questions the professor had set, Alice couldn't help thinking about the way Ottie had crept back to the dorm in her dressing gown but with all her clothes on underneath. At the time, she'd assumed Ottie had been down the corridor in Kelcie and Lexi's dormitory, but now she realised her roommate could just have easily snuck off to meet up with her uncle again. And if that was the case, what did Ottie and Mr Marlowe have to talk about that was so important?

Alice watched the hands of the clock inch forward. Red was expecting her to fail. She needed to find the animal snatcher, not worry about what her roommate was up to. What she needed was a lead . . .

Her head spun with all the different possibilities. Criminals needed motive, means and opportunity, that much she knew from reading Gran's detective novels one Christmas holiday when she was bored. What could the animal snatcher's motive be? The only thing she could think of was money but was that enough? With a sudden wave of sadness, she thought of poor Agent T. Was a seagull worth all that much, especially in a town like Pebblehampton where you couldn't even say 'sandwich' without being swamped by the birds?

"Ugh, she's so annoying," Tim said, shattering Alice's focus. She looked up to see him scowling and followed his gaze. On the other side of the classroom, Ottie was attempting to teach Lexi what sediment transport was, her finger jabbing at the diagrams in the textbook.

"What a teacher's pet!" Tim said. "Always trying to suck up to Uncle Hugo."

"Yeah." Alice nodded. "It is pretty sickening." Ottie was always on her best behaviour in biology, which was taught by Mr Marlowe. But now the headmaster kept popping up in other classes as well and her roommate was dialling up the charm whenever he appeared.

Today it was poor Professor Biddle's turn to have his classroom invaded. Mr Marlowe perched on a stool at the back, watching the rows of students before him like a meerkat studying a desert plain. From time to time, he made a little tick or wrote a brief comment on the fancy tablet he always carried. Fortunately the professor seemed oblivious to the headmaster's presence, radiating his usual blend of lively, if eccentric, energy.

"Ahem!" The headmaster pretended to cough as he strolled towards the front of the room. "Now who can tell me what you're learning today?"

Ottie's arm shot up, her blazer buttons straining as she begged to be allowed to answer her uncle's question. Mr Marlowe glanced around the room, totally ignoring his niece, and eventually chose a quiet boy called Raymond who turned beetroot red. It almost made Alice feel sorry for Ottie. Almost.

~

"I don't know why Ottie's so bothered about impressing her uncle anyway," Tim said at breaktime as he pushed open the library doors. "Professor Biddle's a much better teacher."

"He's the headmaster, I guess," Alice said. "Plus Ottie's mum wasn't exactly the friendliest of people when I saw her. Maybe Ottie is closer to her uncle than her mum? Anyway, I'm glad you decided to forfeit your breaktime slice of pizza and join me. Miss Jessops is really nice and I'm sure she has plenty of books about mental health if you still want to borrow one?"

The librarian was sitting behind the counter covering some new paperbacks in sticky-back plastic and twirling one of her curls absent-mindedly. "Oh, hello, Alice!" she beamed as Alice entered. "How are you?"

"Good, thanks," Alice said, glancing over at the armchair to see if Constance was around, but it was empty. Alice's heart sank. Another day with no sign of the tabby.

"Have you lost something?" Miss Jessops asked, getting up and shaking the creases out of her navy dress. It was covered in tiny green cacti and delicate gold birds swung from her ears.

"I was just wondering if you'd seen the cat," she said. "The tabby one."

"Ah! The grumpy old thing worms her way right into your heart, doesn't she? I've not seen her about today but I'm sure she'll show up. Who's your friend?"

"Oh, this is Tim," Alice said. "Timothy Crossley-Herbert. You've met him before."

"Ah yes," Miss Jessops said. "From what I can remember you were in a bit of a hurry."

"Sorry about that," Tim said, blushing. He glanced at Alice who gave an encouraging nod. "I'm sorry I didn't stick around the other day. I was kind of in a rush. Do you mind if I take another look?"

Miss Jessops smiled kindly. "Help yourself."

While the librarian continued her work and Tim browsed the shelves, Alice slipped away to take a few more newspapers from the mountain in the corner. She was rummaging through the top few editions when a flash of red caught her eye, bright against the beige of the old papers. It was a slim book with a dry, leathery cover. She tugged the small volume loose from the pile and gave the cover a careful stroke. The gold leaf had faded but she could just make out the title: *The Switcher's Companion* by Sir Rudyard A. Jessops.

Alice's heart fluttered in excitement then began pumping at double speed. The school's founder himself had written this book and it was about Switching! She flicked the cover open. To her disappointment, many of the pages seemed to be missing but a handful, though ink-smudged and dog-eared, remained intact.

Alice glanced back at Tim and Miss Jessops. There was no way she could check the book out without them seeing. Neither of them was looking her way. It wasn't stealing if she brought the book right back . . . was it?

Alice slid *The Switcher's Companion* into her blazer pocket.

CHAPTER 17

That afternoon in double maths, Alice's hand seemed to develop a life of its own. She was supposed to be writing out answers to algebraic equations but her hand kept slipping into her blazer pocket and caressing the tatty corners of the little red book. Towards the end of the lesson, Alice realised she hadn't answered a single question and to her total shame, she had to quickly copy Tim's answers before their teacher noticed.

"Sorry, Alice," Tim said. "But I won't be able to help you with your investigation tonight. I've got band practice. Will you be all right?"

"Oh," she said, trying her best to sound disappointed. "I'll be fine. I've got a couple of things to do myself."

After cakes and chocolate milk in the common room, Tim said his goodbyes and Alice went to sit in the quiet of the quad, perching on the edge of the fountain. The buttery-gold light of late afternoon only added to her excitement. Finally she had the chance to get the answers she'd been looking for. She was sure that within the pages of the battered old library book lay the secret to what it meant to be a Switcher. It was time to discover who she really was.

Alice again traced the gold lettering with her thumbnail, breathing in the book's scent of old leather and dust. Carefully she turned the first page.

THE SWITCHER'S HONOUR

1. *Do no harm;*
2. *Protect the world and all its creatures;*
3. *Others before self;*
4. *These maxims must be kept before all others.*

Others before self: those were the exact words Constance had used when she'd told her about the LSPDA! Alice buzzed with excitement. Perhaps, long ago, an animal had first heard the words from another Switcher?

Eager to find out more she turned to the next page, which had the heading 'The Good Listener'. Alice read how you had to empty your head of 'the noise of your mind' if you wanted to truly connect with an animal. Stillness, Sir Rudyard said, was essential, as was 'careful, compassionate listening'. Alice raced on to the next chapter: 'Attuning to Animal Ways'. But there was one section she found rather puzzling.

REST AND RECOVERY

Switching is exhausting work, even for the experienced Switcher. Rest is essential, as is taking the time to recover and recuperate, especially for the novice exploring Switching transference for the first few times. Switchers beware! It is all too easy to fall into the trap of Switching too frequently. Restraint MUST be shown. Pacing oneself is essential.

She knew novice meant beginner so maybe Sir Rudyard was talking about Switchers like her who had been surprised and shocked to learn they could talk to animals . . . and that animals could talk back! But she wondered what he meant by 'Switching transference'. Was that just an old-fashioned way of saying learning to Switch?

She found herself rereading the last few sentences over and over again. The tone scared her. She hadn't considered how often she talked to animals, and why should she have? This was the first she was hearing about pacing herself and showing restraint. Alice wondered why Agent T or Constance hadn't warned her. Perhaps, as animals, they simply weren't aware.

Over in the branches of a beech tree, a pair of house sparrows chattered noisily. Alice turned to listen. She thought about Sir Rudyard's advice, closing her eyes and trying to empty her mind. *Careful, compassionate listening*, she told herself over and over again, focusing on the sparrows' voices. It was so much easier when an animal spoke to her directly. Talking to Constance, Agent T and Red had been like speaking to another human: she could easily follow every word. But listening in to conversations between animals was proving much trickier. The birds chattered so quickly! She tried to harness every spark of energy, steering it so that it was directed towards listening to them.

Alice felt a little lift, a twitch, like someone had turned the volume up a notch, and there were the birds' shrill voices discussing where the juiciest beetles could be found. Alice clapped her hands together in delight. She was so lucky to be able to Switch. But why did she of all people have this gift? As soon as that thought crossed her mind she lost her grip on the sparrows' conversation, their words shifting back to unintelligible chirps. The secret to successful Switching seemed to be in staying quiet, keeping everything inside you still.

Alice turned back to her book, eager for more tips, but the chapter ended abruptly and the book's binding sagged open. The next page was missing and the one after that. She kicked the fountain's stone basin in frustration. Why weren't people more careful with books? She flicked through to the crumpled endpaper and there, scribbled in fountain pen, were six short words: 'Practise your craft, treasure your gift.'

Alice stared at the note. Who had written it? Had Sir Rudyard himself added it as an afterthought? She studied the messy handwriting, the splodge and splatter of ink. It didn't look like the writing of an adult but of someone who hadn't quite mastered the fountain pen. Yes, she realised, that was most definitely a child's writing . . . but whose?

~

"You got a minute?" Tim asked as they filed out of their geography class for break the following morning. "There's something I want to show you."

"Sure," Alice said. The dining hall got far too busy at breaktime for her liking, anyway.

"It's just down here," Tim said, leading her a little way down the photograph-lined corridor to a section of wall where the pictures turned to colour. Alice studied the students' faces, looking out for her gran and her mum among the hundreds of tiny people.

"Look at this one!" Tim said, pointing to a photograph from the year 2000. His finger hovered over the image of one particular girl who'd been squeezed on to the end of an already crowded line. "Who do you think that is?"

Alice stared at the photo of the girl with dark brown hair in a messy bun. She had a book under her arm, and another tucked into her blazer pocket. "It can't be . . ." she mumbled, leaning in for a closer look.

"I knew you'd recognise her!" Tim cried triumphantly. "It's your librarian friend, isn't it?"

"Miss Jessops?" Alice crouched down, studying the photograph. "Yeah, I think it might be, actually."

"That's exactly what I thought," Tim said with satisfaction. "But check this out."

Written in tiny gold lettering at the bottom of the photograph was a long list of student names. Tim found Miss Jessops' row and tapped the very last name in the list. *Veronica Vainwright*, the inscription said.

"Oh." Alice shrugged. "That's odd. I guess it must just be someone who looks a bit like her. It can't be Miss Jessops, anyway – she told me she was never a student here."

"A bit like her?" Tim scoffed. "You said it yourself – that girl's the spitting image of her!"

"But look how small these photos are!" Alice said. "And Miss Jessops is an adult now. People look different as kids, don't they? That girl could be anyone really . . ."

"Yeah, I guess." Tim frowned thoughtfully. "Bit of a coincidence, though, isn't it?"

Over the next couple of days, Alice read and reread *The Switcher's Companion*, carrying it with her wherever she went. She felt a twinge of guilt when she thought about how she'd taken it from the library but she couldn't shake the feeling the book had been destined to find its way into her hands.

The more she poured over the book, the more she came to believe the handwritten note advising the reader to 'Practise your craft, treasure your gift' was a secret message intended only for her. The mystery Switcher – and she was sure now it wasn't Sir Rudyard but someone young like herself – had wanted her to follow their advice.

Whenever Alice got the chance, she listened to the animals and birds around school, whether it was the squabbling rooks who had made the boarding-house roof their home or the tall, sleek horses down in the stableyard.

"Excuse me," she asked a heavy horse with long, feathery fur on his lower legs. "Have you seen Constance the library cat? I can't find her anywhere."

The horse snorted loudly, blasting Alice with his hot breath. "No cats here!" he declared.

"Please," she begged. "Get word to me if you do. It's been almost two weeks!"

The horse whinnied his consent and Alice had no choice but to go on her way. It made her giddy with excitement to think that she was getting better at talking to animals. But the fact that she couldn't find Constance niggled at her like an itchy mosquito bite she couldn't quite reach. Something was wrong, she knew it . . .

CHAPTER 18

"Aren't you excited, Alice?" Tim asked, checking his hand-drawn map as they headed down yet another of the science department's winding corridors. "We're finally getting to do some proper science!"

It was the start of their fourth week at Pebbles and now they were starting to have practical lessons, they were having today's double biology in Mr Marlowe's laboratory rather than his regular classroom. At long last the headmaster might stop waffling on about rules and actually teach them something!

"Of course I am," she said, giving Tim a smile. "I'm just a bit distracted." Alice stifled a yawn – maybe *The Switcher's Companion* was right and all the talking with animals was taking it out of her.

They reached the end of the corridor and stepped through the laboratory door.

"Wow!" Tim gasped. "It's true what they say, then. This school really is minted."

Alice's eyes widened. Rows of shiny new microscopes awaited them and every polished bench housed its own Bunsen burner, tripod and sink. This really was a far cry from her scruffy old primary classroom with its mismatched furniture and cluttered book corner.

"Welcome, welcome!" the headmaster said. "Today you will have the opportunity for some real hands-on learning." He stood at the front of the laboratory, one hand on his equipment trolley like a captain at the helm of his ship. "Dissection."

A groan filled the room but the headmaster carried on, oblivious. Alice looked around at the miserable faces of her fellow students. They'd all been expecting exploding test tubes and colourful combustions . . . not *this*. Only Ottie looked excited at the prospect of pulling apart some poor animal's body. She sat beside Kelcie and Lexi, her eyes trained on her uncle. *How was I ever friends with her?* Alice thought bitterly.

"We will be focusing on the most fascinating of creatures. An oft-overlooked amphibian you will all be familiar with . . ." The headmaster paused, keeping them in suspense. "The common garden frog!"

Mr Marlowe clicked the touchpad on his laptop and an image of a frog was projected on to the board. The poor creature lay splayed upon its back, the skin of its chest and stomach neatly peeled back to display its ghastly pink-and-brown innards.

Kelcie pulled a face like she'd just eaten cat vomit. "Gross."

Ottie frowned at her then turned back to the board.

"Not at all, Miss Maloney, not at all," the headmaster said. "There is nothing gross about science." He swept over to his interactive whiteboard and tapped on the screen. Immediately annotations and notes sprang up. "Pens out, please," he instructed.

Ottie whipped out her fountain pen and began writing furiously. Tim saw Alice watching her and rolled his eyes.

Alice tried to take notes but she kept getting her words muddled up. She found herself thinking of the frog who used to lurk in Gran's back garden, startling her whenever she disturbed its hiding place. The last time it had ribbited at her, she'd dropped the chicken feed all over the lawn! She shifted uneasily in her seat. The poor frog on Mr Marlowe's screen wouldn't be ribbiting again any time soon.

"Come on," Tim whispered, giving her a nudge. "You know what Marlowe's like."

Alice picked up her pencil and attempted to copy the diagram into her exercise book. *Dissection and experimentation are how scientists learn about biology*, she told herself firmly, trying to ignore the uneasy feeling stirring in the pit of her tummy. Even her hero, Beatrix Potter, drew endless pictures of animals to learn about their anatomy.

When everyone had finished, Mr Marlowe clapped his hands. "Time for the good stuff!" he announced. "Up you all come! Collect your equipment from the trolley. Bonus marks for the first pair to bring me a frog heart!"

Alice grimaced. The way the headmaster was making the whole thing seem like a game made her skin feel all tight and itchy. Not too long ago, those frogs had lives of their own . . . It wasn't right that he was treating the experiment like one big treasure hunt. Ottie rushed forward to be first in the queue and slowly other stools scraped back as the rest of the class went to collect their equipment. But Alice's legs wrapped around her stool and refused to budge.

"It's all right," Tim said, putting a hand on her shoulder. "I'll go."

"Now that's strange," the headmaster remarked, rummaging in the drawers of his trolley. "I seem to be missing some of my equipment. My syringes, for one . . . and my test tubes it seems. Well, never mind, at least we don't need them today. I wonder where they've got to, though . . ."

Alice froze like a rabbit in headlights. She could think of one person who might need scientific equipment and would be just the type to steal it – the animal snatcher! She already suspected the missing animals had been drugged and the syringes would come in handy with that but what were the test tubes needed for?

A terrible realisation dawned. If Mr Marlowe's syringes and test tubes were missing then that meant the snatcher had been here inside the school, perhaps in this very lab . . . Her thoughts flashed back to the bottle of medicine in the gardener's shed. Could he have stolen the syringes? Mr Turner had seemed so nice, but appearances could be deceptive and Agent T had warned her to 'trust no one'. Had she been too quick to fall for the old man's excuses?

But there was another possibility. The headmaster could be lying. Maybe Mr Marlowe had taken the equipment from the lab himself . . . What if he was the animal snatcher?

Her muscles rigid with fear, Alice tried to catch Tim's eye across the classroom.

Stay calm, she told herself. *Don't give the game away.*

She kept her eyes trained on Mr Marlowe as he handed a small metal tray, a scalpel and a pair of silver tweezers to each student in turn. After a minute or two, Tim reached the head of the queue.

"Straight in at the deep end, eh, Mr Crossley-Herbert?" The headmaster guffawed, slapping him on the back. "That's the spirit!"

Alice shifted uneasily on her stool. Was she overthinking things or was the headmaster enjoying all this a bit too much?

She couldn't remember ever seeing him look so excited before.

Alice forced herself to take deep breaths. If Mr Marlowe really was the snatcher then no good would come of him knowing she suspected him.

A scalpel landed on the bench before her with a clang and Alice leaped from her stool. "Tim!" she screeched, grabbing his arm.

"Hey, are you all right?" Tim said. "You look like you've seen a ghost?"

"Did you hear what Mr Marlowe said?" she whispered, slowly loosening her pincer-like grip on his forearm. "About the missing syringes and test tubes?"

Tim nodded and then his eyes grew wide as he realised what Alice was getting at. "Whoa! Hold your horses," he whispered back. "I know what you're thinking but there's a million reasons that equipment could be missing. It doesn't mean anything."

Alice nodded, clenching her fists to stop her hands from shaking. Tim was right. One of the science technicians could have moved the syringes and test tubes, or another teacher could have borrowed them. Until she could think about things properly, she just needed to get through the lesson. Mind over matter, as Gran would say. Unclenching her fists, Alice picked up the small tray.

Pinned spread-eagle on a blue paper towel was a frog, a silver spike through each of its tiny, webbed feet. Alice stared at it, paralysed.

"No need to look so frightened, Miss Tonks!" the headmaster boomed from across the room. "It's not going to hurt you!"

From a couple of desks over, she heard Kelcie snigger. "Boo!" she said, waving her frog in Alice's direction.

Alice's anger flared. Couldn't Kelcie see she had more important things on her mind? Alice clamped her lips shut, knowing that if she opened her mouth, she wouldn't be able to stop the words flying out! She hated being laughed at, hated it more than just about anything else, and right now she was all out of patience.

Ottie tutted and took the frog from Kelcie but Alice could tell she was only bothered about her experiment being interrupted, not Alice's feelings. Stinging with anger and hurt, Alice looked down at the frog. Its bulbous eyes stared right back, fixed and unblinking. Alice had a curious feeling that the frog was trying to say something to her. She tried turning away but wherever she looked, the frog's gaze seemed to follow . . .

"Yikes!" Tim whistled, leaning over the tray. "Wish me luck!" He gestured to the frog's stomach with the razor-sharp edge of the scalpel. "That's where the heart is apparently."

"What?" Alice's head was pounding like she'd sat out in the hot sun for far too long.

"The heart," Tim started to explain but she couldn't follow his words. Saliva oozed from her gums, sickly sweet and cloying. If only she had some pondwater, lovely and cool and murky . . .

Pondwater? Yuck! Alice shook her head. Where on earth had that come from?

She heard another burst of laughter and when she looked up, Kelcie and Lexi were gawping at her like oversized goldfish, their mouths hanging open.

"What's the matter with her?" Kelcie said. "Why does she keep doing that thing with her fingers?"

Slowly Alice looked down at her fingers and sure enough, there they were, flapping in mid-air. Swallowing hard, Alice rammed her fists deep in her blazer pockets. How could she have been so stupid? Stimming at home was one thing but she never EVER stimmed in public!

Kelcie and Lexi looked at her again and burst into another fit of giggles. Alice took a few deep breaths, refusing to cry. She didn't want to give them the satisfaction of knowing they'd got to her! "Right, give it here," she told Tim and reached for the scalpel.

The blade hovered just above the frog's lifeless body. "Come on," Alice muttered, urging her hand to do as it was told and slice into the soft green belly. But it was no good. Her fingers wouldn't stop shaking. Her hand brushed cool, damp skin and straight away her vision began to cloud. The bench lurched towards her and the room spun. The silver tray slipped from her hands and skittered across the floor.

"Alice? Are you okay?" Tim asked. His voice sounded muffled as though she was underwater. "You don't look too good . . ."

"I'm f-fine." She brought her fingers up to her eyes, turning them slowly over and over as she tried to examine them. Everything was blurry.

"What's the matter with your hands?" Tim asked, his voice echoey.

"I don't know . . ." Alice rubbed the skin of her fingertips. They were buzzing. She peered at them again, sure she could see them tremble and pulsate. Alice staggered to her feet and reached for the tray, her legs wobbling beneath her like frogspawn.

"Careful!" Tim grabbed her elbow just before she hit the ground. "Mr Marlowe? Mr Marlowe? Alice isn't well!"

"S-sorry," she mumbled, pressing her hands to her mouth, afraid she was about to be sick. Waterlilies danced before her eyes and the contents of her belly sloshed back and forth, back and forth . . .

"Shouldn't we get her to the school nurse, sir?" Tim asked Mr Marlowe as he helped Alice back up on to her stool. "She's looking really pale . . ."

Alice bit down on her hand. It was all she could do not to gag on the stench of rotten eggs that surrounded her. "Can't you smell that?" she said woozily. "It's like stagnant water . . ."

Mr Marlowe glanced down at her. "Go back to the boarding house, Miss Tonks, and have a lie-down. I'll email Mrs Salter and let her know what's happened."

The headmaster then moved on to the neighbouring desk. "Very nice," he remarked loudly, admiring the students' work. "It's good to see at least some of you have a head for science."

Kelcie and Lexi tittered, shooting sly glances in Alice's direction as soon as Mr Marlowe's back was turned.

Ottie got up and for a moment Alice thought she was about to come and help. But then the headmaster glanced in her direction and she sat back down again.

"Ignore them," Tim said, helping Alice to her feet and guiding her towards the door. Alice stumbled out of the laboratory and into the cool, shady corridor. What was wrong with her? She couldn't remember ever feeling so woozy before, not out of the blue like this.

"You're not going to spew on me, are you?" asked Tim, holding her at arm's length.

Alice shook her head. "I'm fine now." She steadied herself against the wall. "Thanks, Tim."

"No problem," he said. "I'd stay but . . ." He gestured back to the laboratory where Mr Marlowe loomed in the doorway.

"It's okay," she said quickly, not wanting to get Tim in any trouble with the headmaster. She tried to give him a smile and he headed back into class.

Once alone, Alice replayed the lesson in her head. Nobody liked dissection but how had it left her feeling so ill? She stared at her throbbing fingers. Something very, very weird was happening to her. This had something to do with Switching . . . but what?

CHAPTER 19

On the short walk back from the science department to the boarding house, Alice realised she'd been completely and utterly stupid. If what had happened to her in the laboratory was due to Switching then she had something in her possession that had to hold the answers.

The Switcher's Companion.

As soon as Alice made it to her dormitory, she rummaged through her bag for the little red book. "Where is it? Where is it?" she muttered, shoving exercise books and stationery out of the way.

Finally she found the book hiding at the bottom of her bag and began to flick through the pages. There had to be something here about what had happened to her, there just had to be. She scanned the pages but there was nothing she hadn't read before, no answers to be found. If only she had the whole book!

"Ugh!" Alice cried in frustration, throwing it to the floor. Hot, angry tears streamed down her face. She was furious with the animal snatcher, whoever they were, furious with herself for not having the answers she wanted, furious with Constance for not being here when she needed her . . .

But then Alice saw it. A slip of yellow paper lying on the rug.

She wiped her eyes and picked it up. It was no bigger than a Post-it and tightly folded. It must have fallen out when she threw the book.

With shaking hands, Alice unfolded the note. She instantly recognised the child's handwriting, scrawled in the same splodgy fountain pen as before.

Signs of Switching:
1. Hot flushes
2. Sweating
3. Muscle cramp/pain
4. Throbbing fingers
5. Obsessive thoughts

Yes, Alice thought impatiently. *I've had all of those symptoms this afternoon but what do they mean?* She reread the list, then reread it again. Suddenly her eyes settled on the title. 'Signs of Switching' – of course! The symptoms meant she was about to Switch, she understood that much, but that didn't make any sense. She hadn't been trying to talk to the frog, and the frog was dead so it couldn't have been trying to talk to her . . .

And then Alice remembered what she'd read the other day. She leafed back through *The Switcher's Companion* to the page about 'Rest and Recovery'. There were those words again: 'Switching transference'.

Alice sat back on her haunches. What if she'd been reading the *Companion* wrong? Sir Rudyard wasn't just referring to talking to animals, he meant becoming one!

The next few hours were a nightmare. Alice desperately wanted to discuss her discovery, but with no Agent T and no Constance she couldn't say a word.

Despite Tim's best efforts to cheer her up, she suffered moodily through dinner and hardly ate a thing. She planned to escape into the woods and find Red the first chance she got. She had no idea whether she could find her way to the clearing again or if the fox would even be there but she had to try. If she couldn't find Red, maybe she'd spot Milo, Henry or one of the other animals from the LSPDA. It had to be better than sitting here doing nothing.

As soon as Mrs Salter dismissed them from dinner, Alice said a hasty goodnight to Tim and rushed back to the dormitory to grab her torch, some warm clothes and *The Switcher's Companion*. She flung open the door, expecting silence, but was instead met with gentle snoring.

"CONSTANCE!"

Alice raced over to her bunk where a small, stripey form was nestled in the duvet. She gave the cat's lean back a shake. "Constance, wake up!"

The tabby stirred, stretched and yawned. "Oh, good evening, Alice," she said sleepily. "I was having a lovely dream." She licked her lips. "Mackerel."

"Constance, you're safe!" Alice cried, scooping the cat up. Her fur was tickly, she stank of fish . . . and she was perfect.

"Put me down!" Constance spluttered half-heartedly but then she nuzzled her head against Alice's chest and was soon licking her affectionately with her sandpaper tongue. Her chest vibrated with a low, happy purr.

"Where have you been?" Alice asked. "I've so much to tell you!"

"Investigating," Constance said. "No one notices a cat hanging around a harbour, it seems. I didn't see that boat you mentioned, though, just the regulars . . ."

"Forget about the boat for a minute," Alice said impatiently. "I think . . . I think I might know who the animal snatcher is . . ."

Constance wriggled free of Alice's grasp and leaped down on to the bed, suddenly alert. "What? Who?"

"Well, I don't know for sure," Alice admitted. "It's actually more of a hunch. But if it is who I think it is then he's been right here under our noses the whole time!" She paused. "I think it's Mr Marlowe. He's been acting really suspiciously . . ."

"The headmaster?" Constance's tail flicked nervously. "How do you know? Are you sure?"

"No," Alice said. "But it all makes sense. He has access to the right equipment, he lives here on site, he knows the local area . . ."

As soon as the words left her mouth, she realised the same was true of the gardener, or any one of the teachers but Constance was already launching into action.

"Oh my whiskers!" the cat exclaimed. "This could be the breakthrough we've been looking for. I have to tell Red. I should go now . . ."

"Wait!" Alice insisted. "There's more."

"More?" the cat cried disbelievingly. "How can there be more?"

Alice held up her battered copy of *The Switcher's Companion*. "I found this in the library. "Constance, why didn't you tell me?"

The cat shook her head as if she had dust on her nose. "Tell you what? You're not making any sense, Alice."

"Tell me the truth about Switching. It's not just talking to animals, is it? It's—"

"Alice, wait," Constance said firmly and there was such a sternness to her voice that Alice fell quiet. "That book.

I've never seen it before, but I've heard of it . . . and I'm sorry, but it's not true."

Alice froze. "What do you mean it's not true? Of course it's true! I'm a Switcher, aren't I?"

The cat sighed. "Yes, you are. You can talk to animals and like I've told you before that's a real honour and not to be sniffed at . . . but you can't do the kind of magic that book talks about. No one can."

Alice glared scornfully at the library cat. "So Sir Rudyard was lying, was he?" she scoffed. "He was making the whole thing up?"

"I . . . I don't know," Constance admitted. "Maybe it was true once, maybe it wasn't, but it's not true now. Everyone knows that." She gave Alice's hand a tentative lick. "I'm sorry."

Alice sank down on to the bed beside the cat. "But Constance, I *felt* it. Today, in biology, I had the symptoms this book describes. We were dissecting frogs and I felt . . . froglike."

Constance draped her head in Alice's lap. "I'm sure you did," she said gently. "You're a kind, considerate girl. You care for animals. But that doesn't mean you can shapeshift. Nobody can."

Tears prickled in Alice's eyes. She'd been so sure. "Are you . . . certain?" she asked, choking out the words.

The cat nodded. "I'm certain. That book's dangerous. From what I've heard, it's got people into trouble before.

I think you should put it away and forget all about it, Alice. Or, better still, get rid of it."

Alice got under the duvet, feeling an icy-blue mix of fear, sadness and anger, and let her tears fall.

Constance wrapped herself around her, and Alice and the cat lay quietly together, Alice sniffling from time to time and Constance purring gently. From the way the cat was licking her lips, Alice wondered if she was dreaming of mackerel again.

Eventually when Alice's tears had dried up, Constance stirred. "I have to go and see Red now."

"No, Constance! You can't go!" Alice protested. She'd only just got the library cat back. Like Constance, Agent T was clever and he too had worked for the LSPDA but that hadn't been enough to protect him. "What if you end up getting taken too?"

Constance butted Alice's arm with her nose. "Thank you for your concern," she said quietly. "But others before self, remember? This is a risk I have to take."

Alice looked at the floor. She'd become strangely affectionate towards the grumpy little tabby.

"Look." Constance sighed. "We have to be practical about this. If you think there's even a chance the headmaster could be the animal snatcher then the LSPDA need to know about it, okay?"

Alice nodded silently, a lump rising in her throat.

"Good," Constance said. "Now I'd better get going before that roommate of yours comes back . . . or worse, that housemistress." The cat shuddered. "A cold fish like her would never have been employed here in the good old days."

"The good old days?"

"When the previous head was here. There used to be school chickens, you know, and goats, until Mr Marlowe got the job last year and kicked them all out." She scratched thoughtfully at one ear. "That makes sense, I suppose, if he is who you say he is . . ."

"I'd never, ever let Mr Marlowe get rid of you, Constance!" Alice vowed. "Pebbles is your home."

Constance nuzzled Alice's hand. "Well, let's not worry about that yet. We've much bigger fish to fry."

"Constance," Alice said finally. "W-what if I can't do it?" The question burst from her lips before she could stop it. "What if I'm wrong about Mr Marlowe like I was wrong about Switching? What if I can't catch the animal snatcher?"

The library cat turned round to face Alice, putting one paw over her eyes to block the creamy light cast by the bedside lamp. "Listen, Thomas was . . . is . . . an excellent judge of character. When he spotted you on the beach, he knew you had a gift that the LSPDA could use. Every animal, however small, has their part to play. The squirrels pass messages. The wood mice make wonderful spies. You, Alice, just need to figure out what your role is going to be."

"That's why I can understand animals, isn't it?" Alice asked. "Because the LSPDA needs me?"

"I don't know how these things get decided." Constance shrugged. "All I know is that you wouldn't be the first person to come to Pebbles and discover they could do something they never could before. Ask your gran."

Alice sat up straighter. "My gran?"

"Hmm. A woman of many talents," Constance said mysteriously, stretching out her paws. "Now I'm at least two sleeps down on my quota for the day, and before I can have them, I need to find Red."

Alice wasn't going to be put off that easily. "What talents has my gran got?" she asked eagerly. "Can she Switch too? She can, can't she?" She tried to imagine Gran talking to animals but she couldn't do it. Gran was just Gran. Boring, lovely Gran.

Constance yawned loudly. It was clear she wasn't going to be drawn into saying any more tonight. "Get some rest, Alice."

"You're so annoying sometimes!" Alice huffed but she still gave Constance's ears a rub.

"Goodbye," Constance purred, jumping up on to the windowsill. "And don't forget what Thomas told you. It's as important as it's ever been, if not more so. Trust nobody, Alice. Not even those who seem to be your friends."

CHAPTER 20

The next morning, Alice woke to the distant sound of the breakfast gong. Hundreds of feet trampled downstairs and cries of "Where's my bag?" and "Hang on, I've forgotten my homework!" filled the landing.

She must have slept through her alarm! Not wanting to miss breakfast, she jumped out of bed and hurried down the hall to the bathroom, steeling herself to endure yet another lukewarm shower.

Alice washed as quickly as she could, trying hard not to touch the cubicle walls. The grouting between the tiles was flecked with black mould that seemed to multiply like fleas. Alice wrung out her hair, wrapped herself in her fluffy dressing gown and was on her way back to her dormitory when she heard the distinctive click-clack of heels outside on the landing, getting closer.

They could only belong to one person – Mrs Salter!

Not wanting a tongue-lashing from the housemistress for getting up late, Alice dived through the nearest door and found herself in the laundry room. The footsteps were getting closer so she ducked behind one of the huge, industrial washing machines, crouching down among the snaking tubes and electrical cables.

A moment later, the housemistress entered, the headmaster at her side. "Why have you been avoiding me?" she hissed. "I've been trying to catch up with you for days."

Holding her breath for fear of making a noise, Alice peeped over the piles of freshly laundered underwear. Mrs Salter had one of Mr Marlowe's hands in hers and was squeezing it tightly.

"We need to take precautions," the headmaster said gruffly. "It is of the utmost importance that our work here remains under wraps." He snatched his hand free of Mrs Salter's grip and began to pace up and down.

Alice leaned in, straining to hear over the sound of a nearby dryer.

"Of course, Hugo," Mrs Salter simpered, her sharp purple nails caressing his cheek. "I'll be more discreet."

Alice had to stick her fist in her mouth to stop herself from gagging.

"If anyone found out I was . . ." Mr Marlowe shuddered.

"The damage to my reputation doesn't bear thinking about."

Alice's ears pricked up. What *were* the headmaster and Mrs Salter up to?

"You worry too much, darling," Mrs Salter purred. "If the students know what's good for them, they'll keep their noses out of our business."

"It's not the children I'm worried about, Arabella," Mr Marlowe said. "Some of the teachers have been asking questions. That professor, for one."

"You can get rid of old codgers like Biddle easily enough," Mrs Salter scoffed. "Keep piling on the pressure and he'll cave. It's early retirement and cocoa for that one."

"I'll do my best," the headmaster said. "Let's get this business over and done with before anyone else pokes their nose in where it isn't wanted. We need to finish what we've started."

Alice gasped. The headmaster wasn't just trying to get rid of all the animals – he wanted to get rid of the teachers too! And what else was he planning?

Mr Marlowe gave Mrs Salter's chalky-white cheek the lightest of pecks. A moment later, the headmaster was gone. Mrs Salter waited a few minutes, craning her neck round the laundry room door to check no one was about. Finally she click-clacked back towards her office.

Alice carefully unfolded herself from behind the washing machine, stretching her cramped legs. Her palms were sweaty and she was breathing fast. Mr Marlowe and Mrs Salter were clearly in cahoots and it sounded like they were planning something much bigger than just forcing poor Professor Biddle into retirement! What if it had something to do with the missing animals?

Checking the coast was clear, Alice darted from the room and made it back to the safety of her dormitory. She dressed as quickly as she could then ran downstairs. As she reached the bottom she skidded breathlessly into Tim, who was on his way over to breakfast.

"Hey," he said, taking off his headphones. "What's the emergency?"

"Tim," she panted. "There's something I have to tell you."

Alice pulled Tim into the library. It was the safest place she could think of.

A group of sixth-form students were packing up their books to go to breakfast so Alice dragged Tim to the far end of the room where the shelves concealed them from view.

"Are you okay?" Tim was looking at her as if she had her clothes on back to front and inside out. "You're acting kind of weird. Is this about what happened in biology yesterday?"

"I'm not supposed to tell anyone," Alice babbled, remembering Constance's parting words: *trust nobody, not even those who seem to be your friends.* "But I have to. I just can't believe it . . ." She paused, waiting restlessly for the last sixth-former to pick up his bag. "I think I've found out who's stealing the animals . . ."

"What?" Tim stepped closer. "How? Who is he?"

Alice shook her head. "Not he, *they*. I . . . I think it's Mr Marlowe and Mrs Salter."

Tim burst out laughing. "Don't be ridiculous!"

"No, you don't understand!" Alice said. "I heard them planning something."

Tim thought about it, clearly not convinced. "Well, I guess it's *possible* . . ." He frowned. "So you just happened to overhear them talking?"

"Yes," Alice said and Tim looked at her quizzically. "Okay, I might have been eavesdropping."

"Spying, eh?" He grinned. "Nice one, Tonks!"

Quickly she filled him in on Mr Marlowe's conversation with Mrs Salter, including the way he'd kissed her on the cheek.

"Ugh!" Tim said, pulling a face like he'd just been forced to swallow a particularly juicy slug. "Marlowe and Salter? What a combo!"

"Tim! Be serious!" Alice snapped.

She crossed her fingers behind her back, praying she was doing the right thing. If Tim was going to be able to help her, he needed to know the full story. "But that's not all."

Tim looked up.

"There's other things I haven't told you. Strange stuff that's been going on ever since I started here. It all began on Welcome Day, when I was down on the—"

There was a loud thud. Alice and Tim looked at one another then peered out from behind the shelves.

"Oh, I'm sorry," Miss Jessops said, a mound of books at her feet and a bottomless cardboard box in her hands. "The blasted thing just gave way."

"Here, let me give you a hand," Tim said quickly. He picked up an armful of books to deposit on the counter.

Alice grabbed a few of the tatty chemistry tomes herself and followed.

"You two are so kind," Miss Jessops gushed. "I'm such a butterfingers sometimes."

Alice looked at the clock. "Sorry, miss. We'd better be off or we're going to miss breakfast. See you soon!"

"Do you think she heard us?" Tim whispered to Alice as they quickstepped it to the dining hall.

"Miss Jessops is in a world of her own," said Alice. "Don't worry. And I'll fill you in on everything else later."

"You might not get the chance," Tim said ominously, for there was Mr Marlowe, red-faced and sweating, marching down the corridor towards them.

"Alice Tonks!" the headmaster bellowed. "I want a word with you!"

CHAPTER 21

The last few students hurrying into breakfast turned back wide-eyed as Mr Marlowe stormed down the corridor, his eyes firmly fixed on Alice. Mrs Salter was in the doorway to the dining hall, ticking the final students off, a sly smile creeping across her face. Alice blinked fast, trying to put the image of Mrs Salter's long purple nail stroking the headmaster's cheek out of her head.

"I'm on to you!" the headmaster raged, spittle flying from his mouth and speckling Alice's cheek. She didn't dare wipe it off. After what she'd heard in the laundry room, who knew what he was capable of? "Sneaking around, trying not to get caught . . ."

Tim tried to edge out of the firing line.

"Not so fast, Crossley-Herbert," Mr Marlowe snapped. "I dare say you're involved somehow too."

"W-w-with what, sir?" Alice asked, her fingers starting to flick. He must have spotted her behind the washing machine. He knew she'd overheard him . . . She rifled through her brain to find a decent excuse but in her panic everything seemed topsy-turvy and back to front.

"Oh, you know, all right! Don't play the innocent with me, young lady. Bringing strays into the school. Encouraging animals to make this their home."

Alice's mouth fell open. Strays? Did Mr Marlowe mean Constance? So this wasn't about her spying on his secret rendezvous with Mrs Salter?

Tim turned to stare at her, a look of total bewilderment plastered all over his face.

Mrs Salter strode over, her heels clattering on the tiled floor. "Don't try to deny it!" Her face was alight with glee. "Cat hair all over your bedclothes! Claw marks on your door! And given the disgusting state of your dorm, I suppose you're in on it too, Timothy?"

"No!" Alice cried. There was no way she was going to let Tim get into trouble for this and besides, the school was Constance's home! She'd lived in the library long before Mr Marlowe and Mrs Salter had arrived.

"What Alice means," said Tim, stepping forward. "Is no, it isn't her fault." He looked at Mrs Salter and Mr Marlowe in turn. "I've had my cat Percy since I was a baby. He's only got three legs but he doesn't let that stop him. He's the most loyal cat in the world. Never leaves my side. I can't bear to be apart from him. It was all my idea. I thought it would be nice to have a pet here at school. Alice was just helping me out."

Alice gawped at Tim, amazed at how easily the lies slipped off his tongue.

"Enough, Crossley-Herbert!" Mr Marlowe held up his hands. "I don't want to hear another word."

Tim fell silent.

Mr Marlowe looked sternly from Tim to Alice. "No. More. Animals. Not now, not ever. From here on in, this school is officially an animal-free zone. Do I make myself clear?"

"Yes, sir," Alice and Tim chorused.

"It's bad enough that the staff let their pets have free rein of the school without students having the same idea! I've told the gardener that dog of his has to go. I'm sure he'd be too only too glad to help –" Mr Marlowe gave a little cough – "*rehouse* any creatures you may have acquired."

Alice narrowed her eyes. What exactly did the headmaster mean by 'rehouse'? Were the gardener and Mr Marlowe somehow in cahoots?

"For too long Pebbles has been crawling with one revolting creature or another. It's not professional. It's not proper. In fact, it's high time that this school smartened up its act." Mr Marlowe straightened his jacket lapels and wiped the sweat from his brow. "Detention. Tonight.

Instead of going to games with the rest of your year group, you can sort out all those old books lying around in the library. Goodness knows why we've kept them when everyone knows the world runs on technology these days! I want that library spotless."

"Detention?" Mrs Salter spluttered as Mr Marlowe strode off up the corridor. "Expulsion more like! Now *that's* a proper punishment."

"Can we be excused, please, Mrs Salter?" Tim asked sweetly.

"Get to class. Now!"

Despite how hungry they were, Alice and Tim didn't need telling twice. "Thank you, miss," they said.

As soon as the housemistress's back was turned, they looked at one another, wide-eyed.

"I told you!" Alice whispered. "Didn't you hear Mr Marlowe? *An animal-free zone,* he said . . ."

"Detention tonight," Tim replied. "Give me everything you've got."

Whistles blew as a game of hockey ended outside the library window. Alice and Tim were half-heartedly restacking the 'Classic Fiction' section, a bag of chocolate cookies at their feet. The library door swung open and Mr Marlowe stalked in. Tim quickly kicked the biscuits under the shelves, out of sight.

"I'm glad to see you're both making amends," the headmaster said stiffly. "I hope you've learned your lesson."

"Yes, sir," they said, trying to sound apologetic. Tim's demeanour was so pitiful he wouldn't have been out of place in the workhouse with a bunch of poor, starving orphans.

"Very good." The headmaster caught sight of Miss Jessops, seated at her counter. "It's about time this place had a jolly good sort-out. Make good use of them, Miss . . ." He wafted his hand vaguely in the librarian's direction as he tried to conjure up her name.

"Jessops," she provided. "Miss Jessops." She looked at him pointedly. "You interviewed me, sir?"

"Ah yes." Mr Marlowe nodded, his cheeks flushing. "Miss Jessops, of course. Very good." He turned swiftly on his heel and hurried out.

Tim pretended to vomit. "What a pompous old . . ."

"Now, now," Miss Jessops said, retrieving the plate of sandwiches and crisps she'd squirrelled away beneath the counter for them. "That's no way to talk about our headmaster, is it?"

Alice thought she saw a smile flicker across the librarian's lips.

"So what have you two done to earn yourselves a detention, anyway?"

"Alice had the audacity to stroke the school cat!" Tim laughed.

"Turns out Mr Marlowe isn't an animal lover," Alice added but she couldn't bring herself to laugh. He'd seemed really furious about Constance being on school grounds. Irrationally furious, you could say . . .

"Well, then!" Miss Jessops winked. "It's lucky I was in such desperate need of help in here. Now I'm afraid I have to shoot off tonight, but if you can water the plants, that'd be lovely. They're looking a little thirsty. And turn the lights off, won't you?"

"No problemo," Tim said, taking a giant bite of cookie. "Got a hot date, miss?"

Miss Jessops blushed. "As a matter of fact I have. It's book club tonight at the church hall."

Tim laughed, spraying wet cookie crumbs all over the table.

Alice kicked him hard under the table. "New boots?" she asked to cover his snigger.

"Why yes, Alice," Miss Jessops said. She stretched out one foot after the other, to show off her black lace-up boots. "Must dash! I'd hate to miss the tea and shortbread."

"Have fun, miss. I'll turn all the lights off," Alice promised.

"Night, miss!" Tim called. "And thanks for the food!"

As soon as the door shut, Tim's face grew serious. "Let's get down to business. Tell me *everything*."

Alice took a deep breath. This was the moment of truth and after all Tim had done for her, he deserved to hear it. He'd just got in trouble with the headmaster to save her neck and he'd stuck by her while Ottie had dumped her the minute the Gruesome Twosome showed the slightest bit of interest.

It was the second time Tim had helped her out in a squeeze and the only time in Alice's life that she'd had a friend she could rely on.

"Okay," she decided. "But first you've got to promise me two things. One, you don't tell anyone – and I mean *anyone* – what I'm about to say. Do you swear it?"

She had to make him see how important this was.

"Yeah, sure!" Tim laughed nervously. "I promise. Cross my heart and hope to die and all that. What's the second thing?"

Alice tilted her head so that for once she was looking squarely at Tim. "That you won't think I'm crazy."

Tim flinched. "I hate that word. In Year Six, Mum had a panic attack when she came to watch the Christmas play. Kelcie said Mum was crazy but she's not, you know. She just feels things more intensely than other people."

Alice felt like she'd been kicked in the stomach. Primary school must have been really tough for Tim. "I'm sorry," she said. "It was a poor choice of words. I don't think your mum sounds crazy, Tim. Not at all." She tried again. "What I meant to say is that if I told most people what I'm about to tell you, they wouldn't believe me."

"Well, I'm not most people," Tim said firmly.

"I just don't want you to think I've made this whole thing up . . ." Slowly Alice began to tell Tim all about the LSPDA and how she came to learn that she was a Switcher, starting right at the beginning with meeting Agent T on Welcome Day.

186

"Wow!" Tim said as she finished, leaning back in his chair. "That's quite the story."

"You do believe me, don't you?" Alice said, scratching at her elbow. "I know it sounds far-fetched but it's true, every single word."

"It's definitely not the kind of thing you hear every day. Talking cats and waving seagulls!" Tim paused, catching her eye. "But you're not a liar and frankly it's too full-on to be made up. So yeah, I believe you."

Alice threw her arms round him.

"Blimey," Tim said, peeling Alice off him. "I didn't think you had it in you."

"Nor did I!" Alice grinned. That was twice now she'd hugged him of her own free will. It was a personal record.

"It all makes sense now," Tim said. "Why you were so worried about the animals going missing . . . I didn't really get it before."

"They're my friends," Alice said. "And they've no one else to help them."

Tim nodded. "Well, let's find this animal snatcher. Whatever it takes!"

CHAPTER 22

"Our case needs to be watertight if we're going to convince people Mr Marlowe and Mrs Salter have been stealing animals," Alice said. "The fact they don't like animals isn't enough."

"Slow down, Sherlock!" Tim said. "Start by telling me everything you know about this animal snatcher."

Alice rummaged in her schoolbag for a pencil and her jotter. "Let's make a list!" She started writing.

<u>What we know about the animal snatcher:</u>
1. Makes animals disappear, probably doesn't like them.
2. Lives locally — or can get to Pebblehampton (and school) easily.

"Didn't you say your, er . . . mates at the LSPDA reckon loads of animals are missing?"

Alice nodded. "I found whole columns of lost pet ads in the local paper too." She added another point to the list:

3. *Committed. Maybe obsessed?*

Tim chewed his nails thoughtfully. "Hides?" he suggested. "Or at least does things in secret."

4. *Secretive — maybe has a hideout. Where?*

"What about that boat we saw?" Tim said, his eyes alight with excitement. "Maybe they're taking the animals some place out of the way."

"But why?" Alice threw down her pencil in frustration. "That's the bit that doesn't make any sense. Without a decent motive, no one's going to believe the headmaster of Pebbles is behind all this!"

"You share a room with his niece, remember?" Tim said. "Why not ask her?"

"Ottie?" Alice scoffed. "Why would she help us? She's more likely to take her uncle's side."

"Then we're just going to have to win her round, aren't we?"

Alice didn't budge. "I'm not sure about this . . ."

189

"No time like the present!" Tim said, leaping to his feet and heading for the door.

Alice sighed. This was going to go horribly, horribly wrong.

"Wait, we promised Miss Jessops we'd water her plants!" She reached for the watering can but Tim snatched it out of her hand.

"Leave that," he said, switching off the lights. "We've got investigating to do!"

The common room was heaving with students. A gang of Year Nines swarmed round a pair of boys in the middle of an arm wrestle, placing bets on who would be first to admit defeat. A large group of Year Eleven students had commandeered the sofas and were glued to a movie where a muscled man on a jet ski was shooting fireballs at a ginormous shark. Finally Alice spotted Ottie at the back of the room, sitting by herself at a table. She was surrounded by textbooks and a tower of cue cards. Alice's heart skipped a beat as she realised that for once Kelcie and Lexi were nowhere in sight.

"Go on." Tim nudged Alice in the ribs. "You start then I'll come and help with the questioning."

"Do I really have to do this?" Alice muttered.

"Do you want to help your friends or not?" Tim said, his eyebrows arched just like Gran's whenever Alice tried to wriggle out of something.

Alice sighed – it was clear that Tim wasn't about to back down. She squeezed her way past the arm wrestlers to Ottie's table, then hovered there awkwardly.

Across the room, Tim was bouncing up and down like he desperately needed the loo. "Get on with it!" he mouthed.

"Can I help you?" Ottie said eventually, without looking up from her homework. "Only I'm pretty busy."

"There's something I've got to ask you, Ottie." Alice sank into the chair opposite her.

With a big sigh, Ottie put down her gel pen and looked up.

"It's about your uncle . . ." Alice mumbled.

"We think he's up to something," Tim said, dropping into a vacant seat. He straddled it, his chin resting on the wooden seat back. "We think you can assist us with our enquiries."

"Is this some kind of joke?" Ottie asked, flicking her hair nervously. Alice glared at Tim. This was a truly terrible idea.

"Maybe you should leave this to me, Tim," Alice said.

Tim ignored her. "Just a few questions, if I may. Would you say that your uncle is an honest man?"

Ottie scraped her chair back. "What?"

"Answer the question please, Miss Marlowe."

To Alice's amazement, Ottie did. "Of course he's honest," she said. "He's a headmaster!"

Tim leaned in, narrowing his eyes. "And would you say your uncle has any secrets?"

"Look," Ottie said, flustered, "I don't know what this is all about but my uncle won't appreciate you nosing around in his business."

"Aha!" Tim cried. "So he does have something to hide, does he?"

"Tim!" Alice hissed. "Stop."

Ottie's bottom lip quivered.

"Does he or doesn't he have secrets?" Tim pressed. "It's an easy enough question."

"JUST LEAVE ME ALONE!" Ottie wailed, her eyes welling up with tears.

Two prefects looked up from trying to police the arm wrestle and started heading over. But before they were even halfway across the room, Ottie had rushed out of the door, sending her cue cards fluttering to the floor.

"Hey! What's going on?" the larger of the two the prefects called. "Is she okay?"

"Migraine," Tim said. "Just needs to go lie down!"

The prefect looked like he was about to say something when the arm-wrestling competition stepped up a gear and a mug of hot chocolate went flying.

"You really shouldn't have done that, Tim," Alice whispered the moment the prefect's back was turned. She started scooping up Ottie's scattered cue cards before they got trampled on. "She's bound to go straight to her uncle and then Mr Marlowe will know we're on to him."

"Oh," Tim said, crestfallen. "I was only trying to help."

He picked up a few cue cards that had landed near him. "Was it a bit much?"

"A bit?" Alice glared at him. "You were quizzing her like she'd murdered someone."

Tim shifted uncomfortably. "My mum watches a lot of cop shows . . ."

"I can tell," Alice snapped.

"Look, I'll make it up to you," Tim said and his big brown eyes looked so earnest that Alice couldn't stay cross for long.

"I'd better go after her," she said, tucking Ottie's cards into her blazer pocket. "See you at breakfast."

"Tell her I'm sorry, will you?"

"I'll try," Alice said. *But I don't think she's going to want to hear it . . .*

CHAPTER 23

Kelcie and Lexi stood in front of Alice's dormitory door, blocking her way.

"If you're looking for Ottie, she's not in there," Kelcie said, her arms tightly folded across her chest.

"She's *really* upset," Lexi chimed in. "She can't stop crying,"

"Ottie can't bear another night sharing with you," Kelcie said smugly. "So Mrs Salter says she can stay in our dorm until something *more permanent* can be arranged. We're just here to collect her stuff."

Alice's heart started to race. "Tim and I didn't mean to upset her," she said. "I wanted to say sorry."

"Best not," Kelcie said. "I don't think she wants to see you."

Beads of sweat sprang up on Alice's neck. That was that, then. Her friendship with Ottie was well and truly over.

Kelcie threw open the dormitory door and together with Lexi, tugged Ottie's mattress down from the top bunk. The girls then piled her pillows and duvet on top.

"We'll be back for her uniform and washbag in the morning," Kelcie said.

"Here," Alice said, taking Ottie's pink pyjamas out of the bedside cabinet. "I guess you'd better take these."

Kelcie snatched the pyjamas out of her hands and threw them down on top of the mattress.

"Tell her I'm sorry?" Alice begged but the girls just laughed.

Kelcie looked up at Ottie's empty bunk and smirked. "Guess we should stop calling you Little Miss Boring . . . You're Little Miss Lonely now!"

"Little Miss Loser more like!" Lexi laughed, slamming the door behind her.

Alice finally gave her fingers the good, hard flick she'd been trying to hold in. No Gran. No Constance. No Ottie. Great.

She sat down on her bed, remembering how when she'd first arrived she'd been worried about sharing a dorm with Ottie. Now she'd give anything to have someone to share with. She glanced up at Ottie's empty bunk and there, caught between two wooden slats in the bedframe, was Stripey. Ottie slept with the toy zebra every night. Alice kneeled on her bed and tugged him free. Maybe if she returned him to Ottie then her roommate would realise Alice really hadn't meant to upset her . . .

Then again, Alice realised, Ottie probably wouldn't want her new friends knowing she still slept with a cuddly toy. Embarrassing Ottie wasn't going to help her case.

"She's left you behind too, eh?" she mumbled, tucking Stripey under her duvet. Lexi was right. She really was Little Miss Loser. Not only was she the only student in the whole school with no one to share a dorm with, she still didn't have a single shred of evidence to tie Mr Marlowe to the missing animals.

Tomorrow, she'd have to find Constance and tell her she was all out of ideas.

The LSDPA were on their own.

"Hello there, Alice!" Miss Jessops called as she trudged into the library at lunchtime the following day. "How's it going?"

The librarian was sat at her desk leafing through a stack of old black-and-white photographs, a pile of yellowing documents littering the carpet around her feet.

"Could be better," Alice said forlornly, glancing over at Constance's empty chair and wondering how she was going to tell the cat her investigation had reached a dead end. "Nothing seems to be going right."

"I always find a cup of tea makes everything okay," Miss Jessops said, getting up and opening the hatch in the library counter. "Why don't you come through?"

Alice followed the librarian into her office. "Have you seen the cat?" she asked.

Miss Jessops shook her head. "No, not for a day or two, actually. Here, grab a chair."

Alice took a seat. "What's all this, miss?" she asked, peering down at the ancient-looking paperwork underfoot.

"Research," Miss Jessops said, nudging the papers with the toe of her boot. She fished out her kettle from among the mass of green leaves and tangled creepers swamping her desk and switched it on to boil. "The headmaster has asked me to make a display for the atrium. Well, more of an exhibition, really."

"An exhibition?" Alice frowned. "What about?"

"His family," the librarian said. "The Marlowe family have been coming to Pebbles for generations. And then of course there's his headship."

"How modest," Alice remarked, clamping a hand over her mouth the instant she realised she'd said it aloud, but Miss Jessops just smiled.

"It's turned out to be quite fascinating," the librarian said. "I never knew Mr Marlowe and his family were so interesting."

Alice's heart quickened. Maybe there was still a chance she could help the LSPDA after all. The librarian's research might have unearthed something she could use . . .

The kettle hissed and Miss Jessops found two enamel mugs. While she was busy pouring the tea, Alice stole a glance at the document at the top of the pile on the floor. It seemed to be an old and very boring set of minutes from a school governors' meeting.

"Here you go!" Miss Jessops passed her a steaming mug. "Biscuit?"

Alice rummaged in the tin until she found a chocolate one, her mind galloping as she tried to work out how she could get a proper look at the papers Miss Jessops had found.

The librarian flopped into her chair, stirred her tea, and began leafing through an ancient-looking book on exotic plants.

"Miss Jessops," Alice asked casually, an idea creeping into her mind. Maybe she wasn't completely done with investigating just yet . . .

"Mmm hmm," Miss Jessops said, her eyes still glued to her book.

Alice knew she'd have to be a lot more cautious than Tim had been interrogating Ottie last night. She tried not to sound too keen. "I was wondering . . . what did you mean when you said Mr Marlowe and his family were interesting?"

The librarian slid a rather tatty bookmark into her book and closed it. "Ah well, Mr Marlowe has been telling me all about his grand ideas for the school. He comes from a very wealthy family, you know."

"Yes, I've heard," Alice said, remembering Kelcie and Lexi gossiping about Ottie's mansion. "What is it the Marlowe family do exactly, miss?"

"Oh," said the librarian, chewing on her thumbnail. "I'm not so sure these days but originally they made their money in fur. Hang on – I've got a picture somewhere . . ." She started rummaging through the piles of paper and mountains of books that were heaped on her desk. "There it is!" She prised out a copy of a grainy photocopy from beneath one of her pot plants. "This is the Marlowe family at Queen Victoria's coronation all the way back in 1838. The girls were good friends with the young queen, I believe."

Alice's ears had pricked up at the mention of fur. She looked at three blond teenage sisters and their white-haired brother, very finely dressed and all with Ottie's sharp blue eyes. They looked painfully serious and extremely elegant.

"And this," Miss Jessops said, plucking a black-and-white photograph from where it was poking out of her desk drawer, "is the famous model and actress Sophia Belmont sporting Marlowe furs just before the First World War."

Sophia was very beautiful with almond-shaped eyes, but Alice squirmed when she saw the silver fox stole wrapped around her neck.

"Hard not to be squeamish, isn't it?" Miss Jessops said. "But you have to remember it was a different time, furs were quite the fashion. Of course, the ban on fur farming hit the Marlowe family fortunes hard."

Alice leaned forward. Could the headmaster's loss of fortune be the motive she was looking for? "When did that happen?" she asked.

"Oh, almost twenty years ago now. Mr Marlowe must have been a young man at the time, still at university." She laughed drily. "It was a hard time financially for the family. That's probably why he went into teaching. I can't imagine he'd have bothered otherwise."

Alice thought about Ottie's gold-and-white trunk and her wardrobe full of flashy dresses. "But the Marlowes still seem pretty rich to me."

The librarian's hands flew to her mouth. "Oh dear," she said. "Please forget I said anything, Alice. I really don't think the headmaster would like me talking to students about his finances."

Miss Jessops looked so horrified that Alice thought she'd better change the subject, and fast. "So what have you decided to focus on for the exhibition?" she said brightly.

"Ah," Miss Jessops said, dunking her digestive and taking a big bite of soggy biscuit. "Now that I can tell you. The clocktower."

"The clocktower?" Alice said, confused.

"Well, of course!" Miss Jessops laughed. "It's the natural choice. If it wasn't for the Marlowe family's *very* generous donation, it would never have been built."

Alice sat up, her brain sparking and whirring. Could she ask another question without arousing the librarian's suspicions? "Miss," she said carefully. "What's kept in the clocktower now?" If nobody went up the old tower these days, it would make it the perfect hiding place.

"Now?" Miss Jessops put down her tea. "Nothing much. It's used for storage, I suspect. Why do you ask?"

"Um . . ." Alice wished Tim was here to bail her out. She hated lying and she was absolutely terrible at it. It always made her feel like she was swimming too far out from the shore, her legs scrabbling desperately away beneath the surface, while above the water she had to look like everything was hunky-dory. A siren blared in her head, warning her to stop now, but she couldn't help herself. This could be her chance to find the missing animals.

"Do you think Mr Marlowe has a key, miss? I was thinking as headmaster he must have keys to all the school buildings . . ."

"Alice," Miss Jessops said with a sigh. "I don't think it's wise to concern yourself with Mr Marlowe's business. I'm not sure he'd like it . . ."

Alice could kick herself! She should have quit while she was ahead.

"Sorry, miss," she said, her stomach churning. Not only did she now have a possible motive, she knew where to search for the missing animals. She glanced at the clock on Miss Jessops' computer. There was only twenty-five minutes of lunchtime left.

She jumped up, pulling on her rucksack. "I think I'd better go now."

"Okay, Alice," Miss Jessops said, returning to her book.

Alice lifted the counter hatch and hurried out of the library to find Tim. There was no time to waste.

CHAPTER 24

Alice stood at the foot of the clocktower, staring up at where
the clouds swallowed the steeple. Tim hadn't been practising
with the school band like he usually did on Friday lunchtimes,
nor was there any sign of him in the common room. Alice
suspected he was poring over some old map with the professor
but she didn't have time to go and look. There was now less
than fifteen minutes until the bell for afternoon lessons. If
she was going to investigate the tower, she'd have to do it
alone.

Wiping her clammy palms on the skirt of her dress, she
approached the huge oak door, engraved with the school's
crest: the gull, the fox, the badger and the hare. The door was
bound to be locked so she walked round the tower's base,

hunting for a window. But they all looked rather narrow and she'd never be able to pull herself through without a leg-up, anyway. Where was Tim when she needed him?

She circled back round to the door, weighing up whether to return after school with Tim. Suddenly peals of laughter sounded behind her. Alice spun round but it was only a group of Year Tens on their way back from lunch.

Alice tried to look like she was waiting for someone in case they wondered what she was up to but they didn't even give her a second glance. Alice looked up at the clock. Ten minutes left.

As the older students disappeared from view, Alice made her decision. The LSPDA were counting on her, and Agent T and the other missing animals might be on the other side of that door, waiting for someone to come and rescue them. Placing both her hands round the neck of the handle – a brass bird blackened by age – she shoved. The wood groaned. She tried again, harder this time. She was about to give up when the door lurched forward, scraping over the stone floor to leave a gap just big enough for her to squeeze through.

Alice let go of the handle in surprise. The school caretaker must have forgotten to lock the door. Either that or the animal snatcher had been here . . .

She hovered at the foot of the stairs in the gloom. Did she really want to do this alone? *This might be where the animal snatcher is keeping Agent T*, she reminded herself. *You owe it to the LSPDA to at least look.* Alice left the oak door as she

204

had found it and began to climb. The steps were so steep that, catlike, she dropped to her hands and knees.

The spiral staircase grew tighter and tighter as Alice crawled her way to the top, the grey stone walls closing in on her. Her head spun, all the breath in her lungs squeezing out until she gasped, dry-mouthed, for air. Maybe this wasn't such a good idea after all . . . She paused beside a slit window on the last few steps and scrambled to her feet. But as she peered outside she instantly regretted it. She was dizzyingly high, the school grounds far below. She wasn't good with heights.

The ticking in her ears grew louder the closer she came to the top. *Not long now*, Alice told herself over and over again. *When I get out of here, I am never stepping foot on a spiral staircase again.*

Just as Alice felt she could go no further and her chest ached for oxygen, she spilled out into the clock room at the top of the tower. It reeked of old feathers and damp. The ticking echoed between the walls like a monstrous heartbeat and Alice pressed her hands to her ears, desperate to muffle the sound.

After the tightness of the staircase, the sudden space felt massive. Alice stood with her back pressed against the cold stone wall, one hand clamped over her nose to block out the stench. Her lungs burned, screaming for fresh air but she gave herself a talking-to. *You're safe. You're fine. It's just an old room.*

Gradually Alice grew accustomed to the ticking. She took her hands from her ears and looked around. She was in a square room with a plaster roof and wooden rafters. Each wall was home to the back of a massive cream-coloured clock face and an identical golden hare chasing time. She imagined that ages ago someone might have worked here or at least popped in now and then to check the clocks were still ticking as they should.

To her surprise, the room was almost empty. The only furniture was a chair and a wooden desk, both blanketed with thick grey dust. Once someone might have drunk their tea here from a flask, done their paperwork at the desk. She fumbled with the desk drawer, yanking it open to discover nothing but a dead spider and two chewed pencils inside.

Old feathers littered the wooden floor and bird droppings, hard and white, crunched beneath her shoes. Above was a flat plaster ceiling and in one corner a rickety wooden ladder led to a trapdoor. A hooked stick hung on the wall. Alice guessed it had once been used to pull down the trapdoor so that the mechanics could be accessed on the floor above and the clock wound up. Now the clock was automatic, no one had cause to climb up there any more. Unless, that is, they were up to no good . . .

Alice used the hook to grab the metal ring on the trapdoor and give it a good tug. It rattled but did not budge. She tried once more but still it didn't open. Alice stood frozen, her ears trained for a yap or a cry, but all she could hear was the constant *tick-tock*, *tick-tock* of the clock.

Perhaps she'd been wrong about the tower like she'd been wrong about everything else . . . If she turned back now, no one need know she'd ever been here. Any secrets concealed at the top of the tower's corkscrew stairs would remain undiscovered but she'd be safe . . .

Alice looked down. Lying on the floorboards beside her shoe was a single black feather. She stooped down and picked it up. As she held it to the light, she recognised it as a crow feather but instead of glossy blue-black, it was a dull and faded grey. The barbs at the tip were crumpled and bent.

Poor thing, she thought, goosebumps prickling on her forearms. *Trapped here alone.* Delicately she laid the feather back where she found it but as she did so, a shiver shot down her arms.

Alice turned to leave but terror wrapped its icy fingers about her neck. She stretched an arm out to steady herself. She felt so dizzy, like a fever had taken hold of her. Her heart lurched and suddenly her head was full of the awful flapping of wings. Feet and beaks scratched at the trapdoor, desperate to be free. It was like how she'd felt when she'd seen the poor frog in biology class, only worse. Alice clutched her head as the crow's terrified *caw-caw-caw* reverberated in her ears.

Something inside her melted and slipped loose, sliding unseen from her body.

For a terrible moment, she was the trapped bird and the bird was Alice. Her wings beat the air and the cold, hard stone walls were unforgiving beneath her peck.

Alice struck her head once, twice, three times. *Stop it!* Her toes wriggled in her shoes, pushing down into the solid wood floor, grounding her. *Stay*, she begged, repeating the word over and over again. Slowly the sound of wings faded away and she felt herself glide back into her own quivering body.

Alice stood panting, conscious only of the need to get out of this place. She shouldn't have come here. She stumbled back to the stairs. Unable to crawl down the way she'd crawled up, Alice had to wedge her outstretched hands against the walls on either side, her eyes almost shut to prevent the staircase from shifting before her.

Alice thought she heard a key turn in a lock and the heavy wooden trapdoor slowly groan open.

Don't be so stupid. There's no one here, she chided, easing herself down another step. *These old buildings always creak and moan.* She turned the bend in the stairs, and was submerged in a pool of blackness. From up in the clock room, there was a soft thud, like feet landing on floorboards. Surely it was just the old cogs clunking away . . . Alice took another step down. Too late, she sensed someone behind her.

Alice let go of her grip on the wall, turning just in time to see two hands shove her. As she toppled forward something told her to spread her shoulders. Her innards seemed to melt and slide. With a pinch and *pop*, feathers burst through her skin and her nose was tugged by some invisible force into a slim, straight beak.

For a split second she was airborne, her tail feathers fanning open. The stairs below her were so steep they were almost vertical but she was safe. Hovering. Birdlike.

Until she fell.

CHAPTER 25

Alice dreamed of steel cages. She felt the slow, heavy creep of dread and the air smelled somehow rotten. When she finally woke, it was to lights that were too bright and the stench of chemicals scorching her throat.

"It's all right, Alice, you're in the sickbay." A middle-aged woman had her hand on Alice's arm and was peering down at her. "How are you feeling?"

"Okay . . . stiff . . ." Alice squinted, shielding her eyes from the light. "What happened?"

She remembered being on the stairs of the clocktower and then lurching forward. And something to do with feathers . . .

"I'd best be off now, Nurse Cullen," a voice said. "Seeing as the young lady's awake."

Alice rubbed her eyes. Everything looked hazy. She blinked rapidly and when she reopened her eyes properly there in the doorway stood the gardener, flat cap in hand, his blue eyes looking hard at Alice. What was Ted Turner doing there?

"Startled you, did I?" he said gruffly.

Alice shifted uneasily, pulling herself up in bed.

"You're very lucky Mr Turner found you when he did," Nurse Cullen said. "If he hadn't, you could have been lying there for hours – days, even." She shuddered. "It doesn't bear thinking about."

"H-how did you know I was there?" Alice asked. She had no recollection of the old man finding her or how she'd been brought to the sickbay.

"I was just heading back to my shed for lunch when I saw the clocktower door open," Ted explained. "I've never known it be unlocked and nor should it so I thought I'd better check everything was as it should be. That's when I found you. Knocked clean out, you were."

Alice looked between the nurse and the gardener, a lump forming in her throat. "Thank you," she whispered.

The gardener scratched his head. "What I can't work out is who unlocked it in the first place." His icy-blue eyes bored into Alice. "Get hold of a key, did you?"

"No!" Alice protested, not wanting them to think she was a thief. "The door was unlocked when I walked past. It seemed . . . interesting so I went to take a look inside. I must have tripped . . ."

"Hmm," the gardener said, pulling on his cap and nodding curtly at her. "Well, just you take care of yourself, Miss Tonks. And keep away from that tower." He said a quick goodbye to the nurse and let himself out of the room.

Alice listened to the shuffle of Ted's boots on the tiles as he limped away down the corridor.

As the door clicked shut, Nurse Cullen scribbled furiously on Alice's notes before letting the clipboard fall back into place against the metal bedframe with a clang. "Interesting, indeed." She tutted. "You could have killed yourself!"

"Sorry," Alice mumbled, pulling the blankets tighter round her. "Have I broken anything?" She peeped under the bedclothes at her legs.

The nurse's face softened. "No need to fret. Nothing broken, though you've had a nasty concussion, Miss Tonks. The main thing for now is that you concentrate on getting better."

How was she not more hurt? All she could recall was toppling forward and then the thud as she crashed down upon the stone floor. There was something she couldn't quite grab hold of, something just out of reach.

"Please don't tell my gran," Alice croaked.

"Not a chance!" Nurse Cullen said firmly. "Your grandmother needs to know."

Alice put her head in her hands. She wouldn't be surprised if Gran came and whisked her away that very day. She'd be worried sick. But she had to stay . . . the LSPDA was counting on her. She couldn't let them down. Her eyes filled with tears.

"Now, now," the nurse said, crouching down beside her bedside and taking Alice's hand in her own. "No harm done. You'll be back on your feet soon. Just no more climbing towers, promise?"

Alice dabbed at her tears. "Okay." She felt a bit dizzy and the flickering bright white strip light overhead was giving her a headache. "Will you let me tell Gran what happened, though? It's my mistake. I want her to hear it from me."

"Let's not worry ourselves about that for now," Nurse Cullen said. "Time for some rest, I think. I'm not sure I like your colour . . ."

Alice lay back on her pillows and snuggled into the duvet but instead of feeling warm, shivers ran up and down her arms as another memory surfaced. The feeling of two hands on her shoulder blades and a hard shove.

Someone wanted her out of the way.

CHAPTER 26

Gran took it even worse than Alice had expected. Alice held the receiver from her ear, wincing as Gran told her exactly what she thought about her decision to go exploring the clocktower alone. It took Alice the best part of an hour to persuade her not to catch the next train down.

"I'm okay," she promised. "It was just a bump on the head."

"Just a bump!" Gran exploded again. "What I can't understand is what you were doing up there in the first place! The tower's been shut up for years, ever since I was a student. I've a good mind to have a word with that headmaster of yours. Leaving it unlocked like that . . ."

"No, Gran, don't," Alice begged. Mr Marlowe was the last person she wanted involved. "It's all my fault."

"Oh, I'm well aware of that, my girl! Tell me again what you were doing up there anyway. I've got a good mind to take you out of that school."

"Please, Gran!" Alice cried. If she went home, who would help the LSPDA? "I'm fine, really. Mr Turner found me."

Gran's voice sharpened. "Mr Turner? Ted?"

"Yes . . ." How did Gran and Ted know one another? Gran had never mentioned him before.

"He's the one who found you?"

"Apparently," Alice said. "Gran, how do you know—"

Gran cut her off with a heavy sigh. "Alice, I want you to tell me the truth. Are you happy at school? You don't have to stay if you're not. I'll come and get you."

Alice hauled the words up and forced herself to say them. "I like it here at Pebbles. In fact, I love it."

Silence.

She'd done it. She'd lied. Alice hated liars and now she was one.

"Hmm," Gran said, but Alice could hear the relief in her voice. "Okay. Let me speak to Nurse Cullen."

When the nurse finally got off the phone, she insisted that Alice remain in the sickbay for the weekend. Alice didn't mind a jot. It meant she didn't have to go back to her empty dormitory and she felt safe here, with Nurse Cullen clucking over her.

A short time later, Mrs Salter arrived with a face like curdled milk. "Like I haven't got enough to do!" she said, dumping Alice's backpack unceremoniously on the floor.

"Thank you, Mrs Salter," Alice said as sweetly as she could bear.

She opened the bag to discover clean pyjamas, her washbag and her Beatrix Potter book. Right at the bottom was Toby. As soon as Alice saw the toy dog's shaggy face, she knew all was forgiven. Only Gran would think of asking the housemistress to bring Toby for her to cuddle.

Alice had everything she needed for a Friday night in. There was only one thing missing: Tim. Why hadn't he come and visited her?

"Well, Miss Alice, I think you're well enough to go back to the boarding house tonight," Nurse Cullen said on Sunday evening when she'd finished checking her over. "I'm sure you'll be keen to get back to your friends."

Alice raised an eyebrow but said nothing. *What friends?* she thought. The whole weekend had passed and Tim still hadn't come to see her.

Outside, the young moon was waxing. The month was almost up. The LSPDA would be meeting again soon and Red would be expecting Alice to make good on her promise. But she felt more uncertain than ever.

What she did know was that her fall in the clocktower had been no accident. Somebody had wanted to stop her sniffing around. But was Mr Marlowe behind it and did he have help?

Gran had reacted strangely when she'd mentioned Mr Turner, like there was some history there she didn't want to mention, and Alice wasn't sure she was buying his story. It was a bit too convenient that he happened to walk by and notice the door ajar just after someone had sent her crashing down the stairs. Was the gardener playing the hero when really he was her attacker? And then there was Mrs Salter . . . did she have a part to play in all this? Given what Alice had overheard that day in the laundry room, there was a chance she could be the headmaster's accomplice.

Alice packed her backpack with a heavy heart, secretly hoping that Nurse Cullen might invite her to stay for a bit longer. Then there was a *rat-tat-tat* on the door and the nurse poked her head round it. "There's a young gentleman here to see you, Alice. Would you like me to send him in?"

Tim! Alice's face lit up. Of course he'd come! She should never have doubted him. "Yes, please, nurse." She had so much to tell him!

A couple of moments later, Tim burst into the sickbay and Alice's smile vanished. His face was tightly screwed up, his nostrils flaring with rage. "How could you, Alice?" he exploded.

"T-Tim, what's the matter?" Surely he wasn't this angry about her going off to the clocktower alone?

"Don't try and deny it!" he snarled. "The WHOLE school's talking about it! They're calling my mum Loopy Lucinda!"

Alice's heart plummeted. "Tim, I didn't tell anyone. I wouldn't do that . . ."

"That's what Ottie tried to say. But everyone's talking about how Mum's lost her marbles and the real reason I had to come back early from that trip at primary school was to look after her! You're the only person who knew about that! At the time, I didn't want Kelcie and Lexi finding out so I told my Year 5 class I was homesick. You're the first person I trusted." Tim was shaking now, angry tears slipping down his face. "That's my mum they're talking about! The things they're saying about her . . ."

"Tim, I promise you I didn't tell anyone," Alice repeated, aghast. Her fingers were flicking and she was too overwhelmed to stop them. How could he think she'd do something like that? Tim was her best friend. He knew her, didn't he? He knew she wouldn't betray him.

Nurse Cullen came hurrying into the room, her face red and her eyes wide. "Whatever is the meaning of this?" she demanded.

Tim glared at her with such ferocity that even the nurse was silenced. "Don't worry," he bellowed. "I'm going!"

Alice tried to call after him but her voice shrivelled up and died inside her.

"I think it is best you do," Nurse Cullen said firmly.

Alice watched as Tim stormed out of the room, his final words a javelin fired right through her heart. "I thought you were my friend, Alice Tonks!"

CHAPTER 27

Alice cried so long and so hard that in the end Nurse Cullen let her stay in the sickbay for another night. By the time the nurse went to do her rounds, Alice's throat was hoarse from sobbing. She'd begged the nurse to ring Gran and let her go home to Foxden but Nurse Cullen just made her a hot chocolate and told her things would get better. Nothing would get better. First Ottie hated her and now Tim. She'd lost her only friend and the only person who could help her find the animal snatcher.

When Alice's meltdown finally ebbed away, she picked up her book and tried to read. It was the closest thing to being at home with Gran, but she couldn't stick at anything and jumped every time she heard a voice float down the corridor, or the wind rattle the sickbay's blinds. Her attention flitted back and forth between wondering how the other students had found out that Tim's mum was ill and worrying that the animal snatcher could appear at any moment, ready to finish the job . . .

Alice knew it was silly as she'd felt perfectly safe before but her confrontation with Tim had really spooked her. As evening closed around her, she pulled the bedcovers higher and higher, looking around warily at the shadows skulking across the sickbay. The tall cabinet where Nurse Cullen kept the medical records was just the right height for someone to hide behind, or they could easily lie in wait under one of the spare beds . . . She didn't feel like the girl who'd ventured to a secret meeting in the woods or gone exploring the clocktower. Now she was just stupid old Alice Tonks who should have kept her nose out of other people's business.

She was just drifting off to sleep when she heard a familiar voice.

"A little bird told me you were here," Constance said, slinking through the window Nurse Cullen had left open for fresh air. "I couldn't understand where you'd gone. Your dormitory's been deserted for days now."

Constance jumped up on to the narrow bed and squeezed in beside Alice, flopping her head over Alice's thigh. The cat felt solid and warm and when Alice stroked the pouch of fluffy podge on Constance's belly, she felt like crying all over again.

"Oh, Constance, everything's such a mess!"

"I'm listening." Constance gave Alice's hand a friendly lick with her rough tongue.

Alice told the cat her discoveries about Mr Marlowe and his family. "When Miss Jessops mentioned the clocktower, I thought I'd better check it out and that's . . . that's when someone tried to kill me," she finished breathlessly.

It was the first time she'd said it aloud.

Constance sat up. "Whatever do you mean, Alice?"

"I was coming back down that horrible spiral staircase and someone pushed me."

Constance turned a couple of circles, her tail flicking back and forth. "Go on," she said.

"I didn't see who it was, Constance. I just felt someone shove me – shove me hard."

Constance didn't try to convince Alice she was mistaken. If you told most grown-ups that someone was out to get you, they'd usually try to persuade you that you were being silly and there was nothing at all to worry about. Constance knew better than that. "A direct attack?" she said. "And on you, a human? That's a really serious development, Alice. I'd better inform the LSPDA at once."

"I don't know it definitely was Mr Marlowe, though," Alice said, hitting the bed in frustration. "It was the gardener who found me and his story doesn't exactly add up . . ."

The cat made a noise like she had a furball lodged in her throat. "Are you talking about Ted Turner?"

Alice nodded.

"Good old Ted," Constance said. "We've been friends for as long as I can remember. He makes a fine fish-paste sandwich."

"Y-you're friends with him?" Alice exclaimed.

"The very best of friends," the cat said. "I've known him since I was a kitten. Surely you don't suspect old Ted? He wouldn't hurt a fly!"

"But he has cages in his shed, and drugs, and he lives on site so he could be the one stealing the syringes from the laboratory," Alice protested. "And what if he didn't really find me? What if he actually pushed me and is just *pretending* that he saved me?"

"Ted Turner is no more the animal snatcher than I am!" the cat chortled. "If you suspected him then why didn't you say anything? I'd have put you straight."

"I tried to," Alice muttered.

"Well, never mind," Constance said diplomatically, suppressing her smile. "The more important thing is whether Ted saw anyone else in the clocktower?"

"I don't think so," said Alice. "He just found me at the bottom of the stairs."

"I still can't believe someone would push an eleven-year-old girl down a flight of stone steps. They must have been desperate. The animal snatcher must have realised you were hot on their trail . . ."

". . . And decided to shove me off it," Alice concluded.

"You need to be vigilant, Alice. Take no risks," Constance said, her paw tightening around Alice's hand. "I should have known something like this was going to happen."

"What do you mean?"

"I was so excited to have a human on our side, especially one with your abilities, that I put you in danger. Forgive me, Alice. I've been a fool."

Alice shook her head. "It's not your fault, Constance. Agent T came back to look for me on my first day to warn me, but I was too wrapped up in being special for once that I didn't really stop and think about the risks I was taking. I just wanted to prove myself to Red."

It had been stupid of her to try to discover Mr Marlowe's hiding place alone. If she'd only waited and asked Tim to come with her, things might have been different. Thinking about Tim made Alice's eyes fill with tears all over again.

"Don't be so hard on yourself," Constance purred. "You were only trying to help."

Alice stroked the cat's soft fur and played with her tufty ears. After a minute or two she asked the question that kept crawling about in the shadowy bits of her brain. "Do you think they're watching me . . . the snatcher?"

Constance didn't answer right away. "I'm not sure," she admitted. "But don't go wandering off. Stay close to your friends."

Alice groaned. "Tim's mad at me, really mad. He thinks I told everyone about his mum being sick."

"Ah yes. I did overhear one or two students not being too kind about his mother earlier on."

"But Constance, I'd never break his trust like that," Alice said. "I know how much his mum means to him."

"Well, I know that, and you know that, but Tim doesn't yet. You're going to have to give him a chance to calm down and remember what you're really like."

Alice sighed. She wasn't a patient person.

"I have to go now," Constance said, ignoring Alice's protests. "The LSPDA need to know what's happened." She jumped down and headed over to the window. "And remember what I said. Better safe than sorry."

Constance sprang up on to the window ledge and then she was gone, lost to the darkness of the gathering night.

CHAPTER 28

Alice let out a sigh of relief. Since the moment she'd emerged from her dormitory that morning, she'd had to put up with a barrage of questions from her fellow students. *What were you doing in the clocktower? Is it true you broke into Mr Marlowe's office and stole the key? Did you really see a ghost up there?*

The nosiness was grating and the stares and whispering made her feel itchy all over but she'd focused her mind on one thing only – making it to 3.30 so that she could get back to the all-important business of catching the animal snatcher. But first she needed to set things right with Tim, who hadn't been in class all day.

Alice headed straight to the common room to try to catch him, taking a seat by the window with a good view of the quad in case he passed by. After a little while, a couple of other Year Seven boys popped in and she asked them to take a message up to his dorm for her. While she waited she devoured all of Felix's lemon biscuits, leaving only a smattering of crumbs on her white porcelain plate. But when Tim still hadn't come down, she decided to go and look for him in the music room.

Alice was just finishing her glass of milk when someone coughed. She looked up sharply.

"How are you doing?" Ottie said, shifting from foot to foot. "I heard about what happened in the clocktower."

"I'm fine," Alice replied warily. She really didn't feel like having another argument.

"Can I sit down?"

"I was just heading off . . ." Alice said.

Ottie's face fell.

". . . But I can wait a minute," she added.

"Thanks." Ottie took a seat opposite Alice and perched on the edge. "I owe you an apology," she said shakily. "I've been a rubbish friend."

"We were never really friends, were we?" Alice said sadly. "Not properly."

"Hear me out, will you?" Ottie pleaded. "I want you to understand why I went off with Kelcie and Lexi."

"Go on, then," Alice said, a little reluctantly.

"It all started with my uncle," Ottie explained. "He told me I had to be friends with Kelcie and Lexi because he wanted their parents as his business associates."

"That's stupid!" Alice said. "How would being friends with those two help him?"

Ottie's gaze dropped to the floor. "My uncle isn't a nice man," she said quietly and the hairs on Alice's arms stood up. "He gets people to do what he wants by blackmailing them. When he couldn't persuade Maloney and Khan Logistics to continue working with him he made me spy for him. Any juicy titbits Kelcie and Lexi let slip, any gossip . . . it all had to be reported back."

Alice nodded. So that had been what Ottie was doing down on the beach with Mr Marlowe the day of the storm!

"Is that *really* why you started hanging around with Kelcie and Lexi?" she said sceptically. "Because your uncle told you to?"

"You don't understand!" Ottie said, two red spots appearing on her cheeks. "He keeps sending that girlfriend of his, Mrs Salter, to check on me."

"So she wasn't looking for me?" Alice asked.

Ottie looked blank. "When?"

"The night I stayed out late," Alice explained. "I saw Mrs Salter in our dorm."

"Oh yes," Ottie said, rubbing the back of her neck. "I had to tell her you had a dodgy stomach from dinner. She came to give me a note from my uncle, but then she noticed you were missing."

Alice laughed shakily. "I wasn't sure what you were telling her, to be honest."

"I'd never rat on you like that!" Ottie cried. "Mrs Salter's always keeping tabs on me for my uncle."

"That's . . . horrible."

"I'm used to it." Ottie shrugged. "In my family, you don't ask questions. You don't talk back. You're expected to just do what you're told. We've two rules: Marlowes never lose and Marlowes stick together. Mother expects me to follow them at all times."

Although Alice felt sorry for Ottie, she couldn't forget the way her roommate had stood by and let Kelcie and Lexi bully her and Tim. That couldn't have been part of her uncle's plan. "And that's the only reason you were friends with them? Nothing else?"

"It was at first." Ottie sighed. "But then I kind of got used to being popular. Hanging around with them felt good in a way . . ."

Alice felt a tickle in the back of her throat. "So you decided you'd rather be one of the bullies than one of us? Figures."

A tense silence descended between the girls like an invisible curtain. Alice glared at Ottie across the table but slowly her anger began to subside. Hadn't she sometimes wondered what it would be like to be popular?

"I wish I was more like you, Alice," Ottie said quietly. "You don't care what anyone thinks."

"That's not true!" Alice scoffed. "I care when people laugh at me. When they're mean."

Ottie put her head in her hands. "I should never have let Kelcie and Lexi treat you and Tim the way they have."

Alice shrugged. "It's okay."

Ottie shook her head. "No, it's not. It's about time I stopped caring so much about what my family thinks and start thinking for myself." She pulled back her shoulders, drawing herself up to her full height, like she'd been dragging around a shotput that she was finally ready to launch. "My uncle isn't the man everyone believes he is."

Alice gulped. *Here it comes.* She closed her eyes. Was Ottie about to confirm her suspicions about Mr Marlowe?

"Everyone reckons he's so clever and so charming but he's a fraud. A fake. All those certificates he has up outside his office? He made them himself. My grandparents even had to bribe the school to let him sit his A levels, he was doing so badly." Ottie grinned. Now she'd started, she couldn't stop. "And that's not all. There was this big scandal at uni too. I heard he almost got kicked out." She leaned in close. "For stealing!"

Alice gasped. Ottie's eyes were sparkling and the colour was back in her cheeks.

"There's more," Ottie continued. "He's up to something. I don't know exactly what but it's shady . . ."

Alice's eyes widened. Was her own roommate about to confess to helping to steal animals?

"That's why I got so upset the other night in the common room when Tim started grilling me. In a funny way, he made

229

me realise how stupid I'd been to fall for my uncle's tricks. He doesn't care about me. None of them do."

Alice gave her temples a rub. "Why are you telling me all this?" she asked, suddenly cautious. What if this was some kind of trap to find out what she knew? Mr Marlowe wasn't above sending his niece to do his dirty work.

Ottie fiddled with the sleeve of her blazer. "Because I trust you."

"And you couldn't have said anything earlier?" Alice knew her autism sometimes meant she missed what people were getting at, but Ottie hadn't even tried to tell her the truth.

"I'm going to make it up to you. Starting now." Ottie pulled a tightly folded piece of paper from her blazer pocket and passed it to Alice.

"What's this?" Alice asked, unfolding the paper. It was a typed sheet, badly photocopied. At the top of the page was Tim's full name. Alice gasped. "This is about his mum. How did you get it?" She leaped to her feet, her anger threatening to spill out again.

"Mrs Salter leaves her office unlocked. Kelcie made me be lookout when she took it from his file. She said it was payback for him upsetting me in the common room." Ottie fiddled with a loose curl of hair. "She thought it'd be funny."

"Funny?" Alice slammed her hand on the table. "This isn't funny. This is cruel!"

"I know," Ottie said. "I tried to tell her not to do it but she wouldn't listen. Even Lexi thought it was too much."

Alice felt like a cobra, coiled up and ready to strike. "You did this to him?" she raged. "You spread rumours about Tim's mum, knowing how it would make him feel?"

Ottie had gone white.

"Tim's mum's a real person, you know," Alice said, jabbing a finger at the photocopy. "She has real feelings. So does Tim."

Ottie could barely drag her eyes off the ground. "I'm really, really sorry, Alice. I knew as soon as I agreed to go along with it that I'd made a massive mistake. I tried to find you but you were in the sickbay."

"Tim thinks it was me!" Alice roared.

"Then I'll show him this," Ottie said. "That way he'll know I was the one who helped Kelcie and Lexi spread those rumours."

"You'd do that?" Alice asked.

Ottie nodded.

"Come on, then," she said. "I think I know where he might be."

CHAPTER 29

"This way," Alice said, marching down the music department's corridor. Ottie trailed behind, fiddling with her hair nervously.

They passed the recording studio crammed with state-of-the-art technology and the chamber where the school's choir rehearsed accompanied by an expensive-looking grand piano. At the end of the corridor, a network of cubbyholes and storage cupboards had been turned into soundproofed practice rooms.

"In here," Alice said, pointing to a dimly lit nook under the stairs. Inside someone was thrashing an electric guitar.

Ottie hesitated outside the door.

Alice wondered if she was going to back out but Ottie knocked once and walked straight in. Alice followed.

Tim stopped mid-chord. "Get out!" he hollered.

"Timothy," Ottie said, sounding at least twenty years older than she actually was. "You need to put that down and listen."

Tim stroked his precious red-and-white guitar protectively. "What's she doing here?" he said, glaring at Alice.

"Alice and I need to talk to you," Ottie said. "You'd better take a seat."

"I've nothing to say to *her*," Tim spat.

"Good," Ottie said. "Then you can listen to me."

Somewhat awed, Tim leaned his guitar against the wall and plonked himself down heavily beside it on the carpet.

It was only now that Ottie's hands began to tremble. "There's something you need to know," she said.

"Did *she* put you up to this?" Tim threw Alice the iciest of glares.

"Not at all. I should have come before . . . You need to see this." Ottie handed Tim the photocopied sheet.

Alice held her breath, her eyes glued to Tim's face, unable to blink.

Tim scanned the paper, his jaw clenching as it slowly dawned on him what he was reading. "Where did you get this?" he said.

Ottie backed away, her confidence gone. "Kelcie, er, took it . . ." she mumbled.

"It's from your school file, Tim," Alice put in. "Kelcie took it from Mrs Salter's office."

"And I let her," Ottie whispered, unable to even look at Tim. "It was me, Kelcie and Lexi who told people about your mum. Alice had nothing to do with it."

Tim was lost for words. "This is . . ." he tried to say. "This is . . . my mum." A single tear swelled and broke, trickling down his cheek.

"Tim, I'm so ashamed," Ottie tried to apologise but stopped. He was slowly crushing the paper in his fist, tighter and tighter, until it was a tiny ball. He flung it on the floor. "I was just angry with you," she said in the smallest of voices. "And I wanted to fit in."

Tim was frozen, still staring at the paper.

"I'll go," Ottie said, her voice now barely a squeak. The door swung shut behind her.

Even though the carpet was grimy with mud from a hundred shoes and smelled faintly of a fizzy orange drink someone had once spilled, Alice plopped down beside Tim and waited the twenty long minutes of silence it took until he was ready to talk. If he was anything like her, he needed space and quiet to recover, not people rabbiting on.

Eventually Tim turned to her. "Well," he said. "Now we're friends again, I've got something to tell you."

"And I've got something to tell you!" Alice said excitedly, pleased to have her friend back at her side. "Ottie's just told me all about her uncle. Apparently he's trying to blackmail

Kelcie and Lexi's family and Ottie reckons he's definitely up to no good here at school."

"Great timing." Tim grinned. "Because I think I've figured out where he's been keeping the stolen animals."

CHAPTER 30

"Are you sure the professor won't mind us being in here?" Alice asked, scratching her elbow as she followed Tim into the empty geography classroom. The last time she'd snuck off somewhere she wasn't supposed to, she'd ended up in the sickbay with concussion.

"No, he's cool," Tim said. "He lets me come and look at his maps whenever I like."

He led Alice to the back of the classroom where the professor housed his private collection of maps in painstakingly organised drawers.

"See this," he said, pulling open the bottom drawer and carefully removing a wafer-thin sheet of parchment. "Professor Biddle says this map is the oldest in his collection.

He thinks it was drawn by a smuggler, maybe even a pirate, back when Pebbles was a big country house. He reckons the map shows a network of passages – one from a cave on the beach back to the school and another going all the way into town. So I've been thinking. What if Marlowe's using these tunnels to sneak away from school without anyone clocking him?"

Tim laid out the map on the nearest desk.

"What am I looking at exactly?" Alice said, leaning in.

Tim scrutinised the map. "There," he said, pointing to the very bottom of the map's curled edge labelled 'cove'. I reckon this might be the entrance to the caves, hidden in the cliffs. Think about it! It's the perfect hiding place!"

"I don't know," Alice said. "This map's pretty ancient, Tim. Even if you're right, how do you know the cave's still there? There could have been a rockfall or something . . ."

"I've been doing some research," Tim prattled on. "None of the newer maps show anything so while you were in the sickbay, I snuck down to the beach to take a look. But by the time I made it there, it was high tide and School Cove had all but disappeared. To get right up to the cliffs, you'd need a boat . . ."

"Like the one we saw," Alice whispered.

"Exactly! We should check it out properly! What do you say?"

Alice shook her head. "No chance. It sounds WAY too dangerous!"

"Oh, come on . . ." Tim pleaded. "Do you want to find these animals or not?"

"Not by ourselves. We should call the police and tell them to have a look. Mr Marlowe sounds really ruthless. Ottie's his niece and even she's scared of him! I don't want to run into him in some dark cave, do you?"

"The police aren't going to listen to two kids who reckon their headmaster's been stealing animals," Tim said. "We're going to have to prove it."

"I still think this is a terrible idea . . ."

"Fine!" Tim whipped the map away and slammed the drawer closed. "You be boring and stay here, but I'm going to wait until everyone's asleep then go and find the cave. I know the professor's got a tide table somewhere . . ."

Tim started rustling through the papers on Professor Biddle's desk and picked up a little yellow book. "Here we are – tonight's low tide is at twenty past midnight."

"You can't go by yourself!" Alice cried. "Look what happened to me when I went to the clocktower."

"Only cos you went without me. It would never have happened if I'd been there."

"Yes, because there's no way our murderous headmaster would have pushed me down the stairs with you there to protect me," Alice said, rolling her eyes.

"Come on," Tim begged. "This could be the final piece in the jigsaw. The evidence we've been searching for . . ."

"Hmm," Alice said. "We can go and look but that's all, okay? We're not going in."

Tim's grin was so wide it took up most of his face. "Cool beans," he said. "Let's do this!"

CHAPTER 31

Clutching her torch, Alice crept towards the stairwell. She couldn't risk waking anyone. She stopped at the top of the stairs, cold sweat clammy on her skin, and checked her watch. Five minutes to midnight.

Keeping to the shadows, she tiptoed down the first flight of stairs, past the boys' landing and down to the common room.

"Coo-ee!"

Alice's heart leaped into her throat.

"Sorry," Tim whispered, stepping out of the shadows. "Didn't mean to give you a fright."

Alice took a long, deep breath and tried to still her trembling hands.

"Better get moving." Tim said. "If this tide chart's right, we've only got a few hours 'til high tide."

"We're just looking, remember?" Alice said. "Nothing more."

"Nothing more," Tim agreed. He headed over to the door that led out to the quad and tried to turn the handle. Nothing happened. He rattled it again but still the door refused to budge. "Rats!"

"Shh!" Alice hissed. "Someone'll hear. Let me have a go." She tried to prise the door open but it was clearly locked. Then she remembered the window Constance had shown her when she'd snuck back into the boarding house after the LSPDA meeting.

Alice let herself into the eerily silent common room, Tim close behind. She crept through the kitchenette area and fumbled with the catch of the big bay window overlooking the quad. The hinges groaned. Alice glanced back over her shoulder, expecting to see Mrs Salter appear in the doorway at any moment. She tugged the window open and was blasted with the chill night air.

She listened again for any hint of the upstairs floorboards creaking or the click-clack of heels on the stairs. Nothing.

"Come on." Alice lowered herself out of the window and slithered on to the flower bed below. They were really doing this.

Tim jumped down after her and landed with a quiet thud, trampling a geranium underfoot. He bent down to prop it up as best he could. "Got to cover our tracks!"

Alice closed the window behind them so that there was just a narrow gap. Then, as fast as they dared, Alice and Tim scurried out into the quad.

The quad was empty but the surrounding school buildings on all sides provided ample hiding places for watchers. Mrs Salter had already almost caught Alice on the night of the LSPDA meeting and this time she was determined not to take any chances.

"Down here," Alice said, ducking into the alley. Quickly they slipped through the darkness. When they reached the end, Alice paused, looking left and then right. "Okay, come on."

As they followed the winding sandy path to the cliffs, Alice's heart pounded in her ears like a drumbeat. Faster. Faster. Mr Marlowe could be lurking, waiting to pounce.

"Alice!" a voice whispered.

Alice almost leaped out of her skin. She looked around, startled.

Tim froze. "What's up?"

"Alice!" the voice urged again.

"Who's there?" Alice said.

"Wh-who are you talking to?" Tim said shakily. He flashed the torch about.

A shadow darted past Alice's feet and she stared after it. There, keeping low to the ground, was Milo, frozen in the beam of the torch.

"Milo, what's the matter?" she asked, dropping down to speak with him.

The hare's skittish eyes flitted between Alice and Tim. "Who's he?"

"A friend," Alice reassured. Gently she put a hand to the hare's long, plush ears and stroked them tenderly. "It's okay, Milo. You can talk to me."

"What are you doing?" Tim hissed.

Alice ignored him. "Tell me what's wrong."

"It's Constance," the hare replied. "She's gone!"

The breath caught in Alice's throat. "The animal snatcher?"

The hare nodded frantically. "Red sent me to tell you. We received word late last night. I've been trying to get close to the school all day but there were too many people."

"Are you sure?" Alice pressed.

"Yes," Milo squeaked. "Our operatives say Constance was last seen rushing through the school garden yesterday evening on her way to the wood. One minute she was there and the next she was gone."

Alice put her head in her hands. This was her fault! Constance must have been on her way to warn Red and the others about Mr Marlowe when she was snatched. She'd always assumed the cat was one step ahead, but no one was safe. Not even clever, sensible Constance.

"The sparrows came to tell us. They've been keeping watch."

Of course the sparrows were with the LSPDA. Why hadn't she thought of that?

"Did they see who took her, Milo?" Alice asked.

"The figure had a hood up but they heard Constance calling for help and saw her being locked in a cage." He paused. "They said she was really frightened, Alice."

Alice's chest tightened at the thought of Constance so distressed. She hugged the hare to her. "I need you to give Red a message. It's very important, okay? Tell him I think I know who the animal snatcher is and that it looks like his hideout might be in a cave off the beach. We're going there now to check it out. Can you do that?"

Milo nodded. "I'll go right away." He nuzzled Alice's hand with his nose. "Good luck, Alice."

The hare turned and bounded off, his long, lolloping strides making short work of the distance back to the school and the woods that lay beyond it.

Alice straightened up. The thought that Mr Marlowe had Constance and might hurt her – might already have hurt her – was too much to bear.

"So you can really do it, then," Tim said, his voice full of awe. "You actually talk to animals."

"Yeah, it's called being a Switcher," Alice explained. "But that's not important right now. Change of plan, Tim. We're going to need to search the cave after all!"

CHAPTER 32

The beach was transformed by night. Far out beyond an expanse of rock pools and driftwood, white crests lapped the sand. The moon was a thick wedge of silver, partially hidden behind the clouds. In the gloom, the cliff steps were treacherous. Tim went ahead, the thin beam of his torch picking out a path, but Alice closed her eyes, relying on instinct as she ran her foot along the sharp edge of each step to feel its drop before carrying on down.

When Alice dared to peep, Tim had already reached the beach. He swung the torch beam in a wide arc from left to right, examining the boulders at the foot of the cliffs.

"Switch it off," Alice hissed. "The light will give us away."

Reluctantly Tim slid the power off, clutching the torch to his chest as he began to weave his way along the cove.

"This way, I think!" He pointed. "On the map the cave was down here to the left. Watch your step. It's slippery."

Alice pushed the thought of seaweed and crusty anemones to the back of her mind, wringing her hands to try to keep them from shaking. There were more serious things to worry about. Constance was out here somewhere, terrified, maybe hurt. The cat needed her to be strong. Alice hoped Constance knew she was on her way. *I'm coming, Constance. Hold on.*

Alice and Tim peered into crevices and under ledges, the moon's dappled glow their only guide.

"What if there is no cave?" Alice fretted. "Constance could be anywhere by now . . ."

"The professor sounded certain," Tim reassured her.

He jogged further along the cove, his trainers squelching in the cold, wet sand. A moment later he called back, "Alice! Alice! Come and look."

Tim was bent low beneath a long, crooked finger of black rock, hooked like a witch's finger, pointing out to sea. As Alice caught up with him, he switched his torch back on, illuminating a small, jagged hole that opened into a wider chamber beneath the cliff.

"Bingo!" he whistled. As he stepped aside to let Alice see, his left foot shot out from under him, skidding across a smooth plate of stone. Tim toppled sideways, his right foot twisting with a sickening crunch.

He groaned in pain.

"Tim!" Alice crouched beside him. "Are you all right?"

The torch lay by his feet, flickering, its glass light cracked. She picked it up and shone the feeble light it offered on to Tim's ankle, feeling as gently as she could for the hardness of bone. "Can you walk on it?"

Tim nodded. "I'll try."

Alice tried to lever him up but as soon as Tim was standing again, one arm wrapped around her shoulder for support, his face twisted in pain.

"Okay, sit down again." She helped him sink back to the sand.

"I'm sorry, Alice!" Tim moaned.

"Are you guys okay?" a voice called from the darkness.

Alice shot round, shining the faint torchlight in the direction of the voice. As the figure drew to a halt inches from where Tim lay, Alice recognised the long blond hair spilling out from beneath a black hood.

"Ottie! What are you doing here?"

"I might have followed you." Ottie smiled sheepishly. "I couldn't sleep and thought I heard footsteps on the landing. That's when I saw you sneaking off. After what I told you, I thought maybe you were doing something about my uncle. Trying to find out what he's up to . . ."

"You thought right," Tim grunted, forgetting he was still meant to be mad with Ottie. "Can you two help me up?" The girls hauled Tim to his feet and propped him up between them.

"Alice," Ottie said, watching her carefully. "What were you doing with that hare back there? It looked like you were talking to it."

Tim and Alice exchanged a look.

"And the words you were using . . . I've never heard anything like that before."

"It's a long story," Alice said.

Ottie waited.

"There's no time now. Could you help Tim back to school? There's something I've got to do here."

"No way, Alice!" Tim said. "It isn't safe."

"My friend's in there," Alice said. "I'm not leaving her."

"Your friend?" Ottie said, bewildered. "And anyway, Tim's right, Alice. It doesn't look very safe. Why don't we wait until morning?"

"She can't wait," Alice said firmly. "It's my job to protect her. If I haven't returned by morning, raise the alarm – the gardener, Ted, will help, I think. I'm going to get Constance back."

Tim peeled his arm away from Alice, grimacing as he tried putting weight on his ankle. "Let her go," he told Ottie. "She needs to do this."

"Be careful getting back to school," Alice told her friends. "I'll see you soon."

Ottie opened her mouth to protest but Tim shook his head.

Carefully Alice scrambled over the rocks to the witch's finger and gazed into the dark, gaping mouth of the cave.

CHAPTER 33

Alice switched on her torch.

Slimy ropes of seaweed snaked across the cave floor. A crab scuttled past, its pincers outstretched. Ahead lay a trail of moon-mottled boulders. Alice glanced back down at the beach. Her friends were now halfway to the cliff steps, Tim's arm draped around Ottie's shoulders. There was still time to change her mind and go after them. Perhaps she could phone Gran and get her to talk to the police . . . But then she pictured Constance locked up in a cage, terrified and alone.

The air tasted salty on her tongue and the chill in the cave seemed to seep into her bones. Skidding on the damp lichen, her outstretched arms grabbing at air, Alice leaped from boulder to boulder. After yet another wobbly landing, she cursed her poor balance and the way her brain seemed to jumble any instruction she sent to her body.

As Alice landed on the last boulder, her heart sank. Before her stretched a pool of midnight-black water, no end in sight. Anything could lurk in its depths.

It's just water, she told herself, her foot hovering above the surface. *You can do this*. She lowered herself into the water, the cold swallowing her up.

Alice waded through the pool, the seawater slapping at her thighs so icy it snatched her breath away. Her teeth chattered and her head ached with the effort of not thinking about what could be hiding below the surface. She almost turned back but the thought of Constance kept her ploughing on.

Her splayed fingers were grazed and bleeding as she stumbled forward, the steep shaft of jagged rock her only guide. *So long as I keep the rock face to the right, it's impossible to get lost*, she promised herself.

The last tendrils of silvery light faded away behind her, leaving Alice with only the dying torch to guide her as she passed through a narrow archway, the rock closing in on either side. As she dragged her heavy legs through the black water, she dared not think of the slippery, sliding things gliding invisibly past her calves. *Just keep going*. Tim had said they had a couple of hours until the tide started coming back in but Alice had lost all sense of time.

How long did she have until the cave started to fill with seawater again?

Gradually the water became shallower, slopping against her ankles rather than her thighs. Alice found herself climbing steeply upwards and finally emerged into a narrow passageway – dry other than the *drip, drip, drip* of water leaking over stone. She stopped to rub life back into her feet and legs and that's when it hit her – a wave of misery so strong it flung her back against the cave wall. In her mind's eye she saw listless paws poking through bars. Parched tongues heavy and fat.

Alice, Alice, Alice. Her name seeped from the rocks and rose trembling from the stone floor. The chill pinched and gripped until finally she wrenched herself free. She forced her mouth to suck in air.

She had felt like this before: a force tugging at her, stealing the air from her lungs and knocking her from her feet. It had happened with the frog in biology and there was something else . . . That memory just beyond her reach. Something to do with the tower . . .

Alice couldn't make sense of these images billowing in her mind but something told her to trust them. Maybe all Switchers felt this way?

Constance and the other animals were close by. She knew it. Alice pushed on, squeezing herself through gaps so tight that she feared the rocks would surely crush her. At one point the only way forward was to drop to her belly and wriggle, her face in the dirt.

The tunnel opened up again and at first Alice thought she was hallucinating, that the faint whispers of light were a mirage, her tired mind playing tricks. However, as she trudged on and the air grew thick with the stench of kerosene, the distant fingers of light grew into the warm glow of lamps. Tim was right! Someone had been hiding here.

Alice turned a corner and was suddenly in a broader tunnel, supported by sturdy wooden beams. It was a crossroads of sorts. She could either continue up the gently sloping broadway or fork off, heading up a second tunnel at a steep incline. Alice chose to stick to the main one, continuing uphill again. Her pulse thudded in her ear, every muscle singing *soon, soon*.

Then she reached it.

A chamber hollowed out of the earth. The air was stale here like it was trapped, rotting. A large table, not unlike an operating table, occupied most of the cavernous space. Lining the far wall were towers of cages, all barred and padlocked, each containing an animal: leaden, hopeless, still.

As Alice stepped forward a hand clasped around her shoulder. "Well, well, well, look what the tide's washed in."

CHAPTER 34

"You?" spluttered Alice.

Miss Jessops twirled and curtsied, holding up the skirt of her sky-blue dress dotted with dozens of black cats. "It's so kind of you, dear Alice, to drop by for my little party."

Alice stood frozen in horror.

The librarian grinned, her dark eyes huge behind their glasses, all the friendliness in them gone.

Alice went to speak but Miss Jessops wagged her finger, hand on hip. "Quiet, please! Silence in the library!" Her laughter was a giddy shriek as she danced in and out of the lamps' orange glow.

"I don't understand . . ." Alice said, staring up at the stacks of cages, with drips hooked up. The animals' glazed eyes stared back. Somewhere among them must be Constance and Agent T. "How could you?"

Miss Jessops hopped from foot to foot, her once pleasant face now cold and sneering. "Not so clever in the end, were you, Alice Tonks? Far too trusting. All it took was some biscuits and kind words and I had you eating out of the palm of my hand. *Tell me what you know, Alice. Have a look in the clocktower, Alice,*" she said gleefully.

The awful truth descended.

"It was you!" Alice cried, remembering the hard shove between her shoulder blades then stone stairs rushing towards her. Bile rose in her throat, sour and putrid. She had fallen right into the librarian's trap.

Miss Jessops snickered. "Guilty as charged!" she said, taking a mock bow. "I was at a crucial stage with my experiments – my life's work. You see for years I've been trying to develop the Super Switcher: a Switcher without fault, without flaw. But I couldn't get the formula quite right. I travelled the world, taking samples, gathering DNA and finally I was almost there, I almost had it. I couldn't risk you blowing my cover, not at this late stage! You left me little choice so I told you what you wanted to hear and off you went on the trail of nasty old Hugo Marlowe and his stolen animals. As if that fool could achieve all of this!"

"You pushed me down the stairs just to shut me up? I came to you for help! I trusted you . . . and you left me for dead!"

"Come now, Alice, you do like to exaggerate! It was just a little a bump on the head," Miss Jessops teased. "I only ever meant to put you off the scent. How was I to know all it would take was one teeny-tiny push for you to show your true colours?"

A memory was returning to Alice, foggy and half-formed. She remembered falling through the air, the stone steps rushing towards her . . .

"Of course, I had my suspicions long before your little tumble in the tower. After all, you're Lizzie Tonks' granddaughter!"

Alice looked up. "You know my gran?"

Miss Jessops didn't answer. She was in a reverie now, her eyes glazed over. "I could hardly believe it when you told me your name but it was when you started sneaking around after the library cat that you really piqued my interest!" She turned to Alice, a smirk on her lips. "Who do you think left *The Switcher's Companion* for you to find? What a pity there were so many pages missing in my old copy! People really should take better care of their books."

Alice felt like she was in quicksand, sinking deeper and deeper . . .

"That day in the tower I saw your talent, your potential." Miss Jessops smiled. It was a leering, hungry smile. "Of course I'd never have pushed you if I'd known what you can really do. All those years hunting and searching for the missing ingredient when actually all I needed was you!"

"Who are you?" Alice demanded.

"Why, I'm sweet Miss Jessops, the cuckoo librarian!" Her sing-song voice echoed round the laboratory. "Happiest watering my pot plants and making nerdy little students a hot chocolate in their moment of need."

She whipped off her spectacles and stomped on them with her boots until the lenses shattered and the frames lay crumpled upon the laboratory's dirt floor.

Alice recoiled. Miss Jessops wasn't just angry. She was dangerous.

"No, Alice Tonks, Miss Jessops I am not. My name is Madame Veronica Vainwright."

That was the name from the photo. Veronica Vainwright. The awkward girl at the end of the line, a book stuffed in her blazer pocket. Tim had been right about her too! She should have listened to her friend, not dismissed him. Alice's brain scrambled to piece together everything she'd just learned. "You didn't answer my question. H-how do you know my gran?"

"Why, your grandmother and I go way back!" A smile crept across her face. "In fact, you could say she taught me everything I know."

Alice's legs wobbled, threatening to give way. "Gran would *never* help the likes of you!"

"Oh, but she did." Suddenly the smile was gone. "Once upon a time, I was your granny's pet project . . . Until darling Lizzie turned her back on me, that is! Then you came along—"

"Alice! Look out!" Constance's voice shouted from a cage at the very top of the stack. But the cat was too late. Madame Vainwright pulled a syringe from her pocket, yanked up her sleeve and plunged the needle down into Alice's bare arm.

Alice put her hand to her skin. Three red dots of blood stained her fingers.

She swayed, her body suddenly too heavy for her to hold up. She tried to call for help but her tongue felt too fat and dry. Alice's brain chugged and whirred, unable to make sense of what was happening. As her legs finally collapsed from under her, the jigsaw piece clicked into place – she'd been drugged.

Alice peeled open her leaden eyes to find Madame Vainwright fastening a tourniquet around the crook of her elbow. The librarian pulled the scrap of old cloth taut, there was a quick scratch and Alice realised she'd been stabbed a second time.

Madame Vainwright drew a full syringe of scarlet blood, holding it aloft and staring at it with eyes full of wonder. "To think this was all I needed," she murmured. "All this time . . ."

As she lay slumped on the cave floor, Alice's memory finally returned to her in full. Feathers bursting through skin. Wings expanding. That day in the clocktower, for a moment, she had transformed into a bird. And then there was that strange experience in the biology lab where she'd felt like she was transforming into a frog. Constance had been wrong. She really *could* change into an animal. And Madame Vainwright knew it.

A sharp tug at her wrists brought Alice back to the present. "I can't have you getting away," the librarian said, binding her hands with a piece of rope. "You're a very valuable asset, Miss Tonks, though luckily for me, an inexperienced one. Not exactly in control of your Switching yet, are you?"

Alice stared foggily up at the cages where one animal after the other was pressing their furry face to the bars. In the furthest cage was Agent T, his wings beating faintly. As Alice's head began to droop, the last thing she heard was the steady, rhythmic pounding of paws on metal as the bars began to shake.

CHAPTER 35

By the time Alice came round, the oil lamp had burned itself out and Madame Vainwright was nowhere to be seen. The drips strung up from each cage door had been refilled. The animals had settled back down in their cages and were sleeping the thick, heavy sleep of the drugged. She felt woozy and she was bound to one of the metal legs of the operating table, the rope so tight that it bit into her wrists, stinging each time she tried to move.

A long bench housed rows upon rows of test tubes, all carefully labelled in Miss Jessops' neat handwriting, except Alice recalled with the sear of betrayal, it wasn't Miss Jessops' handwriting, not really. Miss Jessops didn't exist.

"Constance!" Alice called, one eye trained on the tunnel in case their captor returned. "Constance, wake up!"

Constance's voice was a feeble croak but Alice was so glad to hear it. "You shouldn't have come here, Alice," the cat said. "This is a bad place."

"I'll get us out," Alice promised, trying again to tug her wrists free and wincing as her skin chafed. "Where did Madame Vainwright go?"

"To the school. There's a passage that leads to the library – she goes at night when no one is around. That's how she brought me here. She comes back sometimes with books . . . books and vines. She uses them in her experiments . . ."

Dread tightened its grip on Alice. The librarian's love of plants had seemed so innocent. Just an eccentric hobby. Alice glanced up at the dozens of petri dishes and test tubes. She squinted at the labels but they were just a jumble of numbers and letters – some sort of code perhaps.

"She's obsessed with you, Alice. You're all she talks about. I think she took me because she knew you'd follow. She knows you're a Switcher." Constance moaned again, a pitiful noise. "It's my fault. I should have believed you when you said Switchers can shapeshift. I'm sorry I ever doubted you, Alice."

"None of this is your fault," Alice said firmly. "Help's coming, Constance. Tim and Ottie know I'm here and Milo's gone to get the LSPDA . . ."

"It's no good," the cat whimpered, slumping against the bars of her cage. "It's you she wants – you and your blood . . ."

"Constance?" Alice's heart was beating so fast she thought it might rupture. "Constance! Stay with me! Please stay with me!"

The cat didn't reply.

Alice looked about frantically for a bit of broken glass or a nail, anything she could use to saw through her ropes, but there was nothing within reach. Madame Vainwright was taking no chances.

Alice's anxiety surged until great, choking sobs filled the eerie stillness of the chamber. Her body rattled and shook. Her hands were too tightly bound to stim, she had no soft toy to help calm her and Constance was locked up, unable to lie by her side, warming her.

Alice stared into the gloom, feeling the animals' misery like a current sucking her into the depths. She felt close to shutdown, overwhelmed and exhausted to the point where her body ached to switch everything off. How stupid she'd been to think that she of all people could be a hero.

Suddenly, in the distance, she heard a faint scratching sound. Was Madame Vainwright returning to finish what she'd started? Alice steeled herself.

But it wasn't the animal snatcher.

A rat, brown and plump, scurried along one of the wooden

beams crossing the mouth of the tunnel and down into the chamber.

The rat's single jagged front tooth was sharp and yellow. His fur was matted and caked in mud, his ears dogtoothed. Long ago, some enemy had taken a chunk out of his tail, leaving an ugly pink scar. The rat plopped down before her and rested his paws on his round, podgy belly.

"There you are," he said, looking her up and down. "You really the Tonks girl?"

"Yes," Alice said eagerly. "Are you from the LSPDA? Did Red send you?"

"Ha! Not likely," he scoffed. "Not them snobs. They don't mingle with the likes of me, you know."

"Oh," Alice said, her heart sinking. "How come you're looking for me, then?"

"Long-tailed fella by the name of One-Eyed Simon told me you were down here. You might have seen him about? Sort of . . . squinty?"

Alice shook her head.

"Never mind," the rat said cheerfully. "Truth be told he's a bit of a wrong 'un. Probably not the kind of fella a nice girl like you should be mates with."

I must have hit my head harder than I realised when I fell, Alice thought.

"So if you're not from the LSPDA then who are you?" she said, after a long pause.

"Ebenezer Albert Pinktail." The rat grinned. "I'm a friend of your gran." He held out his paw for her to shake then withdrew it when he realised Alice's hands were bound. "Pleasure to meet you."

"Likewise," Alice mumbled, her head spinning. "Sorry, did I hear you right? Did you just say you were a friend of my gran?"

"Yup," the rat said proudly. "Lizzie's been a friend of the family for donkey's years."

Alice couldn't believe what she was hearing. First Madame Vainwright and now the rat. If she ever got out of this cave, she was going to have to have serious words with her gran! There was clearly a lot she'd been keeping from her.

She eyed the rat's single front tooth. "I don't suppose you could gnaw through these ropes, could you, Mr Pinktail?"

Ebenezer edged closer and gave the ropes a once-over. "Hmm . . . that's Watson Industrial rope you've got there. There's no getting through that in a hurry. Tough as old boots that stuff."

"Would you at least try?" Alice begged. "I've got to get out of here! Madame Vainwright might return at any moment . . ."

The rat stretched his mouth wide, pulling back his lips to reveal a set of blackened gums. "Mylasttoof." He let his lips spring back into place. "Can't be breaking it, I'm afraid. A rat's gotta eat."

Alice groaned.

"No need to look so down in the dumps. You're a Switcher, ain't you?"

"Not a very good one," Alice muttered. "It's only really happened the once . . . and that was by accident! My friend Constance – she's a cat – has been helping me but she didn't think Switchers could still change shape . . ."

"And that, dear girl, is why you should never listen to cats," Ebenezer said, shaking his head. "The problem with felines is they always think they're right. If they ain't seen it with their own two eyes, it can't have happened . . . Us rats, meanwhile, are dreamers. Storytellers. We've got imagination. We remember the old tales." He picked a speck of dirt out from under his claw with the jagged edge of his tooth. "Something some of these fancier animals would do well to remember when they're looking down their noses at us . . ."

"Oh," Alice said. "I never realised . . ."

"Folks don't," the rat said with a deep sigh. "They think all we're good for is sewers and drainpipes. Anyhow, what are you waiting for? Look lively." He gestured to the rope binding her hands with his long, pointy nose.

Alice glanced from the rope to the rat and began to smile. Finally there was someone she could ask about Switching who might actually have some answers. "All right. So how does it work, then? Can I be anything I want to be?"

But Ebenezer wasn't listening to her. The rat's ears had shot up. A moment later, footsteps hurried down the tunnel – and this time they were human.

CHAPTER 36

"Now, Alice!" Ebenezer squeaked. "Switch into a rat!"

"I don't know how!" Alice said desperately. "Everything happened so quickly last time!"

The footsteps were growing louder and the swinging beam of a lamp illuminated the tunnel's mouth.

"Just think ratty thoughts!" Ebenezer urged.

Alice forced her eyes tightly shut. This was madness. How was she supposed to turn herself into a rat? She thought about drains and long tails and cheese (or was that mice?) but it was no good. "I can't!" she wailed.

Madame Vainwright's silhouette, giant and skeletal, appeared in the chamber's entrance. "Honey, I'm home!" she trilled.

"Quickly!" Ebenezer hissed, diving for cover beneath the bench.

Vainwright rounded the corner, a bunch of vines in her hand. Suddenly, from further down the tunnel, came a stampede of paws and the swooping of wings. Madame Vainwright froze. "What is the meaning of this?" she seethed, her expression dark with fury as she turned to see what the commotion was.

But Alice already knew. Milo had done it! He'd fetched the LSPDA.

From out of the shadows, Henry and Red sprang at Madame Vainwright, hissing and snarling, their jaws snapping at the hem of her dress.

The animal snatcher roared: a vicious, rageful cry.

"Hurry! Hurry!" Athena hooted, circling the room as a platoon of wood mice and squirrels led by Milo attacked the bolts on the cages. The animals' fur was damp and sandy. Clever Milo must have told them she'd been heading to find the cave on the beach.

"Run, Alice!" Red shouted. "We'll try to hold her."

Alice was torn. How could she leave the LSPDA to fight her battle? She'd come here to save Constance, not to abandon her.

"Others before self!" Red barked in her direction. "You put yourself in danger to save us animals. Now let *us* help you. Get out of here!"

Madame Vainwright's head jerked up and it was clear she understood every word Red had said. "Not so fast!" she shouted. "That girl's not going anywhere!"

Henry leaped forward, his powerful jaw clamping shut around Vainwright's ankle. She screamed in pain, wrestling the badger with all her might. Her vines were trampled underfoot. As she fell to the floor, Red launched himself at her, his teeth crunching down on her forearm.

"Wake up! Wake up!" Athena commanded, swooping past the cages as the mice and squirrels wrestled the bolts free. As the bolts slid back, Milo leaped up to the first row of cages and whispered pleadingly, trying to coax the animals out.

Alice craned up to see the imprisoned animals. Were the LSPDA too late? She could only make out dark shadows slumped against the cage walls.

Ebenezer scampered over to Alice's bound wrists and began to examine the knot. "Don't just sit there! Try again," he urged, jabbing her with his pointy nose.

Alice made her decision. The LSPDA were risking their lives to give her the chance to flee. Now all she had to do was Switch . . .

Think, Alice, think!

The answer shot into her mind. The visions. Of course! Back in the tower, she'd touched the crow feather before being able to see through the bird's eyes . . .

Although the rope dug painfully into her wrists, Alice stretched out her right hand and ran a finger from Ebenezer's warm nose all the way to the scarred tip of his tail. The rat's coarse fur brushed her finger and a wiry whisker poked her hand. Her fingertips tingled.

Be the rat, she told herself, picturing a drain damp and slimy, and a black pipe clogged with a tangle of fur and chewed cardboard. Alice felt the slip. Just like in the clocktower, something inside her slid away as she imagined life as an animal.

This must be how Switching begins, she thought, her stomach churning and her head swimming. In her mind's eye, she was a rat. She saw herself scurrying along a pipe, her paws chilly and her nose awake to all the delightful smells of the sewers. Ahead was her nest. *Home. Family. Rest. Safety.* Her heart quickened with excitement after a long day's scavenging.

Before Alice knew what was happening, she was sucked sharply downwards. The ground rushed up to meet her with a great whoosh. She was squished like dough pressed flat, her muscles compressed and aching. She opened her mouth to scream . . .

With a loud *pop*, Alice found herself peering up at the ginormous bench. Her paws prickled as strands of black fur sprouted from them. Wait. Paws? Alice looked down and sure enough instead of fingers she had pink toes with sharp claws curling out. The loops of rope lay coiled on the ground.

She had done it. She had Switched!

"Nice one!" Ebenezer congratulated her but Alice just stared in disbelief at her furry body.

With Henry still hanging off one leg and Red's teeth crunching down once more, Madame Vainwright's left hand hunted blindly for the lamp. Her fingers curled round the handle, she pulled back her arm and with a terrible thud smashed it into Henry. The badger flew backwards, releasing her ankle, and landed dazed upon the floor.

Now the librarian's full attention was trained on Red, his teeth still clamped in the soft flesh of her right arm.

"Alice, move!" Ebenezer bellowed, darting towards the passage.

Madame Vainwright levelled a hard kick at Red's stomach. The fox wailed in pain and curled up into a tight ball as she kicked again and again. As the creature fell still, Vainwright dragged herself to her feet and hobbled after the two rats, snatching desperately at them.

Alice bounded across the laboratory, Madame Vainwright stumbling after her. And there, hidden behind one of the bench's metal legs, she spotted it. The syringe, still half full of whatever drug Vainwright had used to send her to sleep. Narrowly dodging the animal snatcher, Alice skidded to a halt. Would this work? It was the only plan she had and it might just buy the LSPDA some time . . .

"What are you doing?" Ebenezer shrieked. "Run, Alice!"

Madame Vainwright lunged forward, her fingers closing around Alice's furry middle. A triumphant smile stretched across the librarian's face. Alice couldn't let this happen. She had to help her friends. Her claws scrabbled for purchase on the earthen floor. Just as she felt herself wrenched upwards, Alice fixed her long, ratty teeth round the syringe and thrust it towards the pale, bony wrist that held her, jamming its needle down into Vainwright's skin with all her might.

This was their only chance. Alice held the syringe in place with her teeth as the liquid inside drained into the librarian's arm.

Vainwright screamed, horror and rage flooding her expression as she realised what Alice had done. Her eyelids flickered. She blinked twice. Then her fingers relaxed and Alice tumbled to the ground.

"Go, Alice!" Red cried, dragging himself up on to all four paws. "Get out of here!"

"This way," Ebenezer wheezed and the two rodents escaped into the tunnel's mouth at a frantic gallop.

Madame Vainwright staggered after them, wobbling and swaying. *Pass out. Pass out. Please pass out*, Alice implored. Hopefully there had been enough drug left. It wasn't good enough for the animal snatcher to be sleepy. They needed her unconscious.

Ebenezer ducked beneath a wooden beam into a rat-sized cranny and Alice followed, narrowly escaping being crushed as Vainwright's body crashed to the ground behind her.

"It's not over, Alice Tonks!" she threatened, her words slurred. "I'll never let you go!" But then the drug tightened its grip and she fell silent.

CHAPTER 37

The two rats climbed steeply up in the pitch darkness, the stench from Ebenezer so distinctly ratty that Alice was able to follow him with her nose alone. The earth pressed down on her, the passageway so tight she couldn't turn or stand. Her ears pricked up and her whiskers twitched, alive to the whole world: water was trickling somewhere close by. Ebenezer paused, sniffing the air before leading them onwards.

"Where are we?" Alice asked after they had been climbing for ten minutes.

"Imagine two main tunnels," Ebenezer said over his shoulder. "One running from the school to the beach and the other going into town. They meet at the crossroads just before the witch woman's chamber."

"Which tunnel is this, then?" asked Alice.

"Neither. This is the Rat Express. Consider it the direct line."

"Where are we going?"

"Hetty's."

"The tearoom?" Alice said, puzzled. "Why there?"

She didn't get an answer.

"Careful here," Ebenezer wheezed, grinding to a sharp halt. He then leaped forward.

Alice sniffed the air where he had just been standing. A faint waft of Ebenezer's cheesy stench still lingered there. A moment later, his voice came again, distant and echoey. "Right, your turn."

"I can't!" But even as Alice said it, her back legs hunched and she sprang forward, leaping through the darkness.

"Simple, see," Ebenezer scoffed as Alice landed beside him on a stone ledge.

"I can't believe it," she said. No human could have made that leap. "I really am a rat."

"Welcome to the club," said Ebenezer. "But if you don't stop jabbering and get moving, you'll soon be a dead rat."

They ran on. Struggling to keep up, Alice marvelled at how fast the rat could scamper, his belly dragging on the ground beneath him. After a while, her whiskers told her that the passage was widening and the air started to smell fresher. They were getting closer to ground level.

"Why are you helping me?" Alice asked.

"You tell me. Must be mad," Ebenezer panted. "Look, your mates in the LSPDA aren't the only ones to honour the old ways, you know, much as they think they are. When One-Eyed Simon said there was a Tonks tied up in the old tunnels, I had to go and see. My old man and your gran go right back. He'd never have forgiven me if I'd left you in there, not with that woman . . ."

"Well, thank you. I know you didn't have to help."

A new smell struck her and a second later her brain said *water, stagnant.*

"Jump!" Ebenezer barked but there was no time. Her feet were already kicking mid-air as she fell after him, down and down into a narrow, upright pipe.

Alice landed with a splash, water flooding her nostrils and her eyes. Instinct told her to kick as hard as she could and her tiny paws powered her through the water. A moment later, she spluttered to the surface of a half-pipe, the metal hard beneath her paws and the water sitting at its base almost up to Alice's whiskers.

"Some warning would have been nice," she huffed, but was surprised to realise she wasn't scared.

"Best we swim this last stretch," Ebenezer told her. "We'll be faster that way."

Alice gulped and snuck a glance over her furry shoulder. Was Madame Vainwright already on their trail? She paddled as hard as she could, her pink toes splaying. The water churned beneath her, oily and grey, splashing her face and whiskers. But she didn't gag or choke. Her rat body was designed for this world.

Minutes passed, maybe more, and then the first spots of creamy light fell before her. But whether it was the light from a street lamp or the early morning sun she couldn't tell. It felt like she and Ebenezer had been on the run for hours, and she had no idea how long Madame Vainwright had kept her prisoner in the cave. By now Tim and Ottie might already be looking for her, maybe Mr Turner too. Guiltily Alice thought of Tim's injured ankle and hoped her friends had made it safely back to school.

"Almost there," Ebenezer promised. "You've done good."

The water gradually got shallower and Alice squinted as she followed the rat up a steep ramp towards the light, which filtered through the thick metal bars of a drain cover. It was the kind of blue-grey glow seaside towns wake to on misty mornings.

"Bit of a squeeze this one," Ebenezer said, sucking in his belly as he wriggled through.

Alice followed him and found herself emerging on to a cobbled street. The kerb was a steep cliff face waiting to be scaled and as a milk float rumbled past, the stones beneath her paws began to tremble and shake.

Ebenezer's eyes were wary, his fur bristling. "Welcome to Pebblehampton. Keep your eyes and ears open. Danger's afoot!"

CHAPTER 38

The shops lining Pebblehampton high street were shut, metal grilles covering their windows. But a couple of people were already up and about. A baker loaded trays of rolls into her van while, further down the road, the milkman's cart buzzed as he continued his round.

Alice stared up at the smart black-and-cream door from the cobbles. Hetty's hadn't changed at all from how Alice remembered it from when she'd visited with Gran. "Are you sure you meant to bring me here? A tearoom?"

"Course I'm sure," Ebenezer replied. "Brought you here specially, didn't I? It's the safest place I know."

The rat knocked three times on the bay window with his paw and then jumped down to join Alice. The frilly blinds were drawn, and a 'Closed' sign hung in the window. Alice hadn't expected to be able to read as a rat but the sign's cheery message was clear: 'We're closed now! Pop back soon!'.

Ebenezer was busy sniffing the door frame. "Nope!" He sighed. "I'm not getting anything."

"It's too early. They don't open until half nine," Alice said, craning her neck to read the opening times written in fancy curls on one of the panes of glass. "And we're rats. No one answers the door to a rat, especially not a café owner!"

"Hetty does," Ebenezer said, and he was right. Keys jingled and the lock turned. A bell over the door chimed. Two navy-blue court shoes appeared in the doorway, belonging to a chunky pair of legs. Alice looked up to see a black dress and white lacy apron. She stepped back to get a better view.

A chubby lady with a round face and greying curls peered round the door. Alice remembered Hetty's bright smile and red cheeks from her last visit.

"Ebenezer!" Hetty cooed. "You're soaked through! Come in out of the cold, you must be frozen. And who's this? A lady friend for you, dear?"

Ebenezer scuttled under Hetty's legs and into the tearoom, Alice following close behind, her paws skidding on the polished wooden floor. The round tables with their heavy linen covers were neatly laid, ready for the first customers of the day. The clock on the wall read twenty to seven.

"This isn't like you to come a-calling so early," Hetty said, closing the door behind them. "I hope nothing's wrong?"

She bent down and to Alice's amazement, Ebenezer hopped into her hand. Hetty scooped him up, holding him aloft so that she could better hear him. Clearly Hetty was a Switcher too. How many Switchers were out there, all looking perfectly ordinary and just going about their everyday lives?

"I've brought the Tonks girl," Ebenezer said. "She was in a spot of bother."

Hetty turned her attention to Alice, squinting at her. "Goodness! Is that really you, Alice dear? Haven't you grown up!"

"I, um . . ." Alice began, amazed that Hetty seemed perfectly unfazed by the fact she was a rat. "Hello."

"Right, well, now the introductions are taken care of, I'd better be off," Ebenezer said, sidling towards the door.

"Come on now, Ebenezer," Hetty said. "Won't you take a nice bit of bacon for your trouble?"

The rat rubbed his paws together. "I am partial to a bit of your bacon, Hetty . . ."

"That's settled, then!" Hetty clapped her hands. "I'm sure you must be peckish too, Alice dear, and there's plenty to go round." She disappeared into the walk-in fridge and returned with a packet of bacon rashers. She fished two out and laid them down before Ebenezer, who jumped on them greedily.

Alice's tummy growled. The raw bacon did look tasty.

Before she could tuck in, the bell above the door rang.

"We're not open!" Hetty cried, hurrying over.

"You didn't lock the door?" Ebenezer exclaimed as he dived beneath the tablecloth. Alice scurried after him.

"I said we're not open!" Hetty flapped. "Go away!" But then she breathed a sigh of relief. "Oh, it's just you two, why didn't you say? Almost gave me a heart attack."

A golden retriever bounded into the tearoom, his tail wagging excitedly as he jumped up to greet Hetty. If Alice wasn't mistaken, she knew that dog . . . Right on cue, a Jack Russell burst through the door. They were the dogs from school!

"What the . . .?" she murmured in disbelief.

The Jack Russell zipped around the room, yapping noisily.

"You might have told me you were coming," Hetty grumbled. "I'd have had the tea ready if I'd known!"

Beneath the tablecloth, Ebenezer's fur puffed up and he began to hiss.

To Alice's amazement, the two dogs started to quiver, their outlines trembling like waves of heat on a summer's day. Their faces caved inwards as if someone had stamped all the air out of a paper bag, then sprang back, human this time. Their furry legs were sucked in and shot back out, wrinkled and liver-spotted.

"Professor Biddle?" Alice gasped, edging out from beneath the fringes of the tablecloth. She stared at the man now standing where the golden retriever had been just seconds before. Could it really be?

The professor straightened his bow tie. "Alice Tonks, if I'm not mistaken?" he said, not at all surprised to be talking to a rat. "Your grandmother *will* be relieved. I called her as soon as I heard you were missing. She's on her way."

The man next to him had shaggy grey hair and wore beige corduroy trousers, patched at the knee, and a checked shirt. "Pleasure to see you again, Miss Tonks," Ted Turner said, his flat cap in hand. "I hope you're feeling better than the last time?"

"Er, hi," Alice said, blinking hard. The school gardener and her geography teacher had just transformed before her very eyes. Balancing on her hind legs, Alice rubbed her temples with her paws.

"We came to rally the troops for your rescue mission," Professor Biddle told Alice. "But it seems you beat us to it."

"How did you know I was missing?" Alice wondered, looking from the professor to the gardener. She still couldn't quite believe they were Switchers.

"Ah well!" The professor winked. "We may have happened upon your friend Timothy hobbling back to the school with the Marlowe girl . . ."

"It's not their fault!" Alice said quickly. "I made them come with me."

Ted Turner laughed. "Funny, they said you'd say something like that." He smiled kindly at Alice. "It took half a packet of Bourbons and two cups of tea back at my shed before they'd

280

tell us where they'd really been. But don't worry, they're not in any trouble. Not with us, anyway."

"And Tim's okay?" Alice asked, remembering the pain he'd been in on the beach.

"Quite all right," the professor reassured her. "We packed him off to the nurse to get that ankle seen to, then came straight here."

Alice breathed a sigh of relief.

"Will someone please tell me what's going on?" Hetty demanded, her hands on her hips.

"I was wondering the same thing."

Alice gasped. There, in the kitchen doorway, stood Gran. She straightened out her waxed jacket and coughed twice. A single blue-grey tail feather floated down to the lino floor.

"Alice?" she said, her gaze flitting between Alice's long ratty tail and her whiskered face. "Is that you?"

A warm tide of relief washed over Alice from her ears to her paws.

For a moment, she trembled and then her furry legs began to stretch. Something tugged sharply at her ratty ears. Her tailbone itched. Her nose ached. Then *pop!* her tail and snout were gone, and her paws were replaced by school shoes.

Alice was human again.

"Gran!" she cried, rushing forward. Gran's arms scooped her up just the way she knew they would. A hundred kisses rained down all over her face.

"My darling girl!" Gran pressed her stubby fingers and calloused palms to Alice's cheeks. "I've been so worried! Thank goodness you're safe!"

Alice sank her face into Gran's jacket, the familiar smell of toffees wafting over her. Her questions could wait. Gran was here. That was all that mattered.

"I'm so sorry," Gran said. "This wasn't how I wanted you to find out."

"I don't understand. I don't understand any of it. I'm a Switcher. I can Switch . . . and you . . ."

"Yes, I can Switch too. In fact, I've just flown in." Gran brushed two downy white feathers from her collar.

Alice pulled back from the hug to stare at Gran in disbelief. She looked just the same as always. Long grey hair pinned scruffily in a clip. Same comfy jeans and red jumper with holes in the sleeve, same green Doc Marten boots. Yet something had changed. Gran wasn't just Gran. She was . . . different. Everything was different.

"I know it's a lot to take in," Gran said. "I'm just sorry I couldn't tell you myself. Oh, Alice, I've been so worried! I came as soon as the professor told me you were missing. How did you know to come here? And whyever did you run away from school in the first place?"

Alice ignored her questions. There was no time to waste. "We've got to go back!"

"Back?" Gran said. "Back where?"

"I haven't got time to explain it all now," Alice said

282

impatiently. "We have to go. It was awful, Gran. The animals . . . Their faces . . . What she did to them . . ."

"Animals? What who did? Whatever are you talking about?" Gran grabbed Alice's arm.

"The animals in the cave!" Alice gabbled. "The ones who've been going missing. I went to find them. The animal snatcher – it was her all along!"

"Who?"

"The school librarian – Madame Vainwright!"

CHAPTER 39

"Madame Vainwright!" Gran's face turned deathly pale. She turned to the other adults for an explanation but they all looked as shocked as she did. "But it can't be! She's—"

"I thought it was Mr Marlowe but . . ." Alice fell silent. Gran's wrinkled hands worried the frayed sleeve of her jumper. She looked old. Old, and scared, and tired. "Are you okay, Gran?" Alice asked, looking around for a chair. She longed to ask Gran how she knew Madame Vainwright but now didn't seem the time.

"Lock the doors," Gran said, her voice trembling. "Be on your guard, everyone."

Ted hurried over to the front door, limping slightly. Hetty's keys were still in the lock and he turned them quickly, before ramming home both sets of bolts. Hetty disappeared into the kitchen, returning with a steaming cup of tea.

"Here, Lizzie, drink this," she said, squeezing Gran's shoulder. "Plenty of sugar."

Gran nodded shakily and took a long sip, then another. Slowly some colour returned to her face.

Ebenezer's whiskers poked out from under the tablecloth. "Good to see you, Lizzie," the rat said, bobbing his head respectfully. "It's been a while."

"Ebenezer!" Gran cried. She bent down and gave the rat's head a friendly pat.

Alice's hands clenched into fists. So Ebenezer had been telling the truth. Why hadn't Gran told her that the Tonkses were friends with a family of rats, either? Alice was beginning to feel like she'd been lied to and not just once. Gran must have lied over and over again.

"It seems this . . . gentleman came to Alice's rescue," Professor Biddle explained.

Gran's eyes flitted between Alice and Ebenezer, like she couldn't quite believe the two of them were in the same room. "So it's you I have to thank for my granddaughter's safety, is it? How will I ever repay you?"

"No need. Pinktails keep their promises, Lizzie, you know that."

Under her breath, Alice gave an indignant *humph*.

Ebenezer edged closer to the half-eaten bacon and began to nibble it.

Gran glanced anxiously at the door. "Veronica's no fool. She'll know Ebenezer brought Alice here. We should get moving."

"She was out cold when we left her," Alice said quietly. "I drugged her."

"Drugged? Whatever next?" Gran shook her head in disbelief. "How long ago was that?"

Alice shrugged. "A couple of hours, maybe more. The syringe was only half full, though. It was all I could find."

"Then we haven't got long until she wakes," Gran said resolutely. "Tell us everything. Right from the start."

"I'll fetch some toast," Hetty whispered, slipping off to the kitchen.

Alice closed her eyes, thinking back to Welcome Day. That had been the beginning of it all. She began to recount her adventure, starting with meeting Agent T on the beach. Hetty soon returned with a tray of buttery toast and a fresh pot of tea. By the time Alice finished explaining how she'd discovered Madame Vainwright in her secret lab and escaped with Ebenezer, the teapot was empty and only a few crumbs of toast remained.

"Well, I never," Ted said, sitting back in his chair. "A Super Switcher indeed! Vainwright's really back, then."

"After all this time," Professor Biddle said. "All these years of searching and in the end, she's returned of her own accord. It's been what – ten years?"

"Eleven," Gran murmured, and Alice noticed she shifted ever so slightly in her seat.

"And right under our nose!" The professor sighed. "I told you – didn't I, Ted? – what a nice young lady the librarian was, though at the time I thought there was something familiar about her. Stupid old fool, I am! I should have known."

"She had us all fooled, professor," Alice said. "I thought she was my friend."

"That woman's no friend," Gran said firmly. "It's my turn to tell you the truth, Alice." She drew a deep breath. "As you've probably realised by now, when I said I was a civil servant, that wasn't quite true . . . I'm actually the Chair of the Switching Board."

"The what?" Alice blinked hard. The room appeared to be spinning.

"The national organisation for Switchers. Most countries have one. As well as helping Switchers in need, it's the Board's job to regulate the British Switching community. We keep everyone in check. Make sure Switchers stay within the rules. Unfortunately Madame Vainwright's been operating well outside those rules for a long time and so it fell to us to look for her."

"All those work trips!" Alice realised. "You were lying the whole time . . ."

Gran swallowed. "I'm sorry I wasn't entirely honest."

"Entirely honest? That's an understatement. You lied to me!"

Alice slammed down her tea, the china cup clanging against its saucer. Gran had a whole second life she'd been keeping a secret all these years. If only she had told her the truth about Switchers earlier, Alice might have been able to guess what Madame Vainwright was really up to. Instead she'd had to find it all out for herself.

She pushed her chair back. "It's bad enough you didn't tell me who you really are but why didn't you tell me that I could do these things? Talk to animals? Shapeshift? I had a right to know!"

"I was protecting you!" Gran said. "That's my job. I'm the closest thing to a parent you've got. It's not an easy life having one foot in one species, one in another. Never knowing quite where you belong. Where you fit in. I should know . . ."

"I'm autistic!" Alice cried. "You think I don't know about not fitting in? I've handled that all my life. I could have handled this. You should have told me."

Gran chewed her bottom lip. "I just didn't want you to suffer the way I did," she said quietly. "Feeling like the odd one out all the time, always having something to hide. Pebbles was supposed to be your fresh start."

"But I *am* different," Alice said. "I've always been different, and I always will be. Autism is who I am. Switching could be too. You should have trusted me."

Tears glistened in Gran's eyes as she reached for Alice's hand. "You're right, my darling. It was wrong of me not to tell you. I see that now."

Alice pulled away.

"I'm hoping you can forgive me," Gran said. "Because the Switching Board's going to need your help."

CHAPTER 40

"I don't know if I can forgive you yet," Alice admitted. "But I'll definitely help. I'm not going to let Madame Vainwright hurt anyone else."

A sad smile played upon Gran's face. "I had a feeling you would."

The professor leaned forward in his chair. "You do understand that this is going to be very dangerous, don't you, Alice?" he said. "Madame Vainwright is not to be trifled with."

"Alice knows that, Walter!" Ted snapped. "Veronica pushed her down the clocktower stairs, for goodness' sake, and just last night she virtually kidnapped her! She isn't stupid." He turned to Alice. "You know what you're taking on, don't you?"

Alice nodded. "I'm the one Vainwright really wants," she said. "We can use that, can't we?"

Gran closed her eyes, deep in thought, her fingers pressed against her nose. "Yes," she said eventually. "But first we need to find a way to flush her out into the open. Ebenezer, I'm going to need your help again. Can you show us the way to Madame Vainwright's cave?"

Ebenezer gobbled the last rasher of bacon and smacked his lips contentedly. "Reckon I can do better than that!" he said. "How's about I get my whole nest keeping watch along the tunnels?"

"Thank you, Ebenezer," Gran said. "Ted, Hetty, Walter – I want you to go to with him and be ready in case she tries to run, though I don't think she will." She grimaced. "Veronica will be holding out for more of my granddaughter's blood. When I give the word tonight, I want you to tell her that I'm willing to negotiate and I'm waiting for her . . . Waiting for her somewhere she'll feel she has the advantage . . ."

"The library?" Alice suggested.

"Good." Gran nodded. "The library."

"She'll never do it!" Ted scoffed. "She'll know it's a trap."

"She will if she thinks there's something in it for her," Gran said darkly, glancing over at Alice. "Tell Veronica I have Alice with me."

"You can't use the girl as bait!" Hetty flung down her tea towel in horror. "Lizzie, she's your own flesh and blood!"

"You think I don't know that?" Gran snapped. "Of course I don't want to put Alice in danger! But we can't risk Veronica getting away, not now she knows a fledgling Switcher's blood is all she needs to rebuild herself. If we don't do this, then Alice will never be safe. Never." She paused. "And I can't let that happen."

Alice felt her bottom lip begin to wobble. She'd assumed Gran had kept her abilities a secret because she hadn't trusted her, but what if she really had been trying to keep her from harm? "D-did y-you know?" she asked. "Did you know that if I learned to Switch then Madame Vainwright would come after me?"

Gran shook her head. "No. I just knew she was out there somewhere, trying to find a way to Switch again and I knew you were safer if you didn't know how special you really are." She sniffed. "I just wanted to protect you, Alice, for as long as I could."

A tear trickled down Alice's cheek and plopped on to her collar.

An awkward silence fell over the room.

"Right," Ebenezer announced. "Come on, you lot!"

Ted Turner and Professor Biddle began to quiver. At first, Alice could only make out a soft blurring at the edges of their fingers and noses but then their faces grew furry and their fingernails turned to claws. Both men sprouted tails and with a whoosh, they were sucked down to dog height. A moment later, there were two audible *pops* and the golden retriever and Jack Russell yapped excitedly.

"Ugh, dogs," Ebenezer groaned, scampering towards the front door. "Hetty, are you coming?"

"Excuse me a moment, gentlemen," she said, stepping into the kitchen.

Alice looked to Ted and the professor, wondering what was going on, but the two dogs just sat on their haunches watching the kitchen doorway, their heads lolled to the side.

A moment later, paws padded on the wooden floor and a bichon frise trotted into the tearoom, its curly white coat puffed up like bubble bath. Alice grinned. "Looking good, Hetty!"

Ebenezer hung his head in shame. "A rat with dogs for mates?" He sighed. "If anyone sees me . . ."

Gran unlocked the front door and Ebenezer scuttled out, followed by the three dogs. "You can count on us, Lizzie," he said. "Just send word when the time is right!"

"Bye, Ebenezer!" Alice called after him. She was sad to see him go. The rat had saved her life.

Gran bolted the door and checked her watch. "Hmm." She frowned. "Switching ordinarily takes years to master. But I can't let you face Veronica without knowing the basics."

Alice fiddled with the grubby cuff of her sleeve, remembering what Madame Vainwright had said in the cave. *Lizzie and I go way back. In fact, you could say she taught me everything I know.* Just how close had Vainwright and Gran been?

"Gran," Alice said, edging over to join her by the door. "How well did you know Madame Vainwright?"

Gran's face darkened. For a moment, Alice thought she was going to refuse to answer but then sighed.

"Come on," she said, pulling out two chairs. "You may as well sit down."

Alice sank into the chair opposite Gran, watching her warily, afraid of what she was about to hear.

"Well," Gran said. "I suppose you could say I was Veronica's mentor. I was the one who taught her everything she knows."

"*You* taught Madame Vainwright?" Alice stared at Gran. "But she's . . . she's evil!"

Gran unfolded a napkin then scrunched it up into a ball. "When I knew her, Veronica was just a girl, barely a year or so older than you are now. It was Professor Biddle who introduced me to her. He thought she could do with a friend."

Alice scoffed.

"Veronica was new to Pebbles," Gran explained. "Lonely. Sad. The professor saw a certain promise in her, I suppose. She was very clever, by far the brightest in her year group."

Alice shook her head in disbelief. "You sound as if you admire her. Like her, even."

Gran smiled a sad smile. "Oh, don't get me wrong! Veronica had her faults, even back then. She was ambitious, prone to jealousy . . . stubborn too. Goodness, was that girl stubborn! But there was also lot to like. She was hardworking. Driven."

"She's a monster who locks animals in cages and performs experiments on them!" Alice exploded. "How can you possibly like someone like that?"

"People change, Alice," Gran said gently. "Veronica wasn't always the way she is now. If you want to help us defeat Madame Vainwright, you're first going to have to try to understand her."

Alice sat back in her chair, fighting the urge to flick her fingers.

"As time went on, Veronica grew more and more resentful of her classmates," Gran explained. "She could never fit in like they could, however hard she tried. Switching was all she had."

Alice scratched her elbow. The girl in the photo had looked a bit awkward but also kind and bright. The type of student she might have been friends with. "What happened to her?"

"I guess you could say her ambition got the better of her." Gran shuffled uncomfortably. "Veronica did things none of us thought possible. Wild things. Incredible things. She liked to push the boundaries. When we tried swimming along the shore as dolphins, she needed to explore the depths of the ocean as a shark. The truth is she hated Switching back and over time, she came to dread it. Eventually human life held no joy for her, no excitement. After she left school and went to university, Veronica spent longer and longer living as an animal. We tried to talk to her, to warn her, but one day she tried to Switch and found she had nothing left. The magic was gone. She'd used it all up."

Alice froze. She'd assumed Switching was forever. She'd already started making plans: animals she wanted to try out, places she wanted to go. Veronica Vainwright must have felt like she'd lost everything. Her whole identity snatched away.

"No wonder she wants my blood," Alice mused.

"Exactly." Gran nodded. "So come on, up you get. We've no time to waste."

Alice slowly got to her feet. What had Gran got planned for her?

"Listen carefully," Gran said. "There's two key skills to Switching: imagination and automaticity. First, you need imagination," Gran explained. She pretended to be deep in thought, her chin cupped in her hand. "The secret is to think beyond the animal's physical features. Appearance won't get you far. What you want to do, Alice, is focus on personality, interests, those sort of things. Habits and routine activities always work well."

"Yes!" Alice said excitedly. "When Ebenezer told me to Switch, I thought about a rat in a drain."

"That's it," Gran said. "The Switcher must strive to inhabit the target. To think as they do. To feel what they feel. I have something to help with that."

She reached into her pocket and retrieved a ball of fur. "Roger's," she said, by way of explanation. "I don't think he'll mind that I've borrowed it."

Alice wrinkled her nose. "Why are you carrying around a clump of dog fur?"

"It's a physical prompt," Gran explained. "An aide, so to speak."

A light went on in Alice's head. "Like in the cave!" she said. "I touched Ebenezer's fur . . ."

"Exactly. But always be sure the imagining process is complete," Gran cautioned. "Rush this stage and you can find yourself in a real pickle."

"Right," Alice said. "Got it."

"Once you've fully mastered imagination, the second skill comes into play. Automaticity."

"What's that?" Alice said warily, opening one eye.

"Automaticity is achieved when you can make the Switch instantly, without control or attention. No thought or hesitation whatsoever and with no physical prompt to help you. We're going to practise these two skills – imagination and automaticity. Get ready, please."

Alice took a deep breath in and out to prepare herself. The handwritten message from *The Switcher's Companion* was at the forefront of her mind: 'Practise your craft, treasure your gift.' She frowned. How had the young girl who had written that heartfelt message become so bitter and tainted?

"We'll start easy," Gran said, holding out the ball of fur. "Switch into a dog."

Reluctantly, Alice took the clump and held it in her open hand. She thought about Roger. His shaggy coat that you could lose your fingers in. His wagging tail thwacking the living-room rug. The way his pink tongue hung out on a hot day. She pictured him squeezed on to the sofa beside her, slowly pushing her out of the way until he had it all to himself. She heard his happy snore and thought *Content. Comfortable. Mine.*

Nothing.

Alice tried again. What had Gran said? Focus on habits. Roger's main habit was snoring . . . snoring and farting! Alice pictured him letting rip. His farts could clear a room!

Suddenly she felt her insides turn to liquid and this time, rather than a gentle slip, it felt more like a slosh as her innards were sucked downwards. There was a *pop*, then a sharp tug and the next thing Alice knew, she had sprouted a thick coat of wiry grey hair. Her tail wagged so fast and so hard she feared it might drop clean off.

"Good," Gran said crisply. "Now back to human form. We won't be attempting animal-to-animal switches quite yet. Let's have a few more tries – but no aides this time."

Next Gran demanded Alice become a horse. Then a sheep. Then a pigeon. Switching was exhausting and as the morning wore on, Gran's requests became trickier and trickier. Alpaca. Hummingbird. Centipede.

Alice gritted her teeth. She was hot. She was tired. And while they were training here, Madame Vainwright could be getting away. "Why are we waiting until nightfall? Isn't it time we got going?" she protested.

"Not yet," Gran said. "I won't put the other students in danger. And you need to be quicker. Veronica won't go easy on you just because you're a child, you know. She still needs more of your blood, remember."

Alice groaned. "Won't you and the rest of the Switching Board be there to protect me?"

Gran stiffened. "We plan for every eventuality."

Alice felt cold all over.

"Wolf!" Gran barked.

Alice refocused, picturing herself tearing through a forest with her packmates, nose to the ground and the scent of blood in her nostrils. A second later, her fangs gnashed and then she was howling, her snout pointing towards an unseen moon.

"Rhinoceros. Stag. Dragonfly." Gran clicked her fingers with each new species and Alice Switched, getting quicker and quicker until she was barely human between each animal and the changes were fluent and swift.

"All right," Gran said gruffly. "That'll do."

CHAPTER 41

The school loomed like a fortress on the cliffside, impenetrable and vast. The main building was steeped in darkness, the two lamps mounted at the top of the marble steps casting a narrow, flickering glow.

Alice was alone again. Gran had sent word via Horace, a nimble nephew of Ebenezer's, that she and Alice would be ready to meet Madame Vainwright at a quarter past midnight. She had then headed to the library to lie in wait for Madame Vainwright. But before Alice could join her, there was something she needed to do. She hurried through the school grounds, hoping that the training Gran had given her would be enough.

She avoided the atrium, wary of coming across one of the teachers on night duty, and instead skirted round the main school building to where the path looped back behind the boarding house.

As she passed through the quad, Alice took a moment to catch her breath. There, looking down upon the school, was the stained-glass window. She gazed up at the fox, the badger, the hare and the gull. Having come to her aid once before, could she count on the LSPDA again?

She remembered Constance's instruction: in an emergency, find the old badger sett below the window. She dropped to her hands and knees, hunting through the grass until she found the D-shaped mound where badgers had excavated the earth below. Her nose located the musty stench of the entrance tunnel before her eyes did.

Alice peered into the hollow. "Hello? Anyone there?" she called.

There was no answer.

Alice tried again.

Still no answer.

What was she going to do? This next stage of the plan relied upon the LSPDA's help!

Suddenly an apparition, white and soundless, glided across the moonlit sky. With the soft beating of wings, Athena the barn owl swooped down, landing beside Alice on the tufty lawn.

"You came!" Alice cried.

With a crisp ruffle of feathers, Athena tucked her wings away and swivelled her heart-shaped head to face Alice.

"The rats said you were on your way," she shrieked, her dark glassy eyes captivating Alice. "I've been looking out for you."

"Thank goodness you're all right! What about the others? How's Constance? Is she okay?"

"She will be, with some sleep and good food," Athena said. "Some of the others aren't so lucky. Red, Henry and the others helped carry those too weak to walk back to safety." The owl pecked at an errant feather. "The animals who were prisoners the longest are still unconscious. The animal snatcher used some powerful drugs."

Alice's anger prickled inside her. Madame Vainwright had to be stopped. "That's why I'm here," she said. "I need the LSPDA's help to end this once and for all. Can you gather as many animals as possible?" Alice glanced up at the clocktower. "In half an hour, that clock will strike eleven. Tell everyone to meet me in the quad outside the boarding house."

The owl nodded and gave a gentle hiss.

"Thank you," Alice said. "There's somewhere I have to be but I'll see you soon."

Athena screeched hoarsely as she flew away, her powerful wings batting the night air. Alice watched her disappear among the canopy of trees, then darted off towards the boarding house.

The front door was locked, so Alice had no choice but to gather a pile of small stones and aim them at her dormitory window, hoping Ottie was inside. The light was out and the curtains drawn. For all she knew, Ottie could have returned to Lexi and Kelcie's dorm but she had to chance it. She couldn't remember which window belonged to Tim and couldn't risk disturbing the wrong boy.

After several long minutes, the dormitory window flew open.

"Tim!" Ottie squealed, turning away. "It's safe to come out. It's Alice!"

Two heads reappeared in the window – one dark, one fair, both grinning.

"Alice!" Tim exclaimed. "You're okay! Where have you—?"

"Shh! You'll wake the whole boarding house!" Ottie hissed. "Hold on, Alice! We're coming down."

CHAPTER 42

Ten minutes later, Alice sat huddled on the common-room sofa with Tim and Ottie, a blanket draped across them all and Tim's crutches propped against the sideboard. It was strange sitting in the dark and talking in whispers but it was great to have her friends back by her side.

". . . And then I came back here," Alice finished, having summarised what had happened.

"I told you that librarian was dodgy!" Tim cried.

"So you're like . . . magic." Ottie stared at Alice in amazement. "I saw you talk to that hare and Tim told me what you could do but . . . you're actually properly magic. You can shapeshift. That's wild!"

Alice nodded. "It is kind of cool. Pretty scary but cool.

Now tell me what you two have been up to." She snuck a glance at Tim's watch, hoping Athena had almost finished rounding up the animals. "But you'd better be quick."

Ottie's eyes lit up. "You're not going to believe it!" she exclaimed. "Professor Biddle and the gardener came to our rescue!"

"Yup," Tim said. "For adults, they're pretty cool." He pulled up his pyjama leg to reveal a tightly wrapped bandage. "Mr Turner gave me ice for my ankle and he even sweet-talked the nurse into not telling Mrs Salter!"

"And that's not all," Ottie chipped in. "Guess what we've got?"

Alice leaned in.

"Look!" Ottie revealed a tablet, flashing it under Alice's nose. Alice recognised it immediately. It was Mr Marlowe's! "Uncle Hugo left his office unlocked and we were able to swipe this." She smiled innocently. "Let's say we've taken it for safekeeping."

"It was all Ottie," Tim said. "She was brilliant."

"Turns out my uncle's not so smart after all . . ." She typed the password G-E-N-I-U-S into the tablet and the screen lit up. "As you can see, he really has been up to all sorts."

"Robbing the school blind, for one," Tim said. "Mrs Salter's in on it too, of course!"

"It's all in here. He must have been stealing since the day he arrived!" As Ottie scrolled through a catalogue of expensive antiques, artefacts and paintings on the screen,

305

Alice recognised the oil painting of the conch shell. There was even an ornate crown, sceptre and orb, like a king or queen would carry. "I guess this is why Uncle Hugo needed Maloney and Khan Logistics. He had to get the goods he's been pilfering from the school out of the country somehow."

"See! I was right after all!" Tim piped up. "Those men in the boat really were smugglers."

Alice and Ottie looked at each other and rolled their eyes.

"We couldn't find anything to do with stolen animals," Tim added. "But I guess that makes sense if it was Miss Jessops or whatever she's called. "So what happens now?"

"Come on," Alice said. "I'll show you."

Alice and Ottie slipped out of the common-room window, then carefully fed the crutches through before helping Tim ease himself out. As they crept into the quad, a dozen pairs of eyes watched them from the shadows.

Slowly the animals stepped out, one at a time. Red was limping slightly but his eyes blazed bright as he nodded in greeting, a vixen and three cubs by his side. Behind him was Henry, along with two older badgers Alice hadn't seen before. Milo loped forward, his eyes darting between Tim and Ottie.

"Friends of mine," Alice said, crouching down to stroke Milo's ears. "You can trust them."

Rabbits, squirrels and wood mice poked their heads up curiously, the rabbits' ears upright as they listened for danger.

A flock of sparrows chattered excitedly while Athena circled overhead. Perched on the nearest bench was a row of seagulls. There was even a toad and two springy frogs.

Alice looked around for Constance and Agent T but they were nowhere to be seen.

"Agent T and Constance are resting," the fox reassured her. "But they send their regards."

Alice smiled but she wished they could be here by her side.

Hooves pounded in the distance, growing louder and louder, until two deer crashed through the alleyway, their rumps bright white in the darkness. "Sorry we're late," the one with antlers said. "What have we missed?"

Tim and Ottie looked around in disbelief as the quad filled with a menagerie.

"Mrs Salter's going to blow her top!" Tim laughed.

"This," Alice said, turning to her friends. "Is Step Two. If the whole school is watching a bunch of animals run wild, they won't notice the Switching Board fighting Madame Vainwright in the library."

"That sounds dangerous," Ottie said. "You're not going to do any fighting yourself, are you?"

Alice smiled, not wanting to tell a lie, and then strode over to the fountain.

"Right," she said, stepping up on to the rim of the basin where everyone could see her. "Listen up."

The animals gathered round.

307

"Thanks for coming tonight. There's been enough hurt and suffering recently. What we need is to keep all the students safely in the boarding house and far away from Madame Vainwright."

"Henry?" Red said. "Can you and the other badgers guard the doors?"

"Got it," Henry replied, shuffling over to his family.

"Watch the housemistress. She can't be trusted. There shouldn't be many other teachers about at this time but some of them live on site in the staff cottages so keep an eye on them too. The headmaster's is the big one on the end. Create as much noise and commotion as you can. We want everyone focused on what's going on here."

Ottie shook herself out of her reverie, running ahead to show Red the way through the common-room window into the boarding house.

Alice felt silky fur brush against her calves. "Well, you heard the girl!" Constance cried. "Snap to it!"

"Constance!" Alice gasped.

As the other animals followed Red, Alice sank down beside Constance on the fountain edge and kissed the tabby all over her furry face. The cat climbed into her lap and licked her hands, purring loudly.

"Oh, Constance!" Alice said, smothering the cat with even more kisses. "You're all right!"

"I am," Constance said, "Thanks to you. And Alice, I'm so sorry. I led you right into danger."

Alice buried her face in Constance's warm coat. "Don't be stupid. There's only one person to blame for all this and that's Madame Vainwright. I'm just glad you're okay."

"So what are you waiting for, Alice?" the cat said, leaping from her knee and settling down on the fountain's edge. "Don't you want to see the chaos unfold?"

"Aren't you coming?"

"I still feel a bit shaky," Constance said. "I'll wait this one out. I've got a good view from here, though."

Alice gave the cat one last kiss, before waving goodbye.

Inside the boarding house, the animals had taken over. Alice stood on the first-floor landing and watched as the deer galloped up and down the staircases. Athena hooted at the top of her lungs, while Red and the vixen had headed straight to Mrs Salter's room on the floor above. Then they started dragging the housemistress downstairs by the fringes of her pink dressing gown.

"What is the meaning of this?" Mrs Salter raged but her voice was lost amid the screech of the owl and the thunder of hooves.

"What's going on?" a student called, flinging open his dormitory door.

"Oh, wow!" another yelled. "You've got to see this!"

Half-awake students poked their heads out of their dorms, rubbing the sleep from their eyes. Animals were running riot over every floor of the boarding house. It was absolute mayhem, just as Gran had instructed. The squirrels were swinging from the lampshades and a group of sixth-formers screamed as mice shot up their legs. A bunch of Year Eight boys were being herded down the corridor by the flock of sparrows.

A prefect, wrapped in his blue-and-white dressing gown, bellowed for order.

Nobody listened.

"I'm guessing this is when you leave," Tim said, appearing beside Alice on his crutches. He panted slightly, worn out by the stairs. It was gone midnight.

"I think so," Alice agreed, her glee at watching bedlam unfold before her evaporating at the thought of Madame Vainwright. "Time for me to slip away."

"Can we help?" Tim asked.

"You are helping," Alice said. "Thank you."

Ottie was leaning over the bannisters, giggling as Kelcie and Lexi were chased down the hall and out into the lobby by a large toad. She turned round when she heard Alice. "Be careful, Alice. We need you back in one piece!"

Alice smiled. "I will."

Downstairs, the common room was bustling with pyjama-clad students laughing and pointing at the frogs hopping all over the kitchenette. One of Red's cubs clambered up on to Mrs Salter's head, pulling at her scrunchie with his sharp white teeth, while the other two growled playfully at one another in a tug of war over her dressing gown's silk belt.

Without anyone noticing, Alice climbed back out of the window and disappeared into the night. It was time for Step Three.

CHAPTER 43

Alice pushed open the library door, like she had a dozen times before.

The lights were on and humming gently. The returns trolley was overflowing as usual. Everything was just as it should be – everything, that was, except for the lone figure perched upon the counter, swinging her booted feet.

"Alice!" Madame Vainwright called. "Nice of you to drop by!"

Alice's skin turned to ice. She balled her hands into tight fists, willing herself to be brave. Madame Vainwright wasn't meant to be here yet. And where were Gran and the rest of the Switching Board? They were meant to be here with her . . .

You can do this, she told herself. She was an expert in masking. She did it every day of her life in order to try and fit in – now more than ever she needed to put on a convincing performance and pretend everything was fine. Alice lifted her head and strode into the library.

"Well, here I am," Alice said. "Just as you wan—"

The words turned to dust in her mouth for there, poking out from between the shelves, were a pair of green Doc Marten boots. Gran's boots. Alice froze. This was most definitely not part of the plan.

Madame Vainwright jumped down from the counter and skipped across the library, barely limping on the leg that Henry had mauled. She was red-cheeked and bright-eyed, far stronger than when Alice had last seen her in the underground laboratory. Her dress was now ebony and her loose, dark curls spiralled down her back, three blood-red roses decorating her hair. Panic ballooned inside Alice. She was all alone.

Vainwright sat down cross-legged beside Gran's body, twirling a strand of hair.

"I'm afraid Lizzie has always underestimated me. I knew there was no way she'd risk her precious granddaughter! And as for sending three old codgers to contain a Switcher with my skills? It's insulting. But thanks to your blood, I was able to *nip* your gran's plan in the bud. Now it's just you and me, Alice."

Alice forced herself to edge forward. Two pinprick dots blossomed on Gran's neck. It looked like a snakebite. With a sickening twist of her stomach, Alice realised that was what Madam Vainwright had meant by nipping her plan in the bud.

She must have Switched. Alice's heart began to race. If Gran had been bitten, she'd need anti-venom and where was Alice supposed to find something like that?

Twin ribbons of red dripped slowly on to the threadbare carpet. Hundreds of students' grimy shoes had tarnished the spot where Gran lay, her kind, wrinkled face lifeless and still. Alice yearned to rush over to her but resisted. Planting her feet firmly on the floor, she told her lungs to breathe and her fingers to be still. Gran had wanted to protect her but now the tables had turned and it was Alice's job to take care of Gran.

Madame Vainwright got to her feet and bounded over to Alice, leaning in cheek to cheek as if sharing some secret with a friend. "I'm afraid I made rather short work of the so-called Switching Board!" She giggled. "Didn't take long, truth be told. It was actually kind of boring. They're too old to put up much of a fight these days."

Alice stood silently, willing every muscle to be still.

Vainwright's face twisted in a snarl. "Lizzie always has to be so *good*," she sneered. "Wanting to give me one final chance to take it all back. Hoping I'd come round. You can see for yourself how that worked out. I took care of her."

Alice stared at the narrow strip of skin right between Madame Vainwright's eyes, refusing to look away, reluctant to give her the satisfaction of knowing she'd won. Life had given her years of practice pretending to be something she was not and neurotypicals never could tell the difference between eye contact and avoidance, truth and pretence.

"Gran would have helped you," Alice said, her voice quivering against her will. "I can still help you."

Madame Vainwright drew closer to Alice. She wore the same lace-up boots Alice remembered her showing off before she went to her book group. Probably another lie. "Your gran's old. Past it. She couldn't help me."

She nodded at the creepers clambering all over the desk and snaking across her office. "It's called the *Boquila trifoliolata* vine. I discovered it in Argentina where they call it the Stealth vine. It's known for its ability to shapeshift and camouflage but I'd been experimenting with it for years and was getting nowhere. The *Boquila trifoliolata*'s clever but not that clever . . ."

Her voice softened, became a purr. "I was lacking the magical ingredient, you see – the catalyst that would trigger the perfect chemical reaction." Her snarl twisted into a smile. "In the end, it was you, Alice – or rather, your blood – that gave me everything I needed."

There was a sharp *pop* and Madame Vainwright Switched into a deer, tall and graceful. Another *pop*. She became an eagle, sweeping across the room, her massive wings and hooked beak inches from Alice's face. A third and she was a lynx, sleek and wily. The cat's intelligent yellow eyes gleamed as she laced around Alice's legs. "There's nothing I can't do now!"

With a screech like nails on a blackboard, Madame Vainwright Switched back to her human form. Alice winced, resisting the urge to cover her ears. Switching back to being human seemed painful for Vainwright, unnatural even.

"I'm just sorry I didn't spot your talent earlier, Alice. All that time, I thought you were an obstacle in my way when really you were the answer I was looking for." She curled her long, slim fingers round Alice's throat, caressing the skin.

Alice tried to back away.

"Brave. Courageous. Loyal. I could use a girl like you." Vainwright's eyes glittered with ambition.

Alice thought of Lexi and Kelcie laughing at her. The anger in Tim's eyes when he thought she'd betrayed him. Ottie abandoning her. Even Gran had lied to her about who she really was. This didn't have to be her life any more. Madame Vainwright was offering her a way out.

"You'd do that?" Alice asked. "You'd teach me?"

"Everything I know," Vainwright promised.

Down on the carpet, Gran stirred, her fingers unclenching. The breath caught in Alice's throat but she made herself turn away. She had to keep Veronica talking.

"I see how little everyone thinks of you, Alice Tonks," Madame Vainwright said. "How they shun you. But I know what you can really do. Look what you've given me already with just a single vial of your blood. Let me help you in return. I could make you powerful. I could make you strong. Don't you want to be great?"

Vainwright sneered in Gran's direction, not noticing her fingers twitch.

Alice quivered with the effort to hide her delight. "My gran will help me be great."

"You don't need her. Lizzie's time is up. The Switching Board's no use to a girl like you. Come with me, Alice." Her hand gripped round Alice's wrist.

Alice stepped forward, her legs shaky and unsure. "A-a girl like me?"

"Alice, no!" Gran cried, pulling herself to her feet.

With an almighty *pop* Gran Switched. A massive brown bear now towered over Madame Vainwright. Its sheer bulk took Alice's breath away. The bear opened its mouth and roared, the sound reverberating off the library walls, filling the space with its rage. Long white teeth gleamed like daggers, spittle stretching between them. With one swipe of its huge paw, it knocked Vainwright to the floor. "Leave my granddaughter alone!"

Vainwright looked up, dazed. Her arm hung limply by her side but she was not down for long. *Pop.* The air crackled. A ferocious Amur tiger circled the bear, its body low and ready to pounce, but Alice noticed it wincing as its front paw brushed the ground. The tiger's tail curled. Its back arched.

Alice's heart was thumping faster than ever before. This was it. She had one chance to get this right.

Both bear and tiger crashed into a shelf of books. Claws scraped. Teeth gnashed.

Alice squeezed her eyes shut. It was now or never.

The air around her scrunched. Alice felt the sharp tug downwards, the ache of being squashed. And then she'd done it. She had Switched. *Latrodectus tredecimguttatus.* The black widow spider. The first creature that had come to mind.

The tiger's mouth closed around the bear's thick neck. Alice had to act fast. Everything relied on the element of surprise. She scuttled forward, scrambling to climb the tiger's furry leg and mount its ginormous back. She shoved her way through the bristles of orange fur, until her jaws could close tight around a piece of the tiger's skin. Then she bit down hard.

The tiger roared.

"Alice, get out of the way!" Gran bellowed as the beast's colossal frame came crashing down.

CHAPTER 44

A half wheeze, half gurgle spluttered from the tiger's heaving chest as it lay sprawled on the floor. The great cat threw back its head, gasping for air. Then its huge face crumpled, its stripes vanishing with an awful sucking sound.

Alice – now human again – buried her head in her hands, not wanting to look at the harm she had caused with one tiny bite. Why had she chosen such a venomous creature to Switch into? She was no better than Vainwright herself.

When she peeled away her fingers, Madame Vainwright was writhing on the carpet, fuzzy and faint around the edges at first but slowly growing more solid. She was drenched in sweat, her face ashen. Her whole body trembled and shook.

Alice stared at her, horrified. "I did this!"

Gran, now human again, slumped against a bookshelf. She wheezed and panted, unable to speak. Her neck had puffed up, the bitemarks now angry red hives, and her face was swollen.

"You did what was necessary," a muffled voice said firmly.

With a low grinding noise, the library counter swung back, revealing Madame Vainwright's trapdoor into the network of tunnels. Professor Biddle hauled himself out of the dark hole in the library floor, brushing the dirt from his face.

Ted's head popped up shortly after. An ugly purple circle was deepening around his eye and his bottom lip was split but he too was soon on his feet. He crossed the library and crouched beside Gran, peering at her neck. "Ouch. Snakebite, I reckon."

"Viper," Gran gasped, her voice tight and sore. "Black triangle head, I think."

Ted shrugged his rucksack off his shoulders, unzipped it and rummaged through the contents. He pulled out a small, heavily creased book entitled *International Snake Catalogue* and quickly thumbed through its pages until he found what he wanted.

"I've just the anti-venom for you, Lizzie, don't you worry!" Ted announced, retrieving a black fabric case. He opened it to reveal two dozen little vials of brightly coloured liquids.

Ted swiftly sucked the contents of a pale pink jar into a syringe, slid his belt free of his trousers and assembled a makeshift tourniquet round Gran's arm.

Next it was Hetty's turn to clamber through the trapdoor. Her right arm was cradled against her chest in a home-made sling, assembled from what appeared to be a man's white cotton vest and a couple of safety pins. She arrived just in time to see Ted jab Gran in the arm and give the wound a little rub.

"Ted's a helpful sort to have around in an emergency." She grinned. "Now don't you worry, Alice, your gran will be right as rain in no time."

"You can never be too careful when it comes to snakes," Ted put in. "It pays to keep a well-stocked collection of anti-venom to hand."

Hetty bent down to get a closer look at Madame Vainwright, who was quaking on the floor. "Not quite so clever now, are you?" she said. "Last time I saw you, you were bringing a rockfall down on our heads. Bit naughty collapsing the tunnel like that, I have to say. But we're made of sterner stuff, us oldies. It'll take more than a couple of rocks to keep us out for the count!"

"I bit her," Alice admitted, her fingers flicking faster and faster as Madame Vainwright thrashed her arms about feverishly.

"Spider or snake?" Ted asked matter-of-factly as he scanned his case for an antidote.

"Black widow," Alice said. "It was the first thing that came to mind. I had to do something. I—"

"Your quick thinking might just have saved the day. No need to feel bad," the professor said quietly. He gave Madame Vainwright a tap with his shoe. "We'll need to call Fearsomes and arrange a pickup for this one."

Fearsomes? Alice had never heard of anything with that name. But before she could ask what it was, Ted was already checking Vainwright over.

"Best we keep her sedated," he said. "Anti-venom plus a sedative should do the trick."

Ted administered the medicine and before long, Madame Vainwright was snoring throatily, the sweaty glaze lifting from her face.

Hetty took a great cumbersome mobile phone from her handbag. It must have been the size of a brick and twice as heavy. Alice watched as she stabbed in a number that had at least five digits too many.

"Hello? Fearsomes? Hetty Button here on behalf of the Switching Board. I need to arrange a pickup for one Veronica Vainwright, please . . . Yes, highly dangerous . . . Pebblewood School, that's right."

While Hetty and Professor Biddle made the arrangements and Ted packed away his medicine, Alice stood over the sleeping librarian, watching her chest shudder with each heaving breath.

Suddenly Madame Vainwright's eyes snapped open, her

gaze fixed on Alice. "I won't forget this, Alice Tonks!" she wheezed.

Alice gasped, darting backwards, but Vainwright's eyes closed as quickly as they had opened and she started snoring once more. Alice ventured closer to Madame Vainwright, nudging her leg, but the woman didn't even flinch. It was as if she'd imagined the whole thing.

"What's Fearsomes?" she asked as Hetty ended the call.

"It's our prison," Hetty explained. "A sort of Switchers' jail with added security. They'll soon have Vainwright safely under lock and key. Here, help me with your gran."

Together, Hetty and Alice heaved Gran up into Constance's favourite armchair and wrapped a woolly throw around her. Alice tucked herself in by Gran's feet and before she knew it, she was sound asleep.

When Alice awoke, bright sunshine like squeezed oranges oozed through the large library windows, and down by the sea gulls dipped and dived.

"Good morning, stranger," Gran said.

Alice looked up. Gran's swollen neck had deflated and the two red dots were little more than pimples. Hetty, Ted and Professor Biddle had left, while Madame Vainwright was nowhere to be seen.

"You've been fast asleep," Gran said. "I didn't want to wake you."

323

"Is she gone?"

"Oh yes," Gran said, stroking Alice's hair. "Veronica Vainwright won't be hurting anyone again, animals or humans."

Alice swallowed. It was hard to believe it was really all over.

"Fancy a quick Switch?" Gran asked, a glint in her eye. "School Bay is beautiful at this time of the morning."

Five minutes later, Alice soared beside Gran on a gust of wind, her white wings taut and agile. They glided over the green clifftops, away from the jagged roofs of Pebbles, past picnickers and daytrippers, over the cliffs and golden sands of School Bay until they sailed atop a sheet of blue.

"Look!" Alice cried, spotting tiny darts of silver glimmering among the waves. "Fish!"

She dived down, swift and smooth, her flight feathers slicing through the air and her tail the perfect rudder. Her feet grazed the water. The shoal of fish scattered beneath her and, with a sudden cry, she thrust her chest up and forward, cresting the breeze.

It was perfect.

Alice landed on the clifftop beside Gran, instantly Switching from a downy young gull to a human. She was alive with the thrill of flying. It had been her first time and although Gran had only let her go the short distance from the library to the coast, it had given her a taste for soaring. She couldn't wait to try it again.

Gran led Alice over to a bench overlooking the cove. The sun glittered atop the waves and they could see right out to sea. Gran held Alice's hand in hers as they watched the pleasure boats sail from Pebblehampton harbour.

"Let's sit here a while," Gran said. "I don't think I'm quite ready to give you back yet." She reached into her pocket and pulled out a handful of toffees, passing one to Alice. "Are you absolutely sure you don't want me to come to school with you and tell your teachers that you've been with me?" she asked.

Alice grinned, thinking of the evidence Ottie had on her uncle's tablet. "I'm sure. I think the teachers are going to have bigger problems than me this morning!"

Gran squinted at Alice. "Hmm. What are you not telling me?"

"Let's just say that Madame Vainwright isn't the only one getting her comeuppance this morning!" Alice laughed. "I'll tell you all about it next time I call, I promise."

"Just you make sure you do!" Gran said. "If you're certain then I'll head back to the Switching Board HQ and start work on my report for the international committee. I'll be sorry not to meet this friend of yours, though. Professor Biddle told me all about him. Timothy, isn't it?"

"Tim," Alice said. "I've another friend too. Her name's Ottie. She helped too."

Gran gave her hand a squeeze. "Well, if it wasn't for you and your friends, Veronica would still be free to do as she pleased and the Switching Board would be none the wiser."

"But if I hadn't gone looking for Constance, Madame Vainwright wouldn't have my blood," Alice said. "She wouldn't be a Switcher again,"

"Enough of that talk!" Gran implored. "We all make mistakes. Mine was not trusting you to handle the truth. I should've known you were more than capable."

"It's okay, Gran," Alice said. "I know you were only doing what you thought was best."

"You've more than proved yourself, Alice," Gran said proudly. "And there's still plenty of work to be done. The Switching Board's going to need you."

Alice sighed. For now, all she wanted was to catch up with her friends and get better at Switching. She'd had enough danger to last a lifetime.

"Your mum would be so impressed," Gran said. "You're the spit of her, you know. Stubborn. Serious. Not afraid to take matters into your own hands. A typical Switcher in fact!"

Alice looked up. "Y-you mean Mum was a Switcher as well?"

"Oh yes," Gran said. "And a very fine one too."

Alice grinned. For the first time, the woman in Gran's photographs didn't seem like such a stranger.

They sat in silence for a while, watching the waves roll in. There was still so much Alice didn't understand, so much to discover and learn, but she could see now wasn't the time for more questions. When the wind picked up and they grew chilly, Alice hugged Gran goodbye. Then she headed back along the path towards the school, the sea breeze propelling her home.

CHAPTER 45

Alice slipped back down the alleyway into school. She was eager to see what Tim and Ottie had been up to in her absence.

When she reached the quad, everything was peaceful. She walked round to the school hall and stared up at the stained-glass window, remembering when she saw it move during assembly. A lifetime ago. Was she even the same person now?

"Hello, Alice."

Alice turned round at the sound of flapping wings as Agent T landed on the grass beside her. His feathers were ruffled, and though he was a bit on the skinny and scraggy side, he looked okay.

Alice found herself feeling a little shy of the seagull. So much had happened since she'd last seen him.

"How are you feeling?" she asked after a moment or two.

"Can't complain!" the gull declared. "Onwards and upwards!"

Alice sat down on the grass and listened to Agent T's story of being lured into a trap on the beach by a particularly plump-looking piece of haddock.

"I really can't thank you enough," he said at the end of his tale.

"You've nothing to thank me for." Alice shifted uncomfortably. "I just did what anyone would have done."

The gull cocked his head to the side. "You're a pretty extraordinary human, Alice."

She looked away. "I couldn't have done it without the LSPDA. Red and the others made it to the cave just in time. Without them, I'd never have got everyone out. They were brilliant last night as well! I've never seen anything like it . . ."

"Milo's quite the celebrity at the minute. He ran like the wind to tell Red you were headed to the cave."

"And there's Ebenezer too," Alice added.

"You're right," Agent T said thoughtfully. "I suppose the LSPDA does have a lot to thank Mr Pinktail for. His help won't be forgotten and the LSPDA always needs new members."

He spread his wings, his feathers fluttering in the breeze. "That cave was awful, Alice. I thought I'd never see sunlight again."

"Me too," Alice said. The memory of the crushing weight of the darkness silenced her for a moment. "Will I see you again soon?" she asked eventually.

"Of course!" Agent T pecked at her sleeve. "We're not letting you off the hook that easily, Alice Tonks!" With a wink he flew off towards the beach. Alice stared after him, thinking how lucky she was to have animal friends as well as human ones.

"You're back, then!" a voice said.

Alice looked up to see Tim balanced beside her on his crutches, Ottie at his side.

"Good to see you're in one piece!" Ottie smiled. "I don't think I could handle sharing a dorm with Kelcie and Lexi again!"

"Let's not talk about the Gruesome Twosome!" Tim rolled his eyes. "There's far more exciting things to discuss. Tell us what happened with the animal snatcher?"

Alice looked at her hands as she thought back to Vainwright writhing in pain from her bite. "She's in a kind of Switchers' prison now."

"Why do you look so miserable then?" Tim gave her a nudge with his crutch. "Haven't you, well, saved the day?"

Alice looked at her two friends. "I had a lot of help."

"So I guess I wasn't dreaming last night," Ottie said. "You really can talk to animals and shapeshift?"

Alice nodded.

"That," Tim announced, "has to be the coolest thing

330

ever. Will you show us?" he asked but Alice didn't get the chance.

Felix came running towards them, his chef's hat askew. "You three had better come quickly!" he called. "There's something I think you'll want to see."

The friends glanced at one another in confusion then followed the chef out to the front of the school, where Kelcie, Lexi and a group of other students had gathered on the marble steps.

A police car was parked on the gravel, its doors open.

"Excuse me! Make way!" Two stern-faced officers led a red-faced Mr Marlowe down the steps.

"There must be some mistake!" he raged. "Don't you know who I am?"

"Oh yes, sir," one of the officers said, keeping a firm grip on the headmaster's handcuffs. "We know *exactly* who you are and what you've been up to."

"He's been robbing the school!" Ottie shouted over the excited chatter of the crowd. "Isn't that right, Uncle Hugo?"

There was a chorus of gasps from the students.

Mr Marlowe glared at his niece. "That's not true!" he roared, his ears flushing a particularly lurid shade of pink.

Tim put a hand on Ottie's arm. "What are you doing?" he warned. "Your mum's going to do her nut when she finds out you were involved in getting your uncle arrested."

"Let her," Ottie said with a shrug. "I'm bored of worrying about what she thinks." She waggled a memory stick in the air. "And besides, with hard evidence, Mother can hardly say I'm lying."

As Mr Marlowe was placed in the back of the police car, a cheer went up from the students. Lexi held up her phone and snapped away, documenting the whole affair. Only Kelcie looked miserable, her face screwed up in a scowl as she stood alone on the outskirts of the crowd. It seemed no one wanted to hang out with her.

"Good riddance to bad rubbish," Tim called out as the police car trundled away down the driveway. "Now can we go and find something to eat? I don't know about you two but I'm starving!"

The rest of the students headed off to lessons but Alice and Ottie hung back to help Tim navigate the steps into school. They were just heading inside when they heard a series of high-pitched barks.

"Wait," Alice said, turning back. "That's a fox!" Immediately she thought of Red. Was he in trouble?

As quickly as Tim could hobble, the trio followed the barking sound down the driveway. At a bend in the road, just out of sight of the main school, someone had parked a sleek black Bentley.

"That's my uncle's car," Ottie said. "What's it doing here?"

The moment the words left Ottie's mouth, the children had their answer. A tall, buzzard-like woman in a rather bedraggled two-piece suit emerged from a hedgerow. She looked both ways and made a beeline for the car. Mrs Salter's high heels sank into the gravel and as she tried to wrestle one of her shoes free, her hastily packed suitcase bulged open, spewing clothes all over the place.

"Trying to get away are you, miss?" Tim shouted.

A blast of wind whipped a pair of the housemistress's knickers into the air. As Mrs Salter staggered after them, a long, whiskered snout poked out from the hedge. Streaking forward, Red grabbed the knickers and ran off down the driveway.

"That fox has stolen my underwear!" Mrs Salter flapped. "Come back, you disgusting creature!"

Just then, a whole pack of animals descended on her suitcase, helping themselves to the contents. Athena swooped down and made off with a single scarlet stiletto while Henry nosed at a satin blouse and Milo lolloped away with one of Mrs Salter's silk scarves round his neck.

"Those wretched animals!" Mrs Salter shrieked.

Abandoning her suitcase, she dived into the car and slammed the driver's door shut. The engine roared to life and the tyres screeched as the housemistress sped away down the driveway.

Alice, Tim and Ottie laughed so hard that their sides ached and tears streamed down their cheeks.

Finally they recovered enough to head back to the school. To their surprise, a young woman with bright auburn hair stood at the top of the steps, a cardboard box balanced upon one hip. She was dressed in a crisp white blouse, black braces and tie and a pair of sharply ironed trousers. She smiled as she saw the trio approach and gave them a wave.

"Who's that?" Alice wondered.

"Dunno," Tim said, giving Alice a cheeky grin before calling over to the woman, "Hey, miss! What's your name?"

The woman came over, extending her freckled hand for them to shake. "I'm not a miss, actually," she said, her green eyes glinting. "I'm a doctor. Dr Ada Jessops. How do you do?"

Alice and Tim looked at one another. The real Miss Jessops!

Tim introduced himself, politely shaking her hand, then Ottie did the same.

Only Alice stood lost in her own thoughts. Dr Jessops turned to her. "And what might your name be?"

"A-Alice Tonks." A little hesitantly, Alice offered her hand to shake. "Are you the founder's granddaughter?"

"Great-granddaughter," Dr Jessops said. "Pleasure to meet you, Alice."

Alice smiled. The doctor had nice dry hands, not clammy at all. Alice didn't even need to wipe her own hand after shaking it, which made a pleasant change. "Are you going to be working here?" she ventured.

"Why, yes, as a matter of fact I am," Dr Jessops said. "I'm your new headmistress." She checked her watch. "And if I'm not quick, I'll be late to my very first assembly – as will the three of you." At that, she strode back up the steps, opened the door and disappeared inside.

"Wow," Tim whispered. "She's a bit different to the last head!"

"Thank goodness!" Ottie said.

Tim and Ottie both headed after Dr Jessops. Alice was about to follow when she felt a silky pelt of fur slink past her legs.

"Hello again, Constance!" she said, bending down to scoop up the cat.

As Constance nestled in her arms, Alice knew her life at Pebbles was going to be all right. Better still, it was going to be an adventure!

ACKNOWLEDGEMENTS

Firstly, to Nicki for endless patience and being the best wife a writer could have.

To Alfred, for keeping me laughing, and for all the cuddles when the edits seemed endless.

To my lovely family and friends for all the support, not just during the writing of this book but always. Imogen, I hope this was worth the wait and that you're not too disappointed!

To Stuart White (because where would we all be without him!) and the fabulous WriteMentor community, for helping, cheerleading and supporting me every step of the way. Writing can be lonely, but it doesn't need to be.

To Lindsay Galvin: the kindest and most generous of writers. Thank you for your writing workshop which started this mad adventure and for holding my hand ever since.

To the ever warm and generous children's book community: readers, librarians, teachers, booksellers, writers, illustrators and industry professionals. Special thanks to Anna Britton, Emma Finlayson-Palmer, Aisha Bushby and Melvin Burgess, for lending me their expertise at various points along the road!

To Lauren Gardner, my superstar agent, for taking a punt on a cat-loving, autistic woman and her boarding school book and for rescuing this story from obscurity. Thanks for your brilliant ideas and excitement, for loving Alice as much as I do, and for sticking patiently with me through all the drafts and wobbles. Thanks also to everyone at the Bell Lomax Moreton family.

To Katie Jennings, editor extraordinaire, for your tireless polishing of my prose and for digging me out of all the plot holes. This book wouldn't have existed without your infectious enthusiasm.

To the whole fantastic team at Oneworld, including, but by no means limited to, Molly Scull, Kate Bland, Lucy Cooper, Mark Rusher, Paul Nash and Laura McFarlane – thank you for getting behind my book and bringing it to life.

Flavia Sorrentino, Ben Summers and Hayley Warnham – thank you all for the amazing artwork and design. You've made this writer exceptionally happy!

Thanks also go to Anna Bowles for her eagle-eyed copyedit and Susila Baybars for her brilliant proofread.

Last but not least, to my readers – thank you. I hope you enjoy it.

ABOUT THE AUTHOR

Like Alice, Emily Kenny is autistic and wanted to write her debut novel about an autistic child protagonist. Emily studied English Literature and Creative Writing at the University of East Anglia, completed an MA in Children's Literature at Roehampton University and was part of the Spark Mentor scheme with WriteMentor. Emily works as a secondary school English teacher and special educational needs co-ordinator and lives in London.